JOCK OF THE BAY

by

R. M. Kain

Publish & Print
www.publishandprint.co.uk

The right of R. M. Kain to be identified as the author of
Jock of the Bay has been asserted by him under Copyright
Amendment (Moral Rights) Act 1988.

All rights reserved.

Copyright © R. M. Kain 2020.

ISBN: 9798670903295

Publish & Print
www.publishandprint.co.uk

It's a strange foreign sun which warms me through,

And stranger birds who sing.

Yet the songs they sing are my love for you.

Always! In everything!

THE AUTHOR

ONE

The Gangster

I sensed, rather than heard, the percussive thump of the mortar bursts. They were coming in disciplined and tight volleys of four from somewhere close to me, penetrating the constant ringing in my ears. I couldn't hear them land but the dust clouds from their impact was turning night into shadowy day and back to night again.

My head was pounding in time to the volleys, reminding me that no matter what had happened, I was still alive. My eyes wouldn't open, my mouth had been hanging open and was filled with the dust. It felt as though I was trying to swallow a cotton ball. I couldn't remember anything of why or how I was there but was filled by the overwhelming sense that it was my fault. That I was to blame. The guilt was paralysing me.

The mortar boys were very close by; too disciplined in their firing rhythm to be insurgents so regular army or perhaps even foreign "advisers". My eyes felt as though they were glued shut, so head injury then, non-fatal but possibly still dangerous and perhaps even fatal further down the line.

I had seen a fair few of those. The debris from a

roadside explosion causing an unimportant head-wound and perhaps some concussion; but the invisible air wave of the blast sneaking through the ears, nose and mouth to rupture blood vessels deep in the brain some of which turned out to be very important indeed.

The medics couldn't scan for those in the middle of parts of the country, which had never had electricity and the helis wouldn't land at any reference where a proven risk of explosive devices on the ground made it too dangerous. By the time the snatch squad arrived the poor bastard had usually gone from celebrating a minor wound to dead on the ground. The dead on the ground had always seemed to me the better option compared to the wreckage of a life left by deep brain bleeds.

My subconscious brain was screaming at me to move and get away, but my trained brain said no-one has spotted you yet. Move slowly and assess the damage first. It would have entertained the mortarmen for weeks if I had sprung up to run only to keel over because the lower end of one of my legs was missing. I know it did me the first time I had seen it. Surprisingly common in this part of the world. The human instinct for survival knows no bounds.

I was on my left side on a soft surface, probably sand. I slowly moved my right hand and was immensely grateful that it appeared to be moving. Encouraged by this I tried to stretch my right leg and the pain shot from my right hip up into my head and down into my toe.

Not good, but better than no feeling. I had been close to a blast before and this was how it had felt, as if I had been hit by a tank. Every movement pushed the pain level up. I could feel a solid surface behind me, on my back. Conscious or not I had rolled into cover as best I could, and the low rise and dust clouds were protecting me from the enemies' sight lines.

I moved to clear my eyes and something thick and sticky crunched under my fingers and rolled away. I had to find my weapon. I must not panic and had to move slowly. I opened on closed my eyes experimentally, slowly and deliberately.

As they cleared, what I was seeing began to inform the decisions my other senses were making. The guilt still lay there, as heavy and paralysing as ever and the pain, particularly in my head, was intensified but eventually familiar shapes swam into focus and back out again. The dust in my mouth began to taste of sour dark rum and my outstretching leg lifted over the arm of the tiny two-seater sofa in my office. Ten years I had been living with these office furnishings and this was the first time I had ever used this sofa.

The thumping in my head continued until I recognised it was not in time to my pulse as was usually the case, but rather was someone hammering on my door with the fleshy side of their fist. Beats of four with pauses in between bursts. My doorbell drilled and whined in a continuous attempt to cause my head to explode like a wineglass in a noise experiment I had done a long time ago in school.

Night turned into day, and back to night as whoever it was stepped back and forward to pound at the door. Someone was in a hurry and was big enough to block the door entirely, shadowing the glass top to bottom and side to side. I had only ever met two men in Cardiff big enough to do that and neither of them was rushing to tell me I had won the lottery.

Barely able to move I stretched through the pain barriers and eased myself into a sitting position, half moving voluntarily, half rolling around like a jetty landed fish. Once up, the gargantuan task of lifting my bowling ball of pain from my chest into its normal position at the top of my neck took a bit of time and caused my eyes to close again.

"For fucks sake John! Open the door!"

Followed by another more urgent volley of mortar fire.

"Open up, you lazy fucker!" Thump! Thump! Thump! Thump!

Driven by the urgency of the shouts and given the courtesy of being called by my name I hobbled erect and limped towards the door.

"Don't make me kick your door in."

I was almost tempted to see him try. My door and frame had come, at enormous expense, from a valley's cannabis factory. The door was bulletproof glass set in a tempered steel frame mounted in a steel and reinforced concrete surround. He would have had more luck kicking in the wall.

"Coming."

I shouted. At least in my head I shouted, what came out was a kind of strangled froggy fart of indeterminate noise. Nothing seemed to be working today except my dreams. When were they ever underemployed?

I leant heavily against the electronic touch pad set away from the door for security purposes and it silently unlocked. As my visitor stepped forward to thump the door again it swung quickly open and he lunged into the room with a shocked look on his face. He did well to stumble in, usually he had to turn his shoulder sideways to get through.

"It was open, you daft twat!"

I hoped that was what it sounded like to him.

"Get dressed the boss wants to see you. Right now!"

I thought I was dressed. My shirt was bunched around my belly and my trousers had been opened at the top for comfort but other than that I was ready for business. My visitor on the other hand had brought with him the stench of Sunday morning. Slightly sweaty socks, half-digested rum, oniony unbrushed teeth hinting at a late-night kebab and the vaguest whiff of a blocked toilet.

I looked down, then somewhat puzzled, looked around the floor. I appeared to be missing a shoe. At least that explained most of the limping then.

"Was it raining last night Den?"

"Absolutely threw it down about half three, why?"

"Thank fuck I thought I had pissed myself."

My sock was leaving big wet footprints around my office. As an ace detective I put together these clues and concluded I had returned home sometime after four, missing a shoe. My quick celebration drink after the ice hockey had gone on somewhat longer than I had planned.

I had arrived home in what my old mother would have called a right state and been too unsteady to make the stairs to my flat. I had simply rested awhile on the couch in my office, perhaps even the smell was me after all.

"I just need a quick shower Den. I will be with you in ten minutes. Help yourself in the kitchen."

My visitor, Big Den, or Denny the Midget as he was known, mainly behind his back, was one of two lieutenants to Marko, the self-styled hardest man in Cardiff.

The other half was Den's brother Donny, the only man I had seen who was bigger than Den. With those two at his side few ever questioned how hard Marko was. Certainly, few survivors. I had my doubts, but I kept them to myself. I didn't want to hurt his feelings.

My office kitchen was small with me in it, but Den was like a giant in a nursery toy as he blundered about, eventually settling on a bottle of water from the fridge and a full packet of chocolate biscuits kept for the posh clients.

"Hurry up then! He's been up all night and is in a bad mood already."

Little did he know that I was hurrying on the inside, but it was just the outside, which was moving in slow deliberate motion. No wonder I didn't attempt the stairs last night I could barely manage them now. Just like pack drill I mentally shouted the rhythm into my stiff and sore legs. Up! one two Drive! one two Grab! one two Up! one two and so on. The stairs seemed like the last two hundred feet of Kilimanjaro had. I was getting old.

The shower woke me up but also made me slightly drunk again. In a hurry I shaved, brushed my teeth and showered all at the same time and as I stepped out a new man, I realised that the previous man had indeed been stinking. Shirt, socks and pants I could understand, but why did my trousers smell so bad. Like the man of action I am, I balled them up and threw them in the laundry basket for Claudia the cleaner to deal with.

I pulled on a clean and freshly ironed Cardiff blue Fred Perry and a natty pair of light-coloured chinos and finished it off sockless with a pair of deck shoes. I had clean socks but given the difficulties I had putting on my trousers, I wasn't going to give the socks a chance to

6

ambush me.

Fewer than ten minutes later I was parade ground fresh and ready for inspection. Den in the meantime had finished the biscuits and was happily eating great pawsful of the honey nut cornflakes as a pastime. I snatched a bottle of water from the fridge before he washed them down and set off through the door, before he had a chance to catch up.

"Cummon! We haven't got all day for you to have breakfast Den!"

I stepped through the door into migraine inducing sunshine which simultaneously dazzled me and laced great bolts of pain through my eyes to the back of my head and out again. Regretting my charge through the door I waited to one side to let my senses recover while Den the midget slid elegantly through. Sometimes, when he thought no-one was looking, that man could move like a dancer.

Right at my door Marko, the hard man, sat in the back of his Range Rover, looking every inch the man who should not be kept waiting, which was of course his intention. The reason he couldn't have just come in existed only in his own head. To me it just made him look a bit of a tosser.

Den held the car door open for me and just to piss Marko off I leant in and said;

"Lovely day, mate. Off anywhere nice, are we? Do I need to bring ice cream money?"

"I ain't never your mate Jock and don't forget it. Just get in. Den take a hike for five!"

Without even a shrug, Den set off up the street to where the Sainsbury Extra would be open. Probably still hungry. He didn't look back.

I got in the back and admired the leatherwork. I

watched Marko as he struggled with my silence. I remember Donnie telling me once that Marko read a lot of self-help books about reading body language and getting your way in negotiations and suchlike. One of his lessons was don't speak first so this was going to be a long five minutes. If he was uncomfortable with my silence, he was very fidgety with my scrutiny. I deliberately slowed my respiration and blink rate and looked at him as if I were memorising him for a photofit.

Like most hard men I knew, and I had known a fair few, Marko was small framed and wiry. He was that mongrel pale brown colour that you see in so many of the inhabitants of Cardiff which could be fifth generation West Indian or half Bangladeshi or even full Lebanese. You just couldn't tell by looking where they were from, the legacy of when it was a thriving dockland, attracting people from all over the world.

He was certainly unattractive and even his expensive porcelain dentistry hadn't disguised his goofy overbite. His skin was pockmarked by some adolescent acne and apart from one long scar from ear to mouth on his left side he had none of the usual scars and chips around the eyes that denote a fighting man the world over.

He was fond of claiming that scar had been handed to him during his fight for the streets of Cardiff and that he had killed the man that gave it to him with his own knife. Several names of people who had disappeared from Cardiff were bandied about as the victim.

To me it looked just like the scar my young cousin had from when he had crashed a stolen car and the bonnet had come through the windscreen with the corner catching his mouth and ripping along his cheek until the jawbone stopped it. Cuts and slashes left clean edges to scars, his appeared raggedy and torn. But what did I know?

To top it all he had the tight curly hair, which denoted some African in his heritage at some point. He had gone grey then dyed it black. When he heard people were laughing at his hair and calling him the Golliwog, he had tried dying it back but had succeeded only in going a mix of orangey brown and grey. I guess he was growing out the brown now.

What I didn't see in his gaze, and never had, was intelligence. Any top kick I had met was bright as well as ruthless, without mercy and conscience certainly, but never without reason. Marko didn't look as if he could work out a train timetable. I upped the stakes and stopped blinking and just stared.

"What the fuck you lookin at?"

I felt like sticking out my tongue and singing Na Na Na Na Na!

"What do you want?"

"Listen. I have a job for you and no matter what happens it is important you understand that you are working for me, reporting directly to me."

"Why did you not just make an appointment and come in like everyone else?"

"I am not everyone else and anyway I have to take you to someone who will tell you what the job is. Once you know; speak to me and I will tell you what to do."

"Two things, I only work for the person who pays me, and no-one tells me what to do."

"Don't be a dick. This could bring a lot of work your way. You look as if you need it."

I knew I shouldn't keep poking this rattlesnake but

the rum still rattling around in me couldn't resist it.

"I manage fine. I think any work from you is probably more trouble than it's worth."

I was tempted to tell him that I had been out celebrating earning a hundred grand last week, but discretion quickly overtook me. I wasn't that drunk then! The last thing I needed was to test how fireproof my fireproof safe was. The cash was all still in there and I didn't want an expensive pile of ash when I opened it.

His eyes hardened. He wasn't used to people answering him back. Maybe he should have kept Dennis handy. Marko just didn't frighten me, but I thought Den could fold me up and put me in his pocket if he wanted.

"Don't get smart with me Jock. I have connections everywhere; Bristol, London, Manchester even Glasgow. Upset me and I could reach your family in Glasgow."

In his head I am sure he thought he sounded like Edward G Robinson see! but in truth it sounded lame even to me. I wasn't even from Glasgow, but I suppose we all sounded the same to him.

"Understand this Marko. My connections are with hundreds upon thousands of trained killers, some of whom owe me their lives Threaten anyone I know, and I will wage a war on you that you would not believe. Thanks for the offer of work but no thanks. Next time you want to speak to me make an appointment like everyone else."

I opened the door and left taking care not to turn my back. The last thing I wanted to do was let him know what else was in my safe, but I thought a bit of insurance might be in order. I couldn't watch my back all the time, or even just those odd occasions when I was sober.

I leant back in for a parting shot;

"Just so we are clear. You keep out of my business and I will keep out of yours. I won't, for instance, ask the Serious Fraud Office to look into the money laundering at Hassam's the dentist."

This was safe to tell him as Hassam had asked all round the mosque and several lawyers how he could get out from under the amount of money Marko was pumping through his business. Any fool could make money illegally. The hard bit these days was keeping it with the sweeping investigative powers of the anti-terrorism laws.

Marko didn't know, and had no need to find out, that I had an entire copy of his weekly cash ledger in my safe including all thirty businesses he used to wash his money, how much each got a week and where the money was coming from.

It was a couple of years out of date but nonetheless represented a powerful weapon should I ever need it. First rule of any war; don't fight. Second rule; win by overwhelming force.

I hoped I never had to even let him know I had the information, but I was confident that if push came to shove, I could finish his whole business with one blow.

I could never tell him that I had come by it from a stroke of the kind of huge good fortune, which had followed me since I came to Cardiff. He probably wouldn't believe me anyway. That little book was what gave me the confidence to laugh in his face. He clearly didn't like it but couldn't think of an adequate comeback.

"If you don't report directly to me, I will finish your business and possibly you for good. I will have the boys burn you out while you're asleep in your crummy flat upstairs. You're just a visitor here you Jock cunt but this is my city and what I say goes. Or else!"

I just laughed and walked away I thought about going into my office but then thought I better hang about where there were witnesses for a while and headed for the back door of The Packet. Sunday morning, the usual crowd would already be in there, if some of them had ever left. I might even find my other shoe. I listened hard but didn't hear the car drive away. Time to stay alert for a while.

As expected, there were about two dozen people in the place despite it being only half ten in the morning.

"Feeling alright this morning Jock?"

"How's the head?"

Knowing smiles were everywhere. I must have popped in for one on the way home last night. The Wig gave me a discreet nod from behind the bar, indicating that he wanted a word at the end of the bar. Here we go, maybe I would find out why I still felt guilty this morning.

"Morning Stevie. Pint of lager please."

The water had rehydrated the rum form last night but not touched my thirst. Maybe a nice slow pint would redress the balance. Stevie leant into me over the bar. I tried hard not to stare at today's wig, which was a natty centre parted wavy auburn model. It would have suited him thirty years ago when he bought it but looked a bit out of place after the ravages of running this twenty-four-hour drinking den for the last decade.

"You have quite a tab from last night, John. Any chance of squaring some of it up this week?"

He should have been a ventriloquist. His lips never moved and no-one else heard him, though no doubt a few were wondering.

"How much are we talking about?"

Genuinely, with no idea.

"Just over four hundred quid."

I thought it was a hearing test the sound arrived so softly. Then he was off to pour my pint and serve the domino school who were taking a refreshment break. No wonder I still felt drunk. Four hundred quid was a lot of rum even for me. Bearing in mind I didn't even remember being there I dreaded to think what I had had. I didn't even think to question it. In my years drinking in here it had never been wrong before.

My pint arrived with a questioning raise of one miscoloured eyebrow.

"Later today Stevie. I am just out on a quick errand just now."

"Maybe you could borrow it off Marko, though his interest rates are a lot worse than mine."

He missed nothing, the old yin, though I had rarely seen him further than the beer garden. He thought I was getting mixed up in something dodgy and wanted to make sure it didn't blow up with him holding a dud IOU.

"Don't worry about that, Stevie, just a bit of a misunderstanding, that's all."

"Be careful with that boy. He is a weasel. He'll have you stabbed in the back soon as look at you. They big ginger brothers have been prowling about all morning. They're usually in bed at this time. You wouldn't want to give them another go at you."

He was worried about me not being in a fit state to repay him!

"It's OK I spoke to Denny this morning. He was quite cheerful once he ate all my biscuits. If you don't mind me asking, what did I break to run up a four hundred quid

13

bill?"

"Nothing. Drinks were on you for about two hours. Wouldn't take no for an answer. I kept the till roll if you want to see it."

"No. It's OK. I believe you. I always have. I'll drop it in later. I'll leave it in an envelope if you're not here."

We both laughed. The only time I had ever been in when Stevie wasn't here was the time the draymen "accidentally" dropped a barrel on his leg, breaking his ankle in three places. Even then I only came over to see what the fuss was. I could hear his swearing three streets away. God knows what the assembly politicians across the Bay made of it.

"If anybody finds a brown leather shoe, please keep it, it's mine."

"I would love to tell you that you weren't wearing it when you came in, but I wouldn't have served you in your stocking feet. Probably fell off during the dancing demonstrations."

I was always fond of roping people into the Scottish country dancing when enjoying the rum.

"Keep an eye out anyway."

I took my pint to the corner furthest away from the dominos. The last thing I needed was to get roped into another session. The first mouthful let me know that I could have sat and drank there all day. I was idly wondering where my shoe could be when an unfamiliar ringtone nagged at me.

It was what my very close friends referred to as the bat phone. A small out-dated folding phone with a number given to a precious few. No-one called me idly on that number. I dug it out of my back pocket and flipped it open

14

just like Captain Kirk. The display told me it was Mrs Peters, the mother of the ginger monsters Donald and Dennis. She had this number from the time I had put Donald in a coma, and I told her she could call me anytime she needed anything. It seemed that moment was now.

Maybe she was calling to warn me the boys were coming for me, but I doubted it. Much as she told everyone she owed me for saving her baby's life she loved her boys more; with a ferocity and devotion I had only seen in Ghurkha troops. She would never betray them. Besides Den was only a minute away. He was smart enough to know where to find me if he wanted.

"Mrs Peters, everything okay. What can I do for you?"

"It's Donald, John. Don't hang up! I'm sorry I had to use my mum's phone, but you wouldn't answer on the work's phones."

That was another thing to add to the shoe. I couldn't remember seeing my phone this morning. All that rushing around. I hoped it was in a forgotten pocket somewhere. I consoled myself with the thought that I had never lost it before. Then I wondered where my jacket was. I couldn't remember seeing it this morning either. No worries, it was either there or lost and either way I couldn't fix it at that moment.

"I wasn't avoiding you Donald, your brother rushed me out the door this morning. I don't have the phones with me. Sorry!"

I thought an early sorry might stop this getting out of hand the way my earlier conversation with his boss had.

"I need a favour, John. I know things didn't go well with Marko this morning, but I have a friend in trouble. He needs someone found and I recommended you. Dai Soldier could not speak highly enough of your ability."

Dai fucking Soldier. I must have had two or three dozen referrals from him over the years and all of them had unrealistic expectations of what I could do. All because of the extraordinary luck, which had followed me about since I had arrived.

In my first days in Cardiff, over a fair few rums, Dai and I had been exchanging war stories. Usual squaddie; where, when, who we had served with. Out of the blue, Dai had asked me to kill his sixteen-year-old daughter's boyfriend. Usual story; she was a good girl devoted to an older junkie bastard who regularly beat her like an old carpet to keep her devotion fresh, building up to turning her out on the street no doubt.

Dai couldn't do anything about it because his daughter would never speak to him again and he thought just beating the guy would just lead to worse beatings for his daughter. I told him just talking like that could get him jailed, far less to a near stranger and told him to forget it. We kept drinking as if it had never been mentioned.

Two days later Dai had turned up at my old office, in the town centre, grinning like a Cheshire cat and plunked five thousand pounds in old rolled up twenties on my desk, winked, and as he walked out said;

"Let me know if that is not enough Jock "

I had picked up the money and followed him down to Mollie Maguires, which was still a pub then.

As I walked in, he had grabbed me in a huge bear hug and whispered, "Thanks" into my ear. I told him I had no idea what he was talking about and he just winked and said, "Me neither!"

It turned out that the junkie boyfriend had been the victim of a hit and run at three o'clock that morning and was not expected to survive. A burned-out stolen car had been found a mile away and police had CCTV footage of three dwarves, or twelve-year olds, running away. As far as I knew no-one was ever charged for the incident. Every time I tried to tell him it was nothing to do with me, he just winked. In the end I had to spend the money and gained a reputation, which still haunted me.

"This isn't business John. It's a personal matter for a friend. Please at least come and see him."

Few can resist a request from a twenty-two stone giant and I certainly wasn't one of them.

"Do you want to meet me in the office in half an hour?"

"I know it's a lot to ask but could you meet him in Chan's. We are there now, and he doesn't want anyone to know he is here."

I had never heard Donny speak so much. Even when his mum had ordered him to thank me for saving his life he had gushed, "Thanks" making it seem like less than one syllable.

I drained my pint with one long, much-needed swallow and set off to Chan's. What else could I do?

And that was how I came to meet and be working for the Namibian.

TWO

The Namibian

It took a fair bit of influence to get into Chan's before it opened at twelve on a Sunday. It took a lot more to have the place to your self. I had seen the dozens of worker ants who cleaned and prepared the restaurant and food for service. God knows where they were or what they had been told.

I hoped for my safety that they were not far away, otherwise I was likely to be locked in a room with Marko and his enforcers, and him in a bad mood. I was relying on the brothers not abusing their mother's trust when she gave them my number. Some bonds you could take to the bank.

Nonetheless, my spine was tingling when I approached the door. I had only a small boning knife from the kitchen in The Packet for company. Not much, but enough if you knew how to use it. I knew. The doors were manned by the two boys, both still in their bouncer's uniforms from the night before, immaculate as ever.

You would have to be mad to look at them and consider that you could take them. There wasn't enough cheap cider in the world for that. They swung the doors open and closed and locked them behind me. The clunking locks did not fill me with confidence, but I pressed on up the stairs. I could hear Donald behind me.

"Thanks John. Appreciated."

Still in the long sentences then. I put my left hand in my trouser pocket where the knife lay behind the outline of my phone. The blade was just short enough to hide in this way. Trained fighters always tended to watch your right hand; experienced fighters stood far enough away to be out of range of both. The brothers fell into both these categories. My hand twitched when the first person I saw was Marko sitting with a bottle of beer as if he owned the place.

As far as I knew Chan's was "looked after" by the Chinese and had no connection to Marko's businesses. Someone was pulling a lot of strings here and it wasn't Marko that was for sure. It could only be the other man then.

Difficult to see in the gloom but a man as black as a man could be. As black as the Earl of Hell's waistcoat as my father would have said. So black, he was almost blue in the half-light. His head was as smooth and shiny as an oiled bowling ball. What light there was bounced around the planes and angles of his magnificent face. He looked for all the world like a bust carved from coal and polished.

Behind him and easily overlooked was his equivalent of Donald. A big dreadlocked West Indian. Same height as Donald, a bit younger and not as heavily muscled but just as fit. If I was going to have to fight my way out of here, then I would have to grab the boss man and threaten him with the knife. I would never manage the three big men; knife or no knife. Where I came from you learned a truth early in your school years. The bigger they

19

are the harder they hit you. That was just as true today as it was then.

I eased my fingers round the handle ready to move, all the while distracting them by moving my right hand wide and away from my body. The boss man smiled and looked as if he was about to speak.

"Told you he would come running. I don't have to ask twice in this town."

We both looked at Marko. I couldn't help myself. The rum was still coursing through my veins.

"I am here as a favour to Mrs. Peters, Donald's mum."

"Who do you think he works for you muppet!! He just does what I tell him."

This time Den didn't look like walking away. He and Donald looked at each other. Marko was too thick to notice. The boss man's smile widened, and he stood and reached for me with his right hand. Dumb move really. If I gripped his right hand with mine the knife would be in my free left hand and at his kidneys or his throat.

"No matter why you came. I am most grateful you could accommodate me in this way. I am delighted to meet you. I am Sunday Smith but please call me Sunny."

"John McLean, but most people call me Jimmy or Jock, whatever suits."

I shook his hand. What else can you do when a man reaches out to you? I made a noise in my throat like two ping pong shots followed by a billiards cannon. He laughed aloud in delight.

"I have not heard that sound since my pampa died many years ago. It delights me that you can speak Nama. Say some more, please."

"Sadly, I speak it so well that I thought it was called Kohekohe. The greeting is all I mastered."

"How did you know I was Namibian my mother always tried to make it less obvious, thus Smith."

"The shape of your head and face and the dark, dark colour. I trained hundreds if not thousands of your people during the troubles there."

"My family fled here to escape the massacres. Which side were you on?"

"As it was explained to me at the time the only way to bet the winner in a three-horse race is to ride all three horses, so we trained all three sides at various times."

Wonderful people. They made the Ghurkhas look like depressives.

I didn't think it prudent to mention that they were also the most bloodthirsty bunch of butchers I ever encountered. From what I saw there were no sides, just groups of people cheerfully hacking each other to pieces over things that had happened even before the white man had set foot on the continent. Absolutely fearless soldiers though and the best close quarters fighters I had ever tangled with.

Marko, undoubtedly feeling neglected in this exchange felt the need to intervene.

"Don't fall for that old flannel. He looked you up after I spoke to him this morning."

It was as if the room froze over. The Namibian's smile faded and without turning around he softly said, "I sincerely and honestly hope for your sake that such is not the case. You were specifically instructed that nothing was to be said which identified me to anyone weren't you? If I find that my name has been mentioned anywhere in this

21

shithole, I will post your head outside your nightclub and leave your entrails for the gulls. So! Did you mention my name?"

Marko looked around pretending to smile but no-one, not even the brothers smiled back. I certainly wasn't going to help him out and the brothers were intent on examining each other for defects. The Namibians head turned painfully slowly towards Marko.

"Well did you or didn't you tell him about me?"

"Of course, I didn't. I didn't, did I?"

That last entreaty was aimed at me. Much as I wanted to target him, I wouldn't tell a lie to do it.

"Go on the three of you fuck off!! I want a word with Mr McLean in private."

Marko trooped away with the brothers dutifully falling in behind him.

"Donald, thanks for organising this I appreciate it. I'll see your mum gets something nice in the post, remember I was never here."

We all seemed a little tense standing around.

"Please Mr McLean take the blade from your pocket and sit down. We don't want you to do yourself a mischief. This is my associate Leonard Duvall. Call him Lenny!"

I hadn't fooled as many people as I had thought, but he wanted me to know that he had trusted me with the handshake. I shook hands with Lenny who treated me to a wide smile as he saw how small the blade was on my knife.

"It isn't the size that counts it's how you use it."

From somewhere behind his back he pulled a filed down machete of some kind and laid it on the table next to my knife. You could have used it to cut down a medium sized tree.

"You white boys always say that!" he said chuckling away.

"Lenny, could you guard the front door please. See no-one gets back in, and check Deedee still has the back secure. Thanks."

I sat in a different prison to the earlier trap, but he was letting me know it was still a cell. He was displaying his trust by leaving both blades where I could reach them.

"John is it all right if I call you John, I am going to rely on your discretion now. I have a problem. It is not in any way business related so you needn't worry about getting involved with criminal activity. Obviously, Marko's heavy-handed tactics have put your back up and I fully understand that.

Unfortunately, I had to ask his help for political and practical reasons. I understand from people I trust that no-one has ever said you were anything less than discreet, indeed Dai Soldier could not have been more enthusiastic about you."

Dai fucking Soldier and his recommendations again.

"Good man, Dai. He served with my cousin. Very much a man's man and a guy whose life frequently depended on making good assessments of people. His thoughts carry a lot of weight with me and what I have seen has backed that up."

Dai fucking Soldier.

"If you don't mind me asking; what did Marko tell you this morning?"

"He told me that no matter what you said, I would be working for and reporting to him."

"And what did you tell him?"

"Basically, to fuck off. I worked for and reported directly to anyone I considered a client and that he couldn't pay me enough to work for him."

"Did he threaten you?"

"Not with anything I couldn't handle."

"I'm inclined to believe you given his demeanour earlier. I understand you put Dennis in a coma a couple of years ago. Was it a fair fight?"

"It was Donald, and as far as the police are concerned, we were mugged. I never intended for him to be comatose. I only hit him twice."

My extraordinary good luck again. It has got me in more trouble than Dai fucking Soldier.

"It must take a lot of resolve to even square up to him far less beat him senseless. Both boys confirm that it was a square go by the way. I am surprised you are still walking about. They both speak very highly of you and your integrity. You must have some skills."

"They would never dare go against their mother. When she was at the hospital the ambulanceman told her that I had saved Donald's life. When he went down, he swallowed his tongue. I pulled it out. She made them both say thanks to me."

"Still I think I would want a small advantage to square up to him. A pump action shotgun perhaps. I don't think Marko has much to threaten a man of your resolve with and that's good. Fifteen years ago, I was a hooker in Bristol. You know what a hooker is don't you?"

I nodded. A hooker in his world was a good-looking young man whose job it was to find and recruit vulnerable underage girls into a life of prostitution. They

24

persuaded them to fall in love with them then steered them down into the spiral of degradation.

He had the look and the charm, no doubt he was good at it. What I was thinking though was that he must have some skills too. To go from hooker to Top Kick in fifteen years was a meteoric rise. Not a man to underestimate.

"Anyway, I was learning the ropes. Meeting at least one girl a month, when I did the unthinkable. I caught the method acting bug a bit too well and fell in love with one of the girls. She was fourteen and got pregnant. Normally this would be good news. An abortion is a bit of an accelerator on that road, but I found I didn't want to do it. She was such an innocent child with family who loved her. She really did deserve better. Most of them don't, you know.

She was a runaway to Bristol. I brought her home to Cardiff, gave her money for the child, even came over a few times to see her and our daughter but by the time she was sixteen and my daughter was two I was moving up a bit.

I had money, but any family would be vulnerable and more importantly make me vulnerable. I knocked it on the head. I did make sure they both had money though. In truth I didn't have much else to spend it on.

Only four people alive know about my daughter; me, her mother, her grandfather and now you. Understand I will do whatever is necessary to keep that number from growing is that clear! Her grandfather had to know in case anything happened that needed my help and until yesterday he hadn't contacted me for years. Yesterday her grandfather called me to tell me that my daughter, Summer, had gone missing. He wanted to know if it had anything to do with me. And thus, to you.

As far as I know no-one knows about her and therefore no-one in my world has anything to do with her being missing. No-one knows better than me that girls go missing every day for a million reasons, real and imagined. What I want you to do is find her and take her home. That is all. I will pay what you ask but in addition I will owe you a favour if you can resolve this for me. If I can fix this quickly then we can all go back to our life just as it was before.

Obviously, her mother is beside herself and expects me to use all my contacts to bring her back. This would make them both vulnerable if they are linked to me and would be a considerable embarrassment to all concerned if our connection was to come out.

I could live easily with that, but I doubt if they, or any of their family, could. I have persuaded her to give me until first thing Wednesday to find her without turning the whole city upside down. Do you think you can work on that timescale?"

"The timescale either will or won't work. I won't know until I start down the trail. Best case she is at a friend's locally and I could have her home tonight. If, however, she has run away to a big anonymous city and she has money, or access to money it could take weeks. As soon as I know you will know. For now, I will report to you at nine, morning and night, and keep you advised of where we have got to. I would expect all expenses to be reimbursed and a success fee dependent on the degree of aggravation I encounter typically five thousand pounds. Other than that, there would be no charge."

He unhesitatingly leant forward to shake my hand

and started to rise.

"Lenny will give you all the details I have, a thousand pounds to be going on with and a phone number for me which will only be live until Wednesday. If you don't have her by then you will see me again when I lay waste to this shithole."

"Please sit down again!"

Like Marko he wasn't used to being told what to do. Perhaps even more so, but he sat anyway.

"What is our cover story for here?"

He looked puzzled.

"Too many people have seen us meet, some of them will soon know I am looking for someone. Too easy a link to make if you intend to keep a secret. Also, Marko has already stuck his curious nose in, and I will be poking around his city. Too easy a question to ask what this has to do with you?"

"What do you suggest?"

"How does Lenny feel about having a sister?"

"Lenny is an orphan. His family were killed in a house fire a fair few years ago now. Anyone who knows him, knows that. You will see that Summer is a very pale brown. Her mum is white, through and through. One of the attractions. Snow White I used to call her."

He thought a long time then answered.

"Deedee, my driver, has two brothers. Building contractors, always working all over. They're a couple of years younger than me but that just makes it more plausible. Deedee's long-lost niece then. It would take weeks to find and ask the boys about it. I'll find them work in Glasgow or somewhere for a couple of months. Hopefully it will be forgotten by then.

I see that you are the man for the job. So! I am here because my best friend's niece is missing, and I am paying for an investigator to help find her. That would make sense. Something and nothing, and nothing to do with the business. Great thinking already!"

"Not missing though, just ran away from home after a fight with her mother. Less dramatic."

"Speaking of background, is there any chance Summer has run away to look for you. Just about the right age to wonder about her dad?"

"Not that I can think of unless her mother has let some things slip. Not as far as I know but I will ask."

"No leave that to me! Just let her mother know I will be in touch this afternoon and that she should trust me. I presume the information is all with Lenny?"

He stood and we shook hands again. He nodded firmly as if to seal the deal and was gone out the back door presumably to brief Deedee on his role. Lenny appeared up the stairs and handed me an envelope.

"There is a grand in cash in there and God knows what else. I don't know what you're doing but good luck. Sonny has been as miserable as fuck since last night. I have written my number on the envelope. If that arsehole Harpo, or whatever, gives you any trouble let me know. I've done harder shits than him before breakfast."

We both smiled at his jokes and nodded firmly. It was infectious, and then he too was off out the back door remembering to pick up his machete and giving my knife a pitying look, on the way out. We both laughed again. Regular comedian that boy. As soon as he had gone the Chan army appeared and ushered me out the front door. It obviously wasn't open yet for the likes of me.

THREE

The Inspector

After detailed consideration taking less than a second, I decided that my first move would be another pint in The Packet. The first one had sharpened me up enough to want, rather than need, a second, and all that talking was thirsty work. I had to have a think anyway, and The Packet was as good as anywhere. It was almost late enough that I could have used the front door but instead I made my way to the tradesman's entrance and, using the secret knock, made my way into the busy bar.

The Wig glanced up and pulled me a pint without me having to ask. He motioned with a dumpy tumbler towards the optic, but I reluctantly shook my head. He shrugged. He had not often seen me refuse strong drink, particularly on a Sunday morning, but it appeared I was going to be a busy boy today if I was going to have anything to report by nine tonight. Better to keep a clearish head, besides I could still feel the glow of last night's rum pounding through my body.

"There's a fair few free drinks for you in the tap after last night."

I think he thought I was skint, that being the only reason I would refuse a drink.

I put the envelope on the stool next to me away

from prying eyes and reached in. Top of the pile was a wad of money. I moved behind the stool as if to sit down and having blocked anyone's view I pulled out a handful and casually stuck the notes into my pocket. As the last drips bled into my pint, I balled up the notes in my pocket until they were hidden in my fist. As the Wig placed my pint in front of me, I reached over to shake his hand with both of mine. The notes vanished quicker than any street magician would have been able to manage, and a curt nod of thanks exchanged.

I couldn't say for certain what had happened, and I was there, so I was confident no-one else could have seen it. The last thing I needed was a reputation for being skint. Who would ever trust me to pay them for information if that got about? In this part of the world reputations followed you about forever regardless of how they were acquired. No-one ever mentioned my considerable good luck when telling stories about me.

I took my seat at the bar with my back to the domino players, this time not to avoid their company but rather their prying eyes. The remains of the wad of money went quickly into my pocket and I pulled the top sheet from the envelope and placed both on the bar where no-one could see. What faced me was a standard school photo of one of the most beautiful young women I have ever seen.

Coffee coloured, flawless complexion and perfect shining teeth topped off by the kind of wide innocent brown eyes with a hint of mischief you see in a host of full-face adverts in every shiny magazine I have ever read in the doctor's waiting room. There certainly weren't any girls like this when I was at secondary school even amongst the staff. If this girl was missing, she could easily be in deep trouble, that was for sure.

I turned the photo over and printed in a neat script were the details I needed;

SUMMER GREGOR
D.O.B. 19.07.05
ADDRESS THE DOWNS, CARDIFF
SCHOOL HOWELLS SCHOOL FOR GIRLS, CARDIFF
VODAFONE CONTRACT
 NUMBER TEXTED TO YOU
 MOTHER SUSANNAH (SUSIE) GREGOR
ALSO VODAFONE CONTRACT
NUMBER TEXTED TO YOU
MOTHER EXPECTING A CALL. BOTH LIVE WITH
STEP-FATHER, GARY.
 REAL GRANDMOTHER DECEASED (SUICIDE) 2012

I turned it back over to look again at that face when the photo and the envelope both magically vanished under the Wig's tea-towel and were spirited under the bar with barely a flick of the wrist. I looked round a second before two familiar figures sat down without ceremony on either side of me, carefully hemming me in.

"Alright John, early start today?"

"Detective Inspector how are you. I could say the same of you. Quiet night last night was it?"

"My big bird here tells me you have had a busy morning. I hoped to have a word with your new partners in crime."

He added a particularly unnecessary emphasis on the final phrase. The entire pub seemed suddenly quiet as the regulars tried hard to listen without appearing to notice what was happening. Their efforts were thwarted when Elvis singing the Wonder of You boomed out of the jukebox indicating that it was now officially opening time. I winked my appreciation to the Wig.

The "big bird "he was referring to was wedged on my left side and was Detective Sergeant Sandra Evans widely known as Sandy because of her name and her short fair hair. I doubt she was pleased at being called a bird, but she loyally stayed silent and squeezed into me a little more than was strictly necessary.

I had coached her women's rugby side for a while now and still refereed many of their matches. I knew she could be a lot more brutal than the gentle squeezing she was currently giving me. You don't successfully police one of the roughest stations in Wales without being able to handle yourself.

"What can I do for you?"

"I hear things, you know. I hear you were spending money like water last night. I hear you met with the biggest gangster in Cardiff and one of the biggest outside of London this morning. What do you think, I think?"

So much for secret meetings. Someone in Marko's team had a tunnel into the police it seemed. Or Chan's team. Or a passer-by with a good knowledge of who's who.

"Buy me a drink and I'll tell you all about it over there!"

I pointed to the far corner table I had been using earlier. My empty pint tumbler still stood there like a friendless alcoholic in a packed pub. Exactly how I felt now surrounded by the police.

"I'll get you a drink, I'm guessing police officers don't have to pay for drinks in a pub as busy as this a minute after it is supposed to open."

The Wig opened his mouth to protest and cause trouble for himself. No doubt he was about to point out that most of his out-of-hours custom were officers from the nearby station, but I stopped him with a glance and a nod to put the drinks on my bill.

He was almost at the table before us with the three drinks, another pint for me, I would have to be careful, a large expensive smelling island whisky for the inspector and a disgusting coloured sugar filled soft drink for the sergeant.

"First of all, these drinks are on me as part of my on-going celebration of the successful completion of a very lucrative case last week, as were the drinks I bought for my friends last night.

Second, Marko put a bit of business my way this morning in the sense that one of his associates needed an investigator to look for the niece of his driver who lives in Cardiff and has run away from home following a fight with her mother. I did not know either of them, and there is certainly no suggestion that it in any way involves criminal activity.

Finally, in twelve or so years operating in this area I have never been involved in any criminal activity and I resent any thought that I would be. I have done both of you personal favours, which have enhanced your professional standing. I did this without any thought of payment or quid pro quo. In your case Inspector I investigated the infidelity of one of your junior officers and resolved the matter without anyone's indiscretions coming to light to the Professional Standards Board."

Sandy Evans nearly spat her drink all over me. It

33

was common knowledge in the Docks Station that Chief Inspector Davies had been shagging the custody sergeant while her man was on traffic. The poor man had hired me to find out what was happening and had accepted my assurances that whilst I could prove with hotel and meal receipts what had been going on, I was unable to provide CCTV or photographic images of her partner or partners without spending a lot more money than he was paying me.

As far as I heard they had agreed an amicable divorce and he was now living happily with a schoolteacher somewhere in North Wales. His ex was still the custody Sergeant down the road from where we sat.

The Inspector gave me what can only be described as an old-fashioned look, but discretion curtailed his curiosity.

"Maybe so, but Lenny Duvall is a very serious player and a dangerous, dangerous man. We wouldn't want him or his type moving into Cardiff. The story is he has killed at least six men we know of."

So not Marko or Chan then, just some local toe rag with a good memory and quick wit looking to earn some brownie points.

"As I said, his driver's niece is a fourteen-year old runaway and he wants to know she is alright."

"Who would she be then?"

"Summer Gregor from the Downs. Date of birth nineteen seven oh five missing from Howells school since Friday evening. Had a fight with her mum about boys and curfews that morning. Almost certainly at a friend's house till it blows over."

He twitched his head to Sandy, and she rose and walked outside the pub already thumbing her mobile. Sent away to check.

"And you're sure that is all this is?"

"Certain."

I swigged from my pint after all the talking and to prevent him asking more questions. It was interesting that he thought Lenny was the top boy. Sonny was a very careful man indeed if he wasn't on the police radar despite occupying such a prominent role.

Sandy walked back with the kind of swagger all good back row forwards have. A kind of athletic indifference to the worries of the masses, sure in the knowledge that repeated applications of brute force could eventually overcome any obstacle.

"Reported at twelve fourteen yesterday, Inspector. Mum thought she was at a planned sleepover with a friend thus the late reporting. Assessed as low risk, no vulnerabilities and with ample resources available to her. Apparently, she contacted her mother before we arrived to say she was safe and well. Uniform left it to see if she would turn up over the weekend. Marked for reassessment and follow up tomorrow morning when her school would be open and school friends would be available for information interviews."

The Chief Inspector swallowed his whisky a lot easier than he had swallowed my lies and turned in hope of a refill. The Wig studiously ignored him until I nodded over and indicated just to bring the one drink. My pint was almost gone but I had a busy day ahead and was already tired from my exertions last night.

"Well cheers guys. If that's all I'm afraid I will have to be off. Lots to do. Incidentally if any of your guys find a brown leather size ten brogue, right foot, anywhere nearby its mine. Just leave it behind the bar. There is a reward."

"It will be my size ten they'll find up your arse if I find out you're pulling my tadger about all of this."

He couldn't hide his disdain. Probably still smarting from the crack about his mistress. Didn't stop him glugging the whisky I was paying for though. Always a man for the last word. As they both left the sergeant broke ranks and turned back as if she had left something behind.

"I'll text you her mobile number later. Usual reward if you can find it."

I was learning from the Wig. My lips hardly moved. Sandy nodded and wagged her finger at me as if making a final point. Well done her.

I looked at the last inch of my pint, calculated the level of my on-going dehydration and thought one more won't make much difference and headed to the bar to round off my latest tab.

As my pint arrived, unasked for, I would add in my defence, it brought with it some thirty pounds worth of change. I regarded the lagers appearance as an omen and set about it as if I were enjoying it.

"That's us square!" said Stevie, his head tilting away from me and his lips not moving. "You gave me forty quid too much earlier."

God bless an honest barman. My envelope was also returned by the reverse of the disappearing trick it had performed earlier, and just as imperceptibly.

"Cheers Stevie. Make this my last, work to do, and on a Sunday as well!"

"You might need this then."

He did his magicians distraction again, looking at

the next customer along the bar, pointing at the gantry whilst slipping my phone and battery on top of the folder.

"I took that off you last night. You were trying to phone your kids. You can do a lot more damage with one of those things than you can with a gun if you're not careful!! You should leave it at home if you're out drinking."

I nodded my thanks and smiled my acknowledgement of the truth of his remarks. Twelve years since they had last spoken to me and that pain ate away at me every day. Pain I knew the drink couldn't cure; but it never stopped me trying. Pain I knew would not have been helped by a drunken early morning phone call. I had tried often enough sober to know better than that.

FOUR

The Volunteer

Retiring to my corner behind the fireplace, well away from prying eyes and ears, I put my phone back together and cleared the call log so I wouldn't have to look at who else I had called. Ignorance is indeed bliss, especially after an alcohol inspired blackout. Ignoring almost all the messages I opened the only one from an unknown number. As promised there were the mobile numbers. I called the mother's number after forwarding the girl's to the Sergeant.

While waiting to be connected I planned my day. I had three targets today;

One: get as much information as possible about her last day. I would be unlikely to be able to speak to many of her school mates until tomorrow so today concentrate on her family and close friends, particularly the one she was supposed to be staying with.

Two: access her peripherals; Facebook, Snapchat any WhatsApp groups etc. so find or trace her phone and collect her laptop from her home.

Three: Sunday is my bread and butter business day so whatever else I had to be back in the office and sober (ish) by four o'clock to allocate the next week's work to my satellite investigators.

"Hello, Ms. Gregor. My name is John McLean and I have been retained to find your daughter Summer."

If it was possible to hear disappointment and despondency in just the breathing over a telephone, I could hear it now. She was virtually sobbing. When number unknown came up on her screen, she must have thought it was her daughter, or someone with very bad news about her daughter. All in all, she was dealing with the disappointment and relief well, I thought.

"I was wondering if it would be possible to see you sometime today, preferably sooner rather than later?"

"Is that all he is doing? Retaining you!!! Why isn't he turning this city upside down to find her? How will you find her? How many men have you got out looking?"

Her questions were coming in a hysterical torrent, rising in pitch and volume as her pent-up tension was finally finding an outlet. I let her run on for a bit whilst saving her number as Snow White in my phone. All my clients get code names just in case I lose my phone.

"If I could just come and see you, we could go over all this."

Time was becoming precious for me and I hated a busy Sunday almost as much as I hated a quiet one.

"I don't want any thugs turning up at my door thanks. I can meet you in the leisure club at the St. David's Hotel if you know where that is?"

Patronising cow making assumptions about me just because of my accent but once again my luck was in.

"I can be there in two minutes, thanks. I have often stayed there. Could you bring Summer's laptop and any spare phones she may have with you please?"

39

"I can't be there for at least half an hour. Can we say one o'clock then. I will be bringing my stepfather with me if that's all right?"

"No problem. See you there at one. Please remember the laptop etc. I'll be sat on the blue stools at the bar and probably the only one drinking bottled Peroni."

I hung up before she could think of anything else to ask me. During our conversation some bastard had snuck up and drank most of my pint. I was pondering how to deal with this dilemma; an inch of pint and forty minutes to kill, when a full pint was magicked in front of me.

"Compliments of the Binman."

His head moving at a very unusual angle to indicate where the said gentleman was sitting.

"Cheers Stevie. Tell him thanks."

I lifted the glass and leaned around the fireplace to salute the Binman who smiled courteously back and tilted his rum towards me. The Binman had never worked for the council neither was his name a reference to the fact that he would eat anything no matter how out of date or mouldy. No, he was called the Binman because as soon as he heard you were throwing something out, he asked if he could have it for his house.

God knew what size his house was, but he had had four three-piece suites and six bed mattresses that I knew about not to mention the countless tables, chairs and ornaments over the years.

I must have been desperate for company to have been buying him drinks last night.

Dilemma resolved I closed my eyes and considered where a fifteen-year old girl might run to. Some of the answers were quite sweet and naïve but some were very dark and disturbing indeed. I was guessing the family, such as they were, could deal with the sweet and naïve solutions leaving me with only the dark and disturbing. Still that was where I lived most of the time, in the dark.

My thoughts were drifting back to a gentle doze when I sensed rather than felt or heard someone sit opposite me. Not wishing to appear startled I slowly opened my eyes.

"That was quick Sandy. Quiet day?"

"Thought you were asleep for a minute there."

She smiled. it was a lovely smile not unlike that of a crocodile looking at his dinner. She had a folded sheet of paper in her hand, which she passed to me with no pretence or artifice. Nothing could have looked less suspicious although she took care to block anyone's view of the transfer with her broad back. I glanced at the map with its three shaded circles representing mobile relay towers. I laughed and placed it in my folder.

"It helped having the provider and of course it is an official enquiry with a case number so there was no need for any back doors or favours and of course the DI has gone back home, or to the golf course so no problem really. I have asked for a call and message history. Call history tomorrow, message later in the week. Will be quicker if the misspers is upgraded tomorrow of course. Lots of flats in that part of Canton. It hasn't moved since Friday evening."

Three "of courses" in the same sentence. Justifying helping me to herself, of course.

"I'll square you up at training on Tuesday if that's okay."

"No problem! Just don't forget."

And she was away as quietly and unobtrusively as

someone her size could be. So much for the expense's monies, almost gone already, less than an hour after getting them. A record, even for me.

I looked at my watch. I had half an hour until my meeting with the mother, I glanced again at the map and figured I could be there and back in twenty minutes. Worth a quick shot at being upgraded from thug to hero.

One of the many great things about The Packet is that taxis queue up at the back door especially for my convenience. I jumped in one and asked to be taken to the heart of those three shaded circles. You don't get many idiots going to her school and what I thought she had done was very clever indeed. I was betting her phone wasn't currently in any flat in Canton.

I thought I knew exactly where to find it,

"The Chapter please Driver; front entrance."

I knew I was making assumptions about young Summer but given her stockbroker address and her attendance at the most expensive school in Wales it was a fair bet that her phone would be as modern, not to say trendy, as possible. It had probably set someone back two or three months of a working man's wages.

Also, like every teenager I knew; okay I didn't really know any, but I had heard about enough of them from their parents. I had certainly witnessed countless of them being all but knocked down whilst glued to their phones. I was confident her whole life was in and on there.

She would have seen enough American television to realise that phones could be traced and tracked. Rather than ditch her most precious possession she had rather parked it somewhere safe to retrieve later, when events had calmed down a bit.

Either that or her cold and decaying body was lying on top of it in some derelict back garden or enclosed lane in the Canton area. My success of yesterday had imbued me with an optimism I rarely felt and even more seldom acted upon. Either that or the rum in my system had bounced back from bleak despair to unwarranted hope. Whichever it was it was worth a tenner in a taxi to check.

The Sunday traffic was light, and we were at the front of the Chapter Arts Centre and Performance Space in under ten minutes. A magnificent old red brick structure, probably a former school, repurposed at enormous public and lottery expense into the kind of trendy arts venue that apparently no British city could now be without. They had managed fine without them for centuries until the deep, deep well of lottery monies eventually found their home in this herd of white elephants.

It was here that the slightly better off came to socialise in the giant bar and coffee lounge. Children were welcome as, thankfully, were aspiring alcoholics. I had drunk myself senseless in here on many an occasion during my early years in Cardiff, in the old bar, before the refurbishment of the building and the gentrification of Cardiff. It had been one of the few places where it was not just acceptable, but de rigeur, to be seen drinking the eight per cent Belgian lager. Perhaps not in the quantities I consumed, but still acceptable, nonetheless.

There was a huge footfall of traffic through the venue from the galleries, cinemas, theatres, dance classes, nurseries and just general family socialising. An ideal place for a fourteen-year-old to sit, playing with her phone and not seem remarkable or even memorable. Even one as attractive as Summer.

Despite what I said earlier I was out of luck today. Fiona, who usually manned the box office, which doubled as a reception was not on duty. A fellow Caledonian, we had socialised a few times without commitment over the years and I was firmly of the delusion that she would have been putty in my hands had she been there.

Instead I got the dreaded weekend volunteer. A man filling his retirement hours until his death with the dream that, by mixing with younger more interesting artists, he was making himself younger and more interesting. Today he only seemed more stressed and grumpier.

I turned my smile down a good two or three notches from lady killer to simple man of the world conspiratorial.

"Hi, I was wondering if my niece's phone was handed in on Friday. It is a top of the range model and here was the last place she remembers using it. My brother in law has grounded her and her only hope of seeing daylight again is if I find it."

Re-organising his face to show me how painful thinking was for him he paused for quite a while.

"Lost property can only be dealt with by the duty manager. She would be too busy to accommodate you just now, its Sunday lunchtime you see. Perhaps if you came back later, or even tomorrow."

Three excuses not to do it and two alternatives, which would be after he had left. The perennial song of the Sunday volunteer. I pantomimed looking around me. The box office and reception areas were entirely bereft of clients. The bar and dining areas on the other hand looked as though there had been a fire drill in a four-storey

44

sweatshop.

"I wouldn't want to disturb her, but it is kind of urgent. If I don't find it here, I am going to have to visit about a hundred shops in the St. David's centre. Could you please check if there was even a phone handed in?"

A further realignment of his features, which seemed to involve rotating his dentures while he considered this.

"There is so much stuff back there. I wouldn't know where to begin and I can't leave here in case there is a safety emergency see."

Progress indeed. Only three excuses on their own that time and a nugget of intelligence. Sometimes I think that I do myself a disservice by not calling myself a detective. Back there could only mean the small back room behind him. The door wasn't even closed.

"What if I call her number and we can see if it rings?"

He gave every appearance of attempting a particularly difficult calculus problem in his head.

"Worth a try, I suppose!"

I pressed the keys on my phone and struggled to hear the ringtone against the clatter of cutlery and hum of conversation. I struggled in vain for there was nothing to hear.

Relieved at having to do nothing the volunteer smiled ruefully but in a particularly irritating self-satisfied way.

"Doesn't look as if it is here."

I looked at my phone and her mobile showed as ringing out. It had been worth a try but maybe I wasn't as lucky as I was feeling. I was just about to hang up when my detective light switched on. She was cleverer that I was, or at least as I was that morning. She would have turned the ring and vibrate options off. Her phone would have been pinging away otherwise from all the frantic calls looking for her.

"Could you look and see if there is a phone lighting up in there?"

Before he could smirk his way to a refusal a tiny hand "accidentally" touched+ my arse. Only one man there would approach me in such a way but for the life of me I couldn't remember his name.

He pirouetted round in front of me like the dancer he aspired to be.

"Johnny my boy, too busy to come up and see me?"

His eyeliner and mascara had smudged a little in the heat and bustle of the lunchtime service. What was his bloody name? I had got him in to meet Ronnie Spector a couple of years ago. I think he envied her make up. Ever since he had served me up a free drink in here under the guise of a taster.

"Martin! How are you?"

It just came to me. Sometimes my brain just needs the added pressure before it kicks into gear.

"Too busy for me at least. It's hard to enjoy a drink when you're surrounded by bairns."

"What brings you in then?"

"My niece thinks she left her phone here on Friday. I was just looking for it. I think it is in the back there."

He looked at me and gave me a knowing wink. I hated that everyone always seemed to know more about me than I did.

"I didn't know you had family down here John. Dial the number and I'll see if I can find it."

He disappeared through the door before I could think of another plausible lie. He could have read the paper front to back for all the difference it would have made. I would have to up my game. I was getting too old to do this when tired; or indeed, after four or five pints.

I thumbed the redial logo and within seconds Martin was back with a thin gold wafer in his hand.

"This would be it then."

I hung up and immediately the screen went off.

The volunteer had had enough of this.

"How can you prove it is your niece's?"

I turned my phone to show him the photo of Summer I had put on my phone to show witnesses.

Martin triumphantly turned the phone in his hand to show a mother/daughter screensaver, which was clearly the same girl.

To avoid doubt I quickly took the phone from Martin and thanked everyone profusely hoping for a smart exit.

Martin walked out with me.

"I presume this is all above board John. I love my job here and that old bastard would love nothing better than dobbing me in."

"Believe me Marty, there will be no comeback on this. Simply a lost phone. You couldn't imagine how much it would have cost to replace. We'll have a few drinks in the week to thank you mate."

I rushed to jump into a taxi that was depositing fares at the front door.

"See you in the week, promise!"

I held my prize tight and flicked the button to open the screen. The same stunningly beautiful face stared back at me as in the school photo. At first glance it appeared to me there was a hint of defiance in the tilt of the chin and set of the eyes that was not there in the school photo. Must be a teenage girl thing.

Alongside her was an immaculately coiffed and made up woman of stunning Scandinavian looks. Summer would look beautiful alongside anyone, but beside this woman she appeared almost ordinary. Perhaps that would explain the defiance. No wonder even Sonny's heart had melted at this woman. She looked no older than twenty now. If it wasn't for the skin tones and hair colour, they could easily be sisters. Now I was really looking forward to meeting her.

Sadly, the phone also had the latest facial recognition security software, so I wasn't going to be able to access it easily, or even today. Theresa, my Cheltenham operative, had worked at GCHQ and had access to a program to open any mobile but she kept it a closely guarded secret. I was happy to accommodate this, as it kept me one step removed from any law breaking. Besides I was reasonably certain it was her husband who carried out the procedure.

Summer had 157 missed calls and 87 texts to open as well as innumerable notifications. If all else failed today I could simply wait in the Chapter for her to appear to claim her phone back. If she intended to ditch it, it would have been in a bin somewhere. She would be back, if only to access those vital notifications she just couldn't live without. At least now I had a medium-term plan to find her, now to work on the short term.

"Mount Stuart Square, please driver, down the Bay!"

Never take any chances with a Cardiff taxi driver; you could easily end up heading gaily down the motorway in completely the wrong direction if you didn't let them know you had a rough idea of where you were headed. Particularly if you sounded like a tourist. Fair game then, apparently.

Less than twenty pounds and I had her phone and would be early for my appointment. If Snow White wasn't impressed by that then God knows what would impress her and with a face like hers, I certainly wanted to impress her. Life should have taught me that nothing good ever comes from trying to impress others.

A quick stop into the office to log the expenses which were swiftly mounting up and put a second SIM card into my phone and a five-minute stroll around the corner and still early for the meeting. I had been using discreet SIM cards in my phone for each case since I had first interviewed Theresa for her job.

She had blithely told me of all the information which could be taken by the government or phone companies from a simple phone number. It was genuinely frightening. It also let me keep a discreet log of my activities on any case, which I could freely show without embarrassment to the client. The embarrassing or illegal contacts all went on my personal number.

FIVE

The Boxer

My day was shaping up as a particularly busy one, so I had contented myself with a small bottle of Peroni, being as close to low alcohol drink as I got on a weekend. I was settled on a stool at the bar enjoying the view, both across the water and the constant stream of well-off, well-groomed and very well–toned bodies on display in a procession to the gym, or fitness and wellbeing centre.

I wondered why they looked as immaculate coming out as they had going in. Another of life's many mysteries, which eluded me. I was just thinking that I should spend more time here when I saw them arrive. Walking briskly along outside the plate glass windows, the two of them, in their way, greatly enhancing the view.

She was smaller than I had imagined but exquisitely proportioned. Without her expensively styled near white hair she would have drawn the eye even in this roomful of sculpted mannequins. With the spotlight of her hair everyone in the bar watched her arrive. Some more obviously than others. Some even gave up on admiring their reflections to cast an envious glance her way.

Her companion was no less impressive. Six foot plus of grace and elegance, star of innumerable TV game and panel shows, still as fit and muscular as he had been when he was cruiserweight champion of the world. Not the whole world, of course, just one or two of the less well-known alphabetti spaghetti world titles, but impressive enough for a Cardiff lad.

His unmarked features gave no hint as to his former profession and he was without question as handsome in the flesh as he appeared on TV. His dockland mongrel heritage had gifted him perfect set of planes, angles and cheekbones. African certainly, but with a hint of the Malay around the eyes; the greatest visual gift given to him by the Cardiff Irish grandmother who had raised him, piercing blue grey eyes. They shone out from his mocha features and made his image mesmerising in close-up.

They both hesitated at the door before easily picking me out as the only customer sat at the bar. There was no chance of this being a private meeting. Every eye in the room followed them to me with more than a few wondering why this gilded couple were meeting a random scruffbag who was drinking alcohol near the gym.

I should have been more switched on earlier and foreseen this happening. It had been a long night and eventful morning but even so I should not have been making mistakes like this. Age was creeping up on me and never more so than when surrounded by such bright young things as these.

The Champ draped a protective southpaw arm around her shoulders and reached forward with his right.

"Gary Gregor. I am Summer's grandfather and

Susie's father."

Despite the obvious affectation of his mock humility, he clearly expected to be recognised. So, I replied as only a Scotsman can.

"I recognise you from somewhere, can't think where. Do you drink in the Docks Conservative Club?"

The barman spoiled our stare off by not letting it develop. I don't suppose you get to work in a five-star hotel without people skills.

"What will it be Mr. Gregor, the usual?"

He reluctantly tore his stare away from me to reply to the barman's adoring gaze.

"Not today thanks Tony, haven't been training yet. Just two green teas for us and another Peroni for Mister uhm"

I deliberately didn't fill the space he was leaving. There was something about his pristine sense of entitlement I didn't take to. Thinking of it I had never liked good-looking men any time in my life. Thank God I wasn't the jealous type.

"Why don't we sit over there?" I said, pointing to the most remote table away at the back of the room and up some stairs to a kind of mezzanine. I had to salvage some vestige of privacy for us now that there was no hope of secrecy.

I strode away before he could respond leaving him to follow or stand impotently at the bar. I could see in the bar back mirror that he didn't like being told what to do. How the fuck did a nobody from Splott get to have such a sense of entitlement and privilege?

Gary "The Ghost" Gregor was one of the three great drunk man myths of Cardiff. Having passed many a working afternoon in various hostelries over the last twelve years I had heard them all. Depending on the age and build of the drinker, Cardiff pubs were filled, usually in the afternoons, by guys in three categories;

The older fatter guys tended all to have been capped by Wales schoolboys at rugby and kept any number of famous household names out of the team before their careers were cut short by injury or rugby politics. There tended to be a huge herd of these as they spanned an enormous age range.

Then there were the younger fitter drinkers, usually in dead-end jobs, working shifts, so free to pursue afternoons in the pub. These had all played football with / against Gareth Bale and had been told by schoolteachers / scouts / managers that they were a much better player than him. By my reckoning Bale must have played every day for ten years to have played against all these guys.

Strangely their careers too had been curtailed by an untimely injury just as they were about to sign professional contracts with academies all over England, except for one guy who had become more and more adamant that Barcelona had wanted him to sign.

Finally, there was the group between those two who had battered Gary Gregor at school, after school or even as an amateur. These tales persisted despite the well-documented fact that Gary had never lost an amateur fight. Like Bale, Gregor must have had little time left for educational work being totally involved in umpteen fights a day especially since he seemed to have lost all of them.

Curiously, this group of fantasists looked as if they may have fought him, as almost to a man, they had faces disfigured by too many fistly collisions. Either that or resorted too quickly to fisticuffs when their stories were challenged.

In any event everyone knew him and clearly, he was used to them bowing before him. The sight of my back moving away from him irritated him and I drew childish pleasure from that. Having been left no choice he virtually pushed Snow White ahead of him as he followed me. He had enough control to ask, "Could you bring those over please, Tony? Put them on my account."

To everyone else it appeared to be a pleasant request dispensed with his usual TV charming smile. My trained ear heard the gritted teeth behind the smile. That just made me smile all the wider. It must be exhausting having to be personable all the time. I couldn't even manage its cousin, pleasant, for any more than half an hour at a time; and often that was a stretch.

Still he wasn't my client to worry about. There was something I just couldn't like about a man who smiled at me. Give me a man who laughed at me, any day.

Somewhat spitefully, I chose a small corner table for two, right at the back of the mezzanine. As first to arrive I took the corner seat so I could watch the room and make sure we were not overheard. This gave Gregor the problem of how to courteously seat Snow White in the one available chair yet still leave room at the table for himself.

A lesser man would have floundered, but I guess his lifetime of charm lessons had taught him how to deal with boorish hosts. Instead of casting about for staff help or standing around like a loose thread, he simply pulled the adjacent table along and sat next to his daughter facing me, smiling again.

I thought it was time to make another effort to take

charge of this meeting, hopefully a better effort than my stunt with the table.

"Mrs. Gregor, first of all let me assure…"

"Mizz."

"Sorry!"

"Mizz. Mizz Gregor. I have never married."

I thought briefly of the joke reply that I had heard her fine I was just sorry; but looking closely I could see how troubled she was. Her eyes were strained and slightly bloodshot and the muscles at the corners of her mouth were rigid with tension. Despite that, this was the face of a woman I desperately wanted to please. I wanted to see how much more attractive she would be with those lips and eyes smiling at me, though I could not imagine how.

"Mizz Gregor"

I added the extra zeds for emphasis

"This morning at around twelve I was instructed by a Mr. Sunday Smith …"

She lifted her head to speak;

"It would be quicker if you let me finish. I will be happy to answer questions later!"

My best schoolteacher voice. Mr. MacDougal would have been proud of me, it sounded just like him.

"I was just going to say that Sonny must really trust you. Not many people know his real name."

"I was instructed to find your daughter Summer Gregor who has been missing from your home since Friday, possibly Friday morning, perhaps the evening. Mr. Smith gave me the autobiography and a recent school photo of Summer."

It was Gregor's turn to twitch. Not much but enough to catch my trained eye. He didn't know about the

55

photo I thought.

I stopped speaking as an elaborate tray of green tea and Peroni was presented to our table. She went to speak but a gentle purse of my lips indicated to her to keep quiet, which she did. I was absurdly pleased that she was watching my lips. Probably not with the same thoughts I had watching hers though.

"Add a drink on for yourself, Tony, thanks."

Ever the charmer, friend to everyone, always buys a drink. I briefly wondered where all this resentment was coming from. Was I jealous because she was squeezing his hand on the table for comfort? Or was it just my usual lager fuelled bitterness and anger at the world in general kicking in a wee bit early? I would have to watch that. Whilst reflecting on the need to watch my drinking I quickly downed the bottom half of my Peroni to allow the bottle to be whisked away. I didn't want more waiting staff interrupting us.

Resisting the need to belch in front of her, it would have appeared uncouth. I attempted to continue, "Bit early in the day for that is it not? How will you be able to drive after two of those?"

"I won't, but then again as I don't own a car it's a bit less of a problem."

"I tried to look you up. You are not a detective. You are not even a former policeman. You are just one of Sonny's cheap thugs. This whole thing is a waste of time. I told Susie we were wasting our time. Let's go!"

He stood dramatically to leave. I was heartened that Susie didn't move. He decided to assert his dominance from the standing position by poking the air with his finger.

"If anything happens to Summer, make no mistake,

I will find you and see that you get what's coming to you. You and all your bloody gangster crew."

I dreamt briefly of just reaching across and snapping his finger between the second and third joint. I saved that dream for another day and simply looked at him with deliberately dead eyes and levelled my voice.

"Understand this Mr. Gregor, when you were younger and fitter you spent your days playing pit a pat with your father, hitting soft pads with gloved hands. At that exact same time, I was learning from world-renowned experts ten different ways to kill a man with a sharpened stick! I continued that education for twenty years. I have never fought a man to knock him out or bloody his nose I have been trained by the very best to fight to kill and to win. I have killed far more men than you have fought so why don't you stop showing off and go and sit at the bar. Mizz Gregor and I have some critically important business to attend to."

I deliberately turned away from him but continued to watch his reflection in the plate glass. If he had made one move towards me, I wouldn't have hesitated to pull his outstretched arm towards me and snap it at the elbow.

With the table between us there would have been nothing he could have done to stop me. I was appalled that part of me wanted this to happen. I was never usually so aggressive. Time to cut back on the rum and imported beers I thought.

"Please wait over there, Dad. All that matters is Summer. I just want to get her home. Please!"

Trying his best to muster some dignity he turned on his heel and walked down the steps towards the bar. Aware that he had his usual audience he smiled broadly and ordered a smoothie in a loud voice from a long way off. Once you could fake sincerity, I supposed nothing on TV was out of reach. As he walked away, I was reminded of my father's verdict on him as a boxer.

"Too fond of his good looks, that boy. If you're going to hurt the best sometimes you have to let them hurt you first."

That was why he was named "The Ghost" and no doubt why he had never won any of the serious titles. Couldn't risk anyone damaging that face. I was smiling about the thoughts of my dad, but a glance showed me she thought I was smirking at this easy victory.

"I'm sorry. I have never seen him behave like that. He is just so worried about Summer. He adores her."

The use of her daughter's name brought a single tear overflowing down her cheek. I had never felt more like cuddling, or indeed cwtching as my new Cardiff vocabulary proclaimed, someone for many years. I was getting softer as I got older. Better get back to business.

"Did you bring her stuff with you?"

Stuff eh? Ever a technical genius I decided not to blind her with too much jargon. Besides, I did not know what else to call the electronic paraphernalia of your modern teenager. It seemed to change every year to a new must have gadget.

"Do you think you will find her?"

The naked desperation of her plea touched me in a place I had forgotten existed. My heart.

"Is she in danger because of Sonny?"

"Is it a matter of money because we can pay?"

"You have no idea what it is like. I can't tell you how often I have called her. There is no reply."

"Have you tried to call her? Perhaps it just us she is avoiding?"

I raised my hand to halt her flow. People were noticing, and she was getting louder as the questions spewed from her. Dreads she had been saving for a couple of days came flowing out uncensored by thought.

"Please let me speak it would be easier and the last thing we need is people noticing how upset you are."

To her credit she did not look round to see who was noticing, neither did she move to wipe away the tear tracks on her face. Then again, I doubted she was giving me any credit for seating her where no one could see her. Still I had at least stayed the tide for a moment and dived quickly in to give her time to compose herself.

"Mr. Smith has asked that I keep you fully informed of my progress so if you could just listen for a moment. As of now I am reasonably confident that Summer is either still in Cardiff or intends to return here soon.

I am also reasonably confident that whatever she is doing is of her own free will and not acting under any duress and is therefore very unlikely to be in any way connected to Mr. Smith's business interests."

I held my hand up again as she gulped a breath to intervene.

"I have undertaken to report to Mr. Smith at nine o'clock tonight and twelve-hourly thereafter and I will not be reporting anything to him that I have not previously made you aware of. I have only one instruction from him; to find Summer and return her safely home. There is no limit to the resources available to me and I must do all that is necessary to achieve that aim. If I am unsuccessful by Wednesday at nine o'clock in the morning, Mr. Smith will try other tactics using the resources of his business empire but for the moment I am to try and keep the matter low key and resolve it quickly. Is all that clear?"

She sniffed and nodded together and before she could speak, I held up my hand again.

"I was instructed in this matter less than an hour ago. I have discovered where and when you reported her missing to the police and am aware that they will take no further action until school reconvenes tomorrow when, if they have the resources available, they may investigate her disappearance further. No doubt your stepfather would be able to exert enough influence to ensure this happens though I have to warn you that without any evidence of foul play it is extremely unlikely that they will make much of an effort to find a runaway teenager regardless of what they tell you."

She was learning by now and I didn't have to hold my hand up. She simply opened and closed her mouth with an enchanting popping noise, not unlike a small baby.

"I know that you have probably called Summer around one hundred and twenty times because I know she had one hundred and thirty-nine missed calls, two of them were from me, a couple no doubt from Mr. Smith, sundry school and other friends leaving the remainder from you."

"How do you know that? Why is she not answering anyone? Something must have happened to her."

Her voice was rising again as her imagination ran away with her. Her nightmares of last night were adapting to incorporate the new information that I knew about her calls. Like a magician I produced the phone from my pocket but far from the tearful gratitude I had thought might deservedly come my way, her face contorted in anguish and the tears overflowed again.

"She would never be separated from her phone unless something has happened to her. Please."

I couldn't help myself. I reached over and put my hand over hers and gently squeezed. The feel of her skin woke me up like the first rum of the day. I wanted to hold her hand for a while yet.

"She left the phone in a safe place. She intends to return for it soon. This is very good news. It means she'll have been in control of her leaving and is comfortable. At the very least we could watch where she left it and simply wait for her to pick it up."

"Are you sure she is safe?"

"As sure as I can be, for now. There is nothing at all to suggest otherwise. If someone had taken her, they would have simply sold the phone immediately, or thrown it in a bin."

In the silence, whilst she gathered herself and tried to claw back the tears, I was acutely aware I was still holding her hand, or if I wanted to be charitable, she was still holding mine. Rather than snatch it away embarrassed I casually reached for the bag of goodies she had brought with her.

There was an iPad, a second phone which was still better than mine, a laptop and two digital cameras.

"Has she been using any of these recently?"

"She is never off the iPad and the laptop is for all of her homework and suchlike. I think she keeps her information in an iCloud account linked to all three. I haven't seen her with that phone since her birthday and I don't think there is a SIM card in it, and I don't think anyone uses digital cameras anymore, but they were in her gadget's drawer at home. I tried to bring everything in case they help."

There was that naked desperation again. It was almost child-like rather than maternal.

"How many of these can you access?"

"The iPad is an old-fashioned figure of four, straight up the middle, diagonal to the left then straight across the other middle, the laptop password is worldchamp all one word (I wonder who thought that up?) but Summer's folders have an additional password. It used to be "notwinter", but she changed it a few weeks ago. Same with the phone. Her new phone is facial recognition and fingerprint protected,"

Having something to focus on; something she could contribute, was drying her tears and edging her away from hysteria. Time to build on that feeling for her.

"What can you tell me about Friday?"

"Just a normal day really. No fights or anything. She got up at around seven, early I know but Dad still goes for a run every morning and no-one sleeps once he is up. We had breakfast. She was quite talkative for a change. Some days we can't get a word out of her. She was talking about her exams and how she might do. She reminded me that she was going straight to Katy's after school to stay the night. She said it was a study night, but even I don't believe fourteen-year olds study on a Friday night. Katy is her best friend. Has been since she started at Howell's. I wasn't concerned because I had had a text from her mum confirming it."

She rummaged in her bag and flicked through her phone to show me the text. It was strange how she saw herself. "Even I" seemed to imply that she was somehow in no real position to judge her own daughter's behaviour. Similarly, the rush to show me the justifying text seemed almost adolescent, more like a friend than a mother. A little niggle crawled into the very bottom of my brain and stayed there. Even her vulnerability wouldn't completely cover it up, but it did go a long way to getting me to ignore it.

I took the eagerly proffered phone from her. The text was unremarkable; headed from Penny (Katy's mum) on Wednesday evening it read;

"All right for Summer to stay on Friday night. Back home tea-time Saturday probably with Katy in tow for your turn."

There was a "No problem" response. I clicked back to the message menu. There were fewer streams than I would have thought a thirty-year-old mum would have. Several headed with "Sophie's mum" or "Eliz. Mum" but not too many personal ones and none from Summer. Even my phone had ten times that number of open conversations at any one time. Now to impress her with my detective skills.

"This a new phone?"

"Yes! I got it two or three weeks ago to use for Summer's engagements. We had a misunderstanding one night when she didn't come in until gone midnight. She and Katy had gone to the cinema after the County Choir practice and Penny had brought them home after they had gone for something to eat."

We were frantic with worry. By the time we realised she wasn't in, it was too late to phone round looking for her. Dad was out, driving round searching for her. Summer was certain she had told us about the plans but neither of us could remember her saying. Her phone battery was dead and neither of us knew Katy's number.

When I was in buying a new phone for Summer's birthday, I got myself one as well just for her use. I mainly use my work one for everything else. I am Dad's manager and personal assistant. It was also a good way to get a list of her friend's parents phone numbers in case of emergencies. We had never really thought of that before. Summer agreed to get her friend's parents to confirm by text when she was going to be out late or staying over. It has worked well recently until yesterday."

The tears which had abated with her dialogue started to fill her eyes again as she mentioned Summer being missing again. I tried to move her along and steer her away from any more crying.

"Did Summer have any boyfriends?"

She pretended to think. She wasn't very good at pretending. Even with her looks she could never have made it as an actress.

"Not in the sense you mean. God no! She had a lot of admirers, of course, she is a very beautiful girl and kind with it, which is just as important, A fair few of the boys in the choir and orchestra, particularly, loved hanging around her and her friends, showing off the way young boys do, but I know her and her friends laughed at their efforts.

We all used to talk about it when her friends were over. I suppose I am a bit closer to their age than their mothers are. Boys and girls are at such different stages at that age, aren't they? Certainly, Summer and her friends didn't appear interested in anyone special. They were scandalised when one of them went out with a boy."

I chose to let it slide for the moment. At least as she spoke the tide went out on the tears. I don't think it even dawned on her that at Summer's age she had already had a child.

"What about you. Any boyfriends? Any men who might have come into Summer's life?"

I added the second bit so that the first question wouldn't appear as flirtatious as it sounded in my head.

"No! Certainly not! I have kept away from all men since Summer became a young lady three or four years ago. My experiences with Sonny made me very suspicious of the motives of men around young girls. I presume he told you how we met?"

I kept as poker a face as I could and nodded slightly. I wasn't going to talk about it if she wasn't.

"I think you must be the first person I have met who knows about us. He must be worried to let that cat out of the bag."

"No-one is going to hear it from me if that's your worry. Mister Smith simply wanted to give me all the information to try to ensure her safe return as soon as possible. In his way, he is as worried as you are about her welfare."

"Besides men, and probably boys for Summer as well, tend to be frightened off by who and what my father was. He is very protective of both of us. He always tries to arrange his work so that we can pick Summer up from her school or activities. She is most definitely his little princess. It is eating him up that she might be in danger. That is why he behaved so badly towards you. I'm sorry about that, I cannot remember if I apologised for him earlier."

"Think nothing of it. I quite understand. Does your stepfather have many visitors to the house; dinner parties, work colleagues, agents et cetera?"

65

"No! No! That is one of his rules. No work in the house. We tend to keep ourselves to ourselves up there. He really believes home is for the family. Has done even when he was world champion and I was his little princess. It seems such a long time ago now. The house is a kind of sanctuary for him away from all of that. A place where he can be himself away from the cameras."

As she stopped speaking, she remembered again why we were there. Her eyes brimmed with tears and dripped slowly down her cheeks.

"You will find her, won't you? She is all I have in the world."

I reached across and squeezed her hand again. It took no great effort. Time to take control, I thought.

"Does she have access to any money, and small things at home she could sell if needs be?"

"She has her own bank account with two hundred pounds a month transferred to it. She usually has it spent in the first week though, particularly recently. She has discovered an interest in more expensive make up and clothes as she has gotten older. That was where most of her birthday money went, on clothes. She also has all my mother's jewellery, some of that is worth an awful lot of money, but she would never even think of selling it. She was very close to my mother as a child."

"How much birthday money did she get?"

"Just over a thousand pounds."

Different world indeed. I had been delighted if I had got paper money of any description; and we still had single pound notes in Scotland until recently.

"Lastly, have you checked her Facebook account, or her friends, to see if there have been any postings or photos since Friday?"

"The first thing we did was private message her friends and their families to see if there is any word of her although they seldom used Facebook now. Apparently, that's more for old folks like us. Her and her friends all used WhatsApp groups for their communications. The encryption on that is much better and we never got her password for that."

Secretly more delighted than I would admit at the "old folks like us" I gave her hand a bonus squeeze.

"The more I hear the more I am certain that Summer is safe and well. That being the case I am certain that I will find her although it will depend on how well she has planned her disappearance how long that will take."

"Why would she plan it? She can't have. She wouldn't hurt us like this."

"Perhaps she is trying to show you that she is growing up, or maybe she is worried about facing up to exams, or maybe she just wants you to show how much you love her by missing her. I don't pretend to know much about teenage girls but here is what I do know:"

We were heading back to hysteria, so I laid a part of it out for her. Listening seemed to stop her crying although not as much as speaking did.

"One: She deliberately left her phone where it could be recovered later.

Two: She set up a false story and alibi in advance about where she would be on Friday, in case she changed her mind.

Three: She probably has money either of her own or by selling jewellery or stuff from your house.

Four: Her friends knew she was going otherwise

67

they would be all over social media looking for her and there is no trace of that. Teenage girls like nothing more than joining in a bit of public drama.

Five: Given all that, I will find her safe and well and it will likely be a race as to whether I can find her before she comes home with her tail between her legs."

She thought about what I said and almost smiled through the tears. I was still holding her hand, or she was still holding mine. Neither of us seemed to mind in any event.

"This is where we go from here."

"Firstly, I need you to tell me where Katy lives then contact Katy's mum and let her know that I will be coming to see her sometime today, sooner rather than later. Don't take no for an answer this won't wait until school opens tomorrow. I'll send you a contact number; text me with the address and the visiting arrangements.

"Then, I need you to go home and pry into Summer's bank records and jewellery collection. I need to know how much money she has and how much she has access to. That includes your and your stepdad's monies. Remember she could have been planning this for weeks. How hard would it be in your house to get your cards or account numbers from the mail? Be suspicious.

"Finally, I need you to believe that she is alive and will be home soon. Your worries are paralysing you both. I know it is difficult but we all must focus on getting her back as soon as we can and for that we need all the information we can get. Draw up a list for me of anywhere she may be, relatives, friends, places you have been on business or holiday. She will almost certainly be somewhere she is familiar with.

"For my part; I will arrange to download her electronics and phones to see if there is anything there to help us. I will speak to her friends, in person, or by telephone. I will liaise with the police once school opens tomorrow and you should be ready to either come there with me or authorise them speaking to me directly.

"I have a team meeting at four, which should take a couple of hours and I will call you by nine tonight to let you know where we are with finding Summer. Is all of that okay with you?"

"What do you mean, team meeting? Surely my girl takes priority over things like that!"

We were heading for tears again. I certainly wasn't going to explain myself to her and her sense of entitlement was truly appalling, particularly as she wasn't even paying. My Sunday conference calls were what drove my business and were cast in stone with my operatives around the country. If we got it right on the Sunday, we never had to speak again all week. I certainly wasn't going to cast that aside for a favour to a friend of an enemy, no matter how tough they were. Then again who would not be sympathetic to those tear-filled baby blues.

"My operatives (blinding her with jargon) in Newport, Gloucester, Bristol, Exeter and Swansea will be doing the donkey work in decoding Summer's electronics. They will also be sifting through them for clues. In addition, one of them will be checking that she has not left the country whilst another will be making sure local police in all their areas have Summer's photo and details and will take the hunt for her very seriously."

"They are all people I rely on for their various skills and expertise. It was one of them who traced and found her phone within minutes this morning. By tomorrow at the latest we will have her call, text and Internet history. The police couldn't do that in a fortnight, these people will have it done tomorrow morning so yes! it is important I speak to them at four."

I think the tone surprised her, but not enough for her to pull her hand away. I could have gotten used to that sensation, she was desperate for something, or someone, to cling to. I gave one final squeeze and my best reassuring smile and stood to leave. She almost smiled back.

"Go somewhere private and call Penny then send me the address as soon as possible. Let's see if we can get Summer home by tomorrow at the latest. I will call you at just after nine tonight to let you know where we are."

I had been deliberately using Summer's name throughout to let her know that she was a very real person to me and to reinforce that it was her daughter we were looking for not some abstract missing person. I hoped that and the smiles were getting through. She still clung on to my hand. It was an awkward moment; I half-hoped she would rise and hug me but instead she looked frantically around for her father who was sat glaring at us from the bar. I walked towards him and leant forward to whisper in his ear,

"Try and keep her on the right side of sensible. I might need her later to persuade Summer home. I've given her a couple of things to do to keep her busy."

He was still unused to being told what to do; but nodded anyway.

"Send me your private mobile number, not your everyday business one, in case the news isn't great, and I can prepare you first. Other than that, I will call at nine-ish with an update as instructed by Mister Smith."

There was no real need for the last part I just wanted to take him down a peg or two by reminding him that he wasn't in control here. Jealousy is a terrible thing but to be honest I was quite enjoying it. It had been a long time.

As I left, I spotted the counter measures. He was easily seen, being the only guy in the bar older than me and less trendily dressed. If he wasn't a retired policeman I would stop drinking for a week! He was doing all he could not to look at me as I left but was too quick to rise after me as I reached the door.

I embarrassed him by turning back to visit the toilet. He had no choice but to carry on past me and out the front door. Although only done for a laugh at his expense, I decided that a toilet visit might be well advised given the amount of beer I had consumed. I took my time to leave him hanging around in the cold wondering if I had slipped out the gym's back door or bar staff entrance, both of which faced out the other side of the building.

When I eventually left by the front door, he had made another mistake, albeit an understandable one. He had gambled that I had come by car and was wandering around the car park. I suppose he also thought it was less conspicuous and visible than simply standing on the pavement peeking around corners. I avoided him by simply walking along the dockside, hidden from his view by the block of very expensive flats and even more expensive furniture shops and hairdressers, sorry beauty consultants.

As I strolled along, I could imagine him frantically checking the bar and then running down the other side of the block to catch up. Don't get me wrong I have been that soldier in other circumstances and whilst I was smiling, I had every sympathy with him. As I walked round the end of the old dock, I caught sight of him rushing around the corner behind me. Time for more fun, I thought. I was enjoying this too much.

There was a children's birthday party going on in the Techniquest Museum and the back doors were open and engulfed by parents frantically avoiding the festivities. In addition, the museum itself was full to bursting with desperate parents and their noisy children finding something to do together on a Sunday before the tactical retreat to the nearby Wetherspoons, or Las Iguanas for the more affluent.

I made a show of reading the notices to make sure he saw me, then nipped in without paying and ran up the stairs to watch his reaction from the first-floor gallery. There were more than enough people about to provide visual cover. He made another mistake. He walked past Techniquest and leant on the railings at the end of the Graving Dock.

He wanted to watch the back door and around the far end of the building in case I simply walked out the front door and kept going. This was stupid because if I had come out and kept going, I would have had to walk past him again, seeing his face for the third time in three hundred yards. Even an amateur would have spotted him, and I was not yet as degraded in my skill set as that.

I left the front door, out of his sight, and crossed the road to the low-rise car park. I hurried now so that I could come up behind him before he got restless and stopped concentrating on the back door. Given his incompetence so far, I didn't think I would have long.

Hurrying along, using the road for speed and to avoid an embarrassing collision on the pavement, I ran around and moved quickly up behind him.

I reached down and yanked one leg up behind him whist leaning my full and considerable weight on him folding him over the railing and leaving him staring into the cold dark water. Only one toe precariously gripped the cobbles to prevent him falling over.

"Who are you working for?"

"Gary! Gary Gregor!"

I wouldn't have liked to go to war alongside him. He gave up his client in a heartbeat without a second thought. I leant back slightly to release some of the pressure.

"Don't follow me again. Work the case any way you want but don't be dancing anywhere near me, understood?"

"What case? I was only to follow you and report who you were meeting."

Somewhat distractingly my phone buzzed twice in my pocket. Hopefully, it would be the intel from Susie and Gary. If it was, I didn't have time to piss about here. I was tempted to just heave him into the dock, but it might have scared the bairns milling about. Either that; or some stupid sod would probably get injured, or worse, jumping in to save him.

"Keep away or the next time it will be the hospital for you. OK?"

I couldn't believe that the stepdad had had the nerve to criticise me knowing he had employed an eejit like this guy. I let him go with a therapeutic shove in the back, which sent him sprawling. By the time he got up I had melted away in the weekend Bay crowds. Just to be sure I nipped into Wetherspoons and had a small rum in the upstairs balcony to make sure he gave up and left.

I took the opportunity to look at the texts. As I expected they were from the Gregors. Susie sent me an address in Radyr, a posh suburb just to the north of the city and a note that she had left a message for Penny on voicemail but had spoken to Katy and they were expecting me before 17.30 when Katy had evensong at the cathedral in Llandaff. Who cared!

The line which caught my attention was her thanking me for my help and urging me to stay safe. I found it strangely touching. It had been a long, long time since anyone cared if I lived or died.

I could not resist replying to the other which simply stated; "This is my private number. DO NOT!!! Give it out to anyone". It wasn't even signed or anything. I was tempted to reply; "who is this?" but contented myself with;

"Your detective has been dismissed. Probably only need to pay him for five minutes."

The temptation of another rum was hypnotic, but time was running short as was my mental capacity. It occurred to me that I had made an enormous mistake. Age was catching up to me.

SIX

The Schoolgirl

I had been so pleased at quickly catching the countermeasures that I hadn't given any thought that it was planned that way rather than as a result of my brilliance. Always plan for the unthinkable if you can. After all there were at least three interested parties looking for this girl. Possibly more if any of Mister Smith's gang fancied racking up a few brownie points.

Any of them could arrange to have me followed and what better way to lull me into a false sense of security than to leave one for me to find. One of the oldest tricks in the book. A good job I wasn't in mine clearance or bomb disposal where this was a standard tactic. Time would tell how stupid I had been.

I ran through where I had been and who I had spoken to so far and could see no great potential for damage. If it was the Gregors, they already knew what I knew and would just be checking that I was always acting in the best interests of Summer. No real problem there.

If it was Mister Smith, again, he would soon know all I knew and would only be checking that I was doing something, so no real problem there either. It was the other two possibilities that raised real problems or me. If it was Lenny or one of the other Bristol lieutenants acting on their own, they would be looking to muscle in on any deal, possibly exploiting any weakness in their boss. Never underestimate the ambition of any second in command. I thought Mister Smith would probably have that in hand, or, could deal with it if I brought it to his attention.

If it was Marko looking to muscle in or hijack my job, then meeting the Gregors in such a public location had been a grave mistake. It had let Marko see who I was looking into and it could be a small step to him working out why. I didn't think he was that smart, but why take the chance. One thing was for sure I would have to make sure I wasn't followed from here on in.

With that in mind I walked round the Bay shops to the front door of The Packet. It was impossible to check if I was being followed because of the crowds so I did only basic drills; stopping suddenly, checking reflections in shop windows to see who else stopped , browsing in a couple of unlikely gift shops and hiding in the racks to see if anyone rushed in to check where I was, that kind of thing.

I didn't spot anyone, but the more I performed the drills the more convinced I was that someone was watching. There had been a time when my life, and that of my colleagues depended entirely on these feelings and I had learned never to ignore them. Acting on them cost nothing, the alternative would have been devastating.

In truth, I was beginning to enjoy flexing my mental muscles in a physical environment for a change. I chatted with the small group of smokers loitering at the front door right underneath the "NO SMOKING IN THIS AREA" sign, then casually went into the pub as I had already done twice that day. Nothing to see there.

I walked straight past the bar ignoring a couple of attempts to catch my eye, hopefully from punters intending to thank me for last night, and out the back door, through the beer-garden cum official smoking area and straight into another of the taxis which always waited there for me. I asked the driver to take me onto the link road and then after half a mile changed my mind and asked him to do a U -turn at the mini roundabout and head back into town on the normal roads.

He looked at me as if I were mad, but a waving twenty-pound note allayed his suspicious nature.

"We're going to Radyr eventually, but I have to make a couple of stops to pick up some money and some flowers first. I just remembered."

As we came back down the road we had just gone up, I watched every car and motorbike. I looked to see if there was anyone looking around in The Packet beer-garden. I stole a quick glance down to the front door as well as we passed the end of the street and spent the trip into town checking the surrounding vehicles at our frequent stops at traffic lights.

"If you go into Canton, please and stop outside the Tesco for a moment. I need to get some money out and nip in the shop for some flowers."

"It would have been quicker on the bypass, my friend."

"It's OK. I was a bit early anyway."

We crawled up through the city centre and headed into Canton. I didn't usually travel this much on a Sunday, but the traffic seemed much, much heavier compared to an hour earlier. I would have to be very careful to be back in the office by four.

"It wasn't this busy earlier, is something on?"

I knew it wasn't the City playing or I would have been at the match and couldn't think that any rugby other than an international match would generate this much traffic.

"The British Athletics Championships at the stadium. There is a lot of coming and going. Apparently, Eastern Avenue is jammed solid."

Typical of Cardiff's planning geniuses, they had allowed four world class event stadia to be built within a one-mile circle in the city centre; rugby, football, athletics and cricket, five if you included the ice hockey and servicing them all were one suburban road in and one urban road out. Naturally, their own offices linked directly to the motorway in both directions by a two and three lane urban clearway.

Too late now to change plan as we edged, somewhat illegally, into Cowbridge Road. The standstill made it easier to spot a follower, or team of followers if you were suitably paranoid. My next manoeuvre should confirm what my gut had been telling me all morning, even though I had ignored it for the first hour or two. Getting old!

In the manner of taxis the world over, my driver simply drove half onto the pavement outside the Tesco Local, ignoring the double yellow lines. The blast of horns from drivers attempting to turn left past him and the knock-on effect of his sudden braking on the traffic behind.

"Please be as quick as you can. I do not know how long I can stay here."

That is what he said, but his manner completely

belied his words as he casually started browsing his phone as an excuse not to have to engage with the drivers squeezing past him. Anyone else stopping would stand out and there was nowhere around this junction where it would have been possible to pull over. And there he was.

A slightly built Asian looking taxi driver trying desperately to find somewhere to stop. No-one else in the car; he didn't know if I was exiting my taxi for good or if he should stick with the taxi. I had seen him in the rank at The Packet and again at the traffic lights at the Millennium Centre in the Bay. He had pulled out in front of us at the bottom of Lansdowne Road. Not without some skills and knowledge then, but an amateur. I had dismissed him earlier because he was alone.

The professional thing to have done would have been to have had at least two passengers. That would have allowed them to disembark to follow me on foot, either alternating the following duties or covering the front and rear of any buildings I entered. Now he was snookered. Nowhere to stop and no idea which direction I intended to travel in. I figured he would just have to sit and suffer, at least until I exited the Tesco store.

I bought the biggest bunch of flowers I could find in the small store and detoured round and added a small potato peeler for the bargain price of 50 pence from their essentials range. As cheap a freedom as I could purchase. As a precaution I also ostentatiously took a couple of hundred from the cash machine; both to reassure my own driver and give me a chance to look at the reflections in the window to see where my shadow had gone.

He had opted to simply stop on the double yellow lines on the other side of the junction. If we were to turn left, he would have had nowhere else to go. It was a tempting strategy but would have taken us deeper into the heavy traffic heading for the Athletic Stadium and I was already conscious of the time pressure.

I stuck with my original plan and using the crowd of pedestrians waiting to cross as cover I slipped alongside the taxi and drove the potato peeler into his back tyre. It made a very satisfying bang and to emphasise the point I walked to the front and let the driver see me do the same to the front tyre.

He did not even get out to demand an explanation, confirming his guilt. Up close I could see that he may not be an Asian as I had thought but could have been any number of Mediterranean or mongrel races. I noted the taxi number and registration and strode purposefully back to my taxi whose driver appeared somewhat apprehensive as I drew alongside his cab, fearing I was some sort of nutcase bent on disabling Cardiff's taxicab fleet.

He was relieved as I got quietly into the back and waved the cash I had withdrawn at him.

"My ex paid him to follow me and find out where my new missus lives!" I told him.

He nodded understandingly, though still slightly fearfully.

"Do you know him?"

"I see him around. He works mainly over in the Ely area. I think that is where he lives. I don't often see him with fares. He does a lot of deliveries I think."

Marko it was then. Deliveries was cabbie code for drug couriering.

"There is an extra twenty in it for you if you don't tell anyone where we go. Is that OK?"

"No problem!"

"Let's go to Radyr Golf Club then."

I thought it best to park somewhere inconspicuous and walk back to my destination. You can't tell what you don't know after all. A taxi wouldn't be noticeable in a big car park either, if I could persuade the driver to wait for me. Radyr would not be an easy place to find a taxi on a Sunday and time was pressing in on me.

With the nonchalance of a professional driver, he simply swung out without looking, cut across two lanes of braking and hooting traffic and accelerated through the two red lights whilst green man observing pedestrians stopped and swore at him. With that fanfare, we set off for Radyr. The traffic was noticeably thinner and thankfully we made good time to the golf club.

"Could you wait here for me please? I will be no more than half an hour. Leave the meter running and there will be another bonus in it for you."

He weighed up the chances of getting another fare out here and the time he would take to fight through the traffic empty and grudgingly nodded.

"And remember no telling where we are. Turn your radio off if necessary."

I doubted he would. The radio was the biggest part of his livelihood. I couldn't blame him. With that agreement, I set off out of the car park and down the hill. I didn't have far to go. I had seen Katy's street two roads down. A hotchpotch of Scandinavian wet dreams with gorgeous views down the River Taff to Cardiff and beyond. From here, I could easily see Flat Holm the old fortress island in the Severn Channel. I wondered how the residents around here felt about the council's plans to swamp the

81

area with over ten thousand new homes in the coming years.

Not my problem, nor ever likely to be, as homes around here would undoubtedly start at around a million pounds; or did before the development plans. Thinking about it, I probably could afford it now, but there was no public house in Radyr. Who would want to live in a place without a pub? The very idea baffled me.

Every house in the street was immaculately maintained, beautifully manicured and coiffed lawns and shrubbery and any stray weed on the driveways or paths would have died of loneliness and abandonment. Up close the great coloured slabs of the walls glowed in the reflected sunshine and the stainless-steel frame and windows gleamed and sparkled without a stain or smear. If there hadn't been a path leading to it, I would have struggled to locate which panel was the front door so discreet were the fittings.

Despite the enormous slabs of glass looking down on me as I walked to the front door no-one seemed to be moving to answer the door. Probably didn't want to make the house untidy by living in the front section with its breath-taking views. Imagine all your neighbours being able to see you slobbing around in your PJs, or worse. Is that really a home?

The doorbell was a modern high-tech wireless camera connected to the Internet. Thinking about it, the entire house was probably Wi-Fi remote enabled. If only these people knew that the more Wi-Fi devices there were on a property, the easier it was to hack into the entire system. iPhone cameras, for instance, are notoriously easy to hack.

I never forgot the photograph of Mark Zuckerberg, the Facebook founder, in his offices and all the computer screens in the image had a piece of black insulating tape over the built-in cameras and microphones. If he couldn't solve the problem, that was enough of a hint for me.

I pressed the button, smiled into the lens and despite feeling quite smart in The Packet earlier, felt very much like a beggar going door-to-door in this environment. The best flowers in Tesco seemed like a very small accolade indeed here. Nonetheless I mentally braced myself into charming mode. How hard could it be to charm a housewife bored rigid living out here in this pub free wilderness.

The door opened suddenly and soundlessly. Why wouldn't it in this precision-built perfection? No creaking floorboards or warped frames here I wouldn't think. It would not be tolerated any more than the weeds would, or indeed a car more than three years old. I wasn't quite taken by surprise, too old a hand for that, but was shocked by the beauty of the woman who materialised from behind the door. She was stunning.

My original thought of using the corny but charming "is your mother in?" dried to dust in my mouth. This woman could easily have been in her early twenties. Her naturally (as far as I could tell) blonde hair was casually tied back into a loose ponytail yet fell into an immaculate arrangement in the way that only the most expensive haircuts could. Her un-made-up (as far as I could tell) face could have graced any beautiful people gathering anywhere and her eyes and smile sparkled and danced. I could simply have looked at her all day.

If I had a woman like this in my home, I wouldn't

need windows. The view of her alone would be enough to delight me endlessly. She made Susie Gregor look like a washerwoman in a nineteenth century pictograph.

Twice in a day already I could have fallen into forever love. Either this was the luckiest day of my life to date or I really did have to start expanding my romantic liaisons again. I suspect it was a bit of both. Thinking about it, it was indeed a long time since I had sought out female companionship. Desperation probably did strange things to your perception of beauty, but not in this case. Aware I was starting to stare, she saved me from my own awkwardness by holding out her hand, "Mister McLean, Penny Price. Come in, we have been expecting you."

Given how she looked, she was probably used to people staring, or even gawping, and was practiced in smoothing around the ragged social etiquette.

"Are those for me? Thank you so much. They will brighten that dark corner perfectly; just let me find a vase for them."

I couldn't see a dark corner anywhere in the vast open plan space, but then I doubt I most men would see anything except her, when she was in a room. Having been a touch fazed by her appearance I thought it best to say nothing until I had regained my bearings. I hoped I might appear inscrutable and mysterious and therefore a touch more interesting to her. I pretended I was looking around in a professional rather than social way.

"Thank you for not laughing. I do find the Penny Price jokes a bit tiresome, I have had them all my life."

Originally quick-witted, but seemingly becoming slower by the day I had not even noticed nor thought to pass a comment. Too busy trying to describe the exact shade of grey in her eyes, which I had settled on as midsummer cloud. That is what comes from reading too much English poetry, or perhaps paint catalogues. I was not so slow as not to notice the hint that Price was her maiden name. So, no Mister Price then! Hope springs eternal, at least it does in English poetry, if almost certainly not in the paint catalogues.

I decided to forego the charming approach, as that boat appeared to have sailed, and moved straight into the smooth professional. I would have said suave but in this house, I still looked like a vagrant; around her I looked like a vagrant who had been dragged in through the rear garden hedges by a particularly vindictive horse.

"I understand you know why I am here Mizz Price?"

"Please call me Penny, and it is Mrs. Price. I know it is confusing, but my husband's name was also Price, so when we married, I didn't have to change my name. Lucky really."

I didn't believe anything a creature as perfect as this did could be attributed to luck. Then I had a real head slapping moment.

"PRICEPENNY! Of course."

I had blurted it out without thought of how it would sound like a star struck child.

"I'm sorry. I thought you knew. I suppose that sounds a bit arrogant to you, but most people round here know me; then again you are clearly not from around here."

She genuinely smiled as if it was a pleasant change to meet someone who didn't know who she was. I could have lived on the warmth of that smile through a very, very long, cold winter. Pricepenny was one of the fixtures of all

85

South Wales high streets; an ethical, cruelty free cosmetics and pharmacy chain, they had revolutionized health foods, medicine and toiletry provision in the area in the nineties, long before the Poundlands and their ilk had been invented.

It was remarkable for having been started by a twelve-year-old podgy girl in her parent's garage to help her and her friend's emerging body and nutrition issues. By the time she had gone to university she was a millionaire with a chain of shops. She had sold a controlling interest for a vast fortune because she had become disillusioned at the commercial exploitation of her dream of helping others.

Instead of retiring she had launched one of the biggest charitable institutions in the country, still assisting youngsters with body issues; a boom "industry" since the advent of the Internet. And here she was; looking every inch a twenty-five-year-old when she must have been in her mid-forties. Perhaps it really was time for me to start looking after myself a bit better. She was around my age but could have comfortably been my daughter. Not that I would know what my daughter looked like now.

I decided to stick with the enigmatic and professional.

"I am truly sorry to disturb your Sunday like this, but as you can appreciate Mizz Gregor is worried witless about Summer. She just wants to know that she is alright."

"Yes. I am sorry, what must you think? Me standing here flirting with you when a child is missing. You don't think anything has happened to her, do you?"

Like I said, getting old, I hadn't even realised that we were flirting. I didn't dare look up at her in case I blushed at the thought. It had been a long time since I had blushed as well!

"I am reasonably confident that she is still alive and well, if that is what you mean. Other than that, who knows how much trouble a teenager can get themselves into these days."

I risked a glance up and saw that she was laughing at my discomfit, betrayed by a hint of a smile and a sparkle to her eyes which I doubt she could have stopped; or faked for that matter.

I would probably give up drinking to be a true co-conspirator in her amusement. Second time today I had thought about giving up drinking for the right companion. I really was going soft. I hadn't managed it when I had the most forgiving of partners; what made me imagine I would manage it now!

Perhaps the sadness of that thought flashed unbidden through my eyes, or maybe she was slightly ashamed of her teasing, but whatever she saw or felt made her glance quickly away.

"Would you like a drink; tea, coffee or some wine perhaps?"

I would have liked nothing better than sitting with her; perhaps with a nice Rioja, and wasting away my Sunday afternoon, trying to see that amusement in her eyes again, but time was flowing past and time was quickly becoming my enemy.

"Ordinarily you would need a very good bouncer to prevent me sitting in a place like this with such attractive company, but time is wearing on, and finding young Summer might just be time critical before she manages to run too far."

Very subtle and suave. What worked in Kiwi's late-night lounge, clearly wasn't going to melt much ice here, but it had been so long I wasn't sure what else I had. It was as if a light had gone out in her head. My clumsy compliment was clearly well below the usual standard of flirting she enjoyed. I was, at least, certain that she both received and enjoyed compliments every day. What gorgeous multi-millionaire didn't?

I matched her hardening features to at least let her know I wasn't either intimidated or disappointed by her cooling mood. She could not know that failure with women was a very comfortable and familiar battleground for me. Possibly that was my trouble. Almost certainly, on reflection.

"I'm sorry. Susannah and Gary must be going out of their minds. When Katherine told me you were coming, I thought it was a bit of an overreaction. They were frantic last month when they forgot the girls were going out one night. I see from your face that this is not a trivial matter. If someone like you is worried, then so should they be. Katherine is expecting you. Would you like me to call her down?"

There was a lot in her words to process and unfortunately, I focused on the wrong end of the statement. What did she mean someone like me? How did I appear to her that leant weight to my opinions? I should have been listening instead of worrying how I appeared. I did, however, process that Katy was upstairs somewhere, presumably in her bedroom. I motioned to go up the stairs.

"Would it be alright if I spoke to her in her bedroom? She may feel more comfortable there."

"I don't know if that would be appropriate. I know she was nervous about meeting with you. I could call her down and we could all have a coffee in the diner."

None of this was going to plan. I wanted the girl to be comfortable in her own space and free to speak in private with me. I doubted if either of those would apply down here with her mother fussing around making the coffee. Captain Decisive to the rescue I strode towards what I imagined were the stairs up, though they appeared only as spars of wood winding from the wall. No safety rails here.

"No! It's okay. I will leave the door open. Really, I just want a quick chat with her about Friday, hopefully that will be enough to stop the police from having to see her tomorrow. If she needs you, she can always shout down."

As I hoped the throwaway police reference gave her pause for thought and I used the time to mount the stairs. I was only three slabs up when a head appeared at the top.

"It's alright Mummy, I may as well get this over with. I don't want to get into any more trouble because of her."

She emphasized the "her" with a contemptuous toss of her head. They clearly studied drama at the posh school. I did hear the "more" in her sentence though, steering me towards an approach to break the code of omerta between teenage girls. As I headed up, I was thwarted from appearing athletic and elegant by the odd spacing of the steps, too large to climb two at a time and too short to run up without appearing as if I was practicing a tap-dancing routine. Still too concerned about how I looked I pretended to look at my phone to account for my slow pace.

I was almost at the top when what I had missed occurred to me. I would like to blame the lager or the rum, but I think I was just having an increasing number of dense days recently. Alcohol may indeed kill off the brain cells gradually after all. I turned back and was pleased that she was still watching me. I pretended not to notice the concerned look on her face and told myself it was probably awe at how elegantly I had climbed the stairs without falling over, or even off, the bloody things.

"When you said that Katherine told you I was coming, surely you had a message from Susannah, Summer's mum as well?"

My voice bounced around the tiled walls and marbled floor and, even to me, sounded authoritative and manly. She smiled directly at me and it was as if the sun had suddenly appeared through the glass skylight directly over my head;

"Oh no! No-one has my number. I don't give it out to anyone otherwise I would be inundated with calls. Anyone who wants to speak to me goes through the charity and works numbers. I never bring those home with me at weekends. Only my secretary and of course Katherine have my mobile number. Katherine knows better than to give it out to anyone. If she had rung the house telephone, we would have heard it. We have been in alone all day."

I thought the unasked alibi was a bit unnecessary; perhaps she was still rattled by the police reference, but I was pleased at the slight stress on "alone" as if it were a coded message for me. She must have noticed my Fred Astaire ascent of the staircase, which I finished with a flourish for good measure.

Katy was standing in what I presumed was her room doorway, awaiting my arrival. In any classroom in the world she would have been a pretty girl, in any classroom I had inhabited she would have been beautiful but sat between her mother and Summer she would have felt like Quasimodo.

Her perfect straight, white teeth and tousled auburn hair would endure forever but at this moment in her life she was carrying the couple of extra pounds which would transform into a voluptuous figure in a year or two, but which overshadowed all her confidence at present. In addition, even the best and most expensive concealers from her mother's cabinets could not hide the outbreak of teenage acne on her dusky forehead.

Again, time would heal this and leave her skin as flawless as her features but what it wouldn't do would be to eradicate the sullen childish pout from her face, the moody slump from her shoulders or the entitled whine from her voice. If she wasn't careful these could scar her beauty forever. I was tempted to tell her that what she needed was a couple of years in the army but thankfully my recruiting sergeant days were long behind me in the rear-view mirror.

As with Marko earlier, I stood and looked but was determined not to be the first to speak. In this case it was to emphasise that I was going to be the adult in our conversation. I didn't really need to dominate in this way as I could see that she realised how much trouble my last exchange with her mother could put her in. The longer the silence stretched, the lower her chin sunk on to her chest in the universal body language of submission in the animal kingdom. I continued to stare.

I had stared battle-hardened squaddies into submission, but I was not sure that the former navy captain who had taught me the technique would have been proud of me using my skills on a teenage girl. She cracked quickly.

91

Her chin came up suddenly and pointed defiantly at me. The defiance sparked in her eyes lending them a yellow tinge of fire and her mouth tightened the pout into a sneer.

"You might as well come in; if you can tear yourself away from Mummy Dearest!"

She turned and walked into a bedroom, which was bigger than my flat. She didn't know yet that she had used the clear resentment of her mother to mask her guilt over her friend but once she learned to control her manipulation, she would be an effective opponent. I supposed that was true of all women; they seem to be born with that duality at their core.

The room was so big that it had room for two sofas as well as a huge bed and a massive desk and associated bookshelves. The colours were pinks and pastels and the draperies were lacy and diaphanous but there didn't seem to be too much girlie about this space. It certainly could never be described as a boudoir. There were no photos or posters either on the walls or on the surfaces. From what I remembered of teenage girls they loved their posters. Perhaps time had moved on from then, or I had, or posh girls might be different.

"I don't have long, Katy. Do you prefer Katy or Katherine?"

I took a seat on one of the sofas as if it were my right and motioned her to sit as if we were in my office.

"Your friend, Summer, might be in a bit of danger. My only aim in this is to find her and help her. I think you could know how to do these things and I would appreciate it if you could assist me."

"Most people call me Kat. Only my parents call me Katherine and only Summer calls me Katy, after the books;

"What Katy Did Next." It's sort of a private joke."

Her defiance did her credit, but the trembling lip and shuffling eyes told me all I needed to know. She knew where Summer was, and it would take but a moment to break her into a flood of tears and release the information. I didn't know if I wanted to go that far.

Rich and spoiled or not she was still only a bairn. There was something else, there in her face, but there was so much going on and it was hard to read. If the lunchtime conversations I overheard in my office doorway were anything to go by most teenage girls were a seething mass of resentments and slights at the best of times. Another mistake.

I didn't know whether to go good cop or bad cop; favourite uncle or my dad. I had already been a favourite uncle that day so went straight to my dad. It wasn't too much of a stretch if truth be told, probably my greatest failing as a father was that my dad was the only example I had.

"Don't piss me about Miss Price! I have Summer's phone!"

I pulled it from my pocket and laid it on what I supposed was an occasional table. Too much daytime television for me, I think.

"I know about the fake "Mummy Dearest" phone and her texts arranging dates!"

I laid my phone next to Summer's and opened the message from Snow White supposedly to Kat's Mum.

"I know about the boy. Or should that be boys if I include you, as well!"

This last one struck home. Her face turned visibly crimson even under the layered concealer and foundation. It seemed to swell up and the pressure was forcing tears to roll down her cheeks leaving tiny channels. Even the bright Mrs. Price, it seemed, couldn't make waterproof foundation.

"Tell me what I need to know now, and I may not have to take this information to the police before they question you in school tomorrow. All this would be enough for them to take you out of your class and down to the station for questioning."

I looked grim enough for her to imagine that would mean being led from the school in handcuffs though I was not even certain the police would even investigate far less visit the school.

The mention of the police did, at least, galvanise her. Her chin shot up from her chest and her eyes widened although I wasn't quite sure if it was fear or excitement in them. She almost looked drunk!

"Why would the police come?"

"You know why!"

I was not blinking now. Staring straight at her. I let anger flare into my eyes and set my mouth in its grimmest line.

"Under-age girls, older boyfriends!"

Bingo! Score one for the detective. Not that creditworthy really; whoever heard of teenage girls with younger boyfriends after all, but given my poor performance so far, I took any ego boost I could get. Based only on the overheard conversations I flew another balloon.

"Pictures!"

Bingo again! This time it really was fear. She looked at Summer's phone. She couldn't help herself.

"So! Don't piss me about Katherine otherwise all

94

of this is going straight to the police and your parents. No more posh school, no friends, boys in jail for child pornography. That is what the charge would be; or one of the charges at least. Any idea how child molesters are treated in prison?"

There was a real horror there now. She shrank back onto the sofa as far away from me as she could travel. There was still something else in her expression though and this time I could see it a bit better. There was a smugness underneath the fear and loathing. A child-like satisfaction. I couldn't figure it out, but it wasn't a typical grown-up reaction at all.

To further assert my dominance and keep her compliant I half rose and leant over towards and above her. She cringed. I don't think I had ever seen anyone cringe before. The hidden expression vanished into straight fear. I deliberately shot my hand out and snatched her phone from her. She flinched and cried out softly. She didn't want her mother to hear and come up.

I laid her phone alongside the others on the table.

"Tell me now where Summer is and who she is with and I won't have to open these up and let everyone see the messages, photos and videos."

Of course, I had no real idea how to open them up. Of the three I struggled with my own from time to time, but the threat was enough to turn the tears into a steady stream. The chin dropped again, hopefully for the last time. I really didn't have the stomach for bullying wee lassies. If I had caught anyone treating my daughter like this, I would have happily left them looking as if they had been run over by a truck. I had to remind myself my daughter was approaching her thirties now, not the gauche teenager I remembered.

"Please don't. Everyone would hate me even more if they saw what I had done. Please! I will do anything."

Her eyes, swimming in tears, rolled up to look at me appealingly. I may have been wrong, but I think she hoped the look was seductive to go with the do anything entreaty. It was all I could do to maintain my grim demeanour.

"Let's start at the beginning; Where is she?"

"She's with Mo."

It was a very sullen response, more in keeping with how I expected young daughters to behave. She did everything except stamp her feet and toss her head, though in all probability it would come to that soon. I left a silence for her to fill. Once they start talking it's usually best not to interrupt them.

"He was my boyfriend first, but his friend Alfie really fancied me and is much nicer looking anyway and we have such a great time when we are together, and I think Mo was cheating on me anyway. There was this time..."

My training said not to interrupt but I had an instinct she was on a long and not very helpful verbal journey. I was aware the clock was ticking, and I wanted to be back in the office as soon as possible.

"What is Mo's full name?"

"I don't know, I really don't. I know it is Mohammed and that my boyfriend, Alfie, calls him Slim; but that's all I know."

She glanced up nodding her head to convince me of her truthfulness. She may as well have been wearing an "I am a Liar" tee shirt. It would have been more persuasive. I was undecided on whether to push her further. There was very little smug cleverness in her evasion but quite a lot of fear. I hoped the fear wasn't of me.

"Show me Mo on your phone!"

Short, sharp and back on track. She reached across as if it was a trap of some kind; trying to reach her phone with just her fingertips. I picked it up and handed it to her. I could hear the ticking clock but was aware that I didn't want to miss anything. I had a feeling that perhaps I already had.

She quickly opened her phone and selected an album of photos. I noticed that she had to put a password in though even from the other side of the table I could see it was simply in the form of the letter K; 1474248, I might need that later to access her other media.

"That's him with me, in one of his shops."

It was said with pride. There were no worries or concerns in her voice.

The photo was taken in a small phone shop. Kat was sitting on the counter, in her school uniform, doing her best to look as sexy as a fourteen-year-old could manage. Not as much of an effort as she had just made with me though, I thought. Behind her, whispering into her ear was a young Pakistani man with the high cheekbones and long nose of the Pathan. He was undoubtedly very handsome with a slightly cheeky flash of white, white teeth. I would have said he was in his early thirties.

"He has a lot of businesses. That is just one of his small shops. His restaurant is huge."

She reached over and moved the album forward one photo with a flick of her finger.

"That's us in his car."

The same spider's smile; it seemed to be aimed at the photographer though. His arm casually around Kat in a

97

gesture of ownership rather than affection. A White
Mercedes convertible with the roof down and praise be to
Allah The Mighty and Merciful the registration number in
full view.

Personalised naturally, in order that no-one could
know the age of the car. SAL11M. As a last resort this
would make finding him easy. As unobtrusively as possible
I opened the DVLA app on my phone and put in the
registration. In moments there it was; Salim Akhtar
Mohammed with an address in Cyncoed, a good suburb of
Cardiff, not the best but still very good, nonetheless.

I was aware she had continued speaking, some
story about going down to the local resort of Porthcawl in
the car but something she had said had tickled my
subconscious mind.

"Who took the photo?"

"I told you! Summer! That was when she started
causing trouble between Mo and me. That trip. She is
welcome to him! I hope the two of them get into so much
trouble for this. They deserve each other. We hadn't
properly broken up when she started hanging around his
shops. He wanted me to run away with him first, but
Summer thought it would have been mad. Now look what
she has done. I think she just wanted him for herself! She
has always been a selfish cow."

Once she started there was no stopping her. Where
I saw a child; she undoubtedly saw a grown woman with
the full range of entitlements that implied. I was torn
between letting this spoilt rich kid sink into the mire of her
own sense of importance and rescuing the child drowning
in the insecurity of always being the plain one.

In a much different way, I knew exactly how that

felt. I had never served or trained with officers from my kind of background. That lingering sense of inadequacy could scar your whole life if you let it. I decided to throw her a lifeline.

"Show me Alfie!"

I said the name with as much contempt as I could. Not as much as he deserved as it turned out. She went through the same transparent password ritual on a different album and with a mixture of defiance and pride showed me the resultant photo.

A balding Pakistani man around forty appeared. Tall for a Pakistani and with the heavily muscled physique of a weightlifter or bodybuilder his eyes were too close together, his smile too white to be real at his age and what hair he had was dyed a very unnatural black.

"He is such a laugh. He is the manager at Mo's restaurant. And he's super fit. He calls me his princess and treats me like a queen. Boys my age are only interested in rugby and shouting insults at everyone…"

"Not another word now!!"

It was said in my best parade ground order voice. I stilled my features into the grim reality and drove all the anger burning in me from my eyes. This was not going to be a negotiation.

She sat back. I do not think anyone had ever exerted disciplinary authority over her. Presumably the big fees bought you persuationists rather than orderers. If I had to guess I would think the absentee parents were too guilty about their neglect to fill the role either. I turned her phone towards her.

"This is wrong!!! Not just illegal! Wrong! You know that. That is why you are embarrassed and crying.

99

The way you feel now will change. Maybe not today or tomorrow but soon and when it does you will look at these and feel just as ashamed and worthless as you do now. This is only making the problem worse. Do you understand?"

She nodded without looking up. The little girl again. Given my success bullying this poor child so far, and my hundred per cent record with wild guesses I took a flyer on another, guessing at what was clouding her expressions, knowing it could undo all my work so far if I was wrong.

"Give me the drugs now!"

Her head snapped up; hate swirling through her tears. Confident of being right I simply held my hand out and waited in silence for her head to drop again and the defiance to drown in her misery. That was what was making it difficult for me to read her expression. She had been using before I arrived; perhaps even because I was going to arrive.

I was expecting a small bag of weed or perhaps even a couple of packs of cocaine but when she rummaged around in the unicorn pyjama case at the bottom of her bed and produced a carrier bag full, I was astonished.

"Here!!!"

She practically threw the bag towards me. Ever cool I plucked it one-handed from mid-air. I placed it open end towards me on the table between us. She was full on sobbing now. Buying some time, I walked around her and checked there was no-one around her door before firmly closing it. This was not a good time for Mum to join in.

"Are you keeping these for a friend, or have you been selling them?"

Sob! "I have sold a" sob! "a few" sob "but only at" sob! "one party" sob! sob!

I left the silence while I thought about how much of this child's life I wanted to ruin.

Sob! Sob! "Alfie" a huge flurry of sobs "will want the money for those" almost a wail now "if I don't give them back" finishing off with a noise I cannot even describe but certainly one I have never heard a man make.

I came to a decision based solely on what I would have wanted someone else to do if they had caught my daughter in this position. Again, I had to remind myself that my daughter was no longer fourteen but was approaching thirty now. Grimmest face possible now.

"Look up at me now Kat! You cannot imagine how much trouble this puts you in. This is young offenders and then jail time territory. This would not be getting back at your family or friends it would ruin you forever. Do you understand?"

"Look up at me. Do. You. Understand?"

She nodded slightly. Her face was destroyed now the make up a streaky mixed palette of blacks, browns and greys. Where her own coffee coloured skin was visible it was so pale it was almost grey. She was beginning to understand that I was serious.

"Are you going to be sick?"

Concern in my voice, the good cop putting in a belated appearance.

She tried to say no but the action of shaking her head brought a reaction. She burst past me and through a door at the back of her room. I should have known there would be an en-suite. I could clearly hear her vomiting through the door that she had not had time to close. I walked over to it, intending to close it and give her some privacy and dignity to come back with, but then thought

101

better of letting her out of my sight line. I had just destroyed her entire world; I didn't want to risk how desperate she might become.

"Wash your face and when you come back out, we will try and find a way out of this mess for you."

Splash! "It's you!" Splash, retch vomit, splash "You are the mess." Splash, splash.

"Just clean up and get out here or you are on your own."

Bad cop coming back without any effort from me. I used to be good cop by nature. What was happening to me?

I whiled away the wait browsing through the carrier bag. It was a real assortment. There was a bag with about a half pound of weed; a half a bar of foil wrapped resin, at least couple of hundred violet tablets stamped with a scimitar which I presumed were MDMA or ecstasy in a freezer bag, forty or fifty separate gram wraps of white powder which was probably cocaine, a few Loctite bags with a greyish crystal in which I did not recognise but might be amphetamine in its modern form and various bottles of medical Oramorph and perhaps one with a dropper of LSD. A real chemist's shop. I would have thought that two or three of these in combination would be enough to kill an adventurous teenager.

She watched me from her toilet doorway as I put it all back into the bag.

"You can keep it all if you don't tell anyone about it."

She had scrubbed her face almost raw but was still a deathly grey colour. She was standing against the doorframe in a parody of her mother's easy seductive stance.

"Get over here and sit down!"

She did as she was ordered. She struggled to keep her face up and towards me, but I gave her some credit for the effort. The tears and vomit were not far away but she was using a piece of toilet roll to continually mop her nose. I say toilet roll based on my own habits; she probably had a choice of tissues and wipes in her bathroom.

"This is a different league to shagging a couple of old men!"

Cruel but necessary from the bad cop. I didn't want her big trouble allowing her to forget about her little ones.

"Some of the stuff in that bag could kill one of your friends. If that happened there would be no road back for you. Do you understand?"

She was beginning to.

"If you were caught with even a small part of this amount you would be looking at least at seven years. Do you understand?"

"But it's only for…"

"There is no only. It is possession with intent to supply. Do you understand that?"

A nod was all I was going to get. I settled for it.

"Your old men friends are exploiting your age and your resentment of your parents and your friends. They have no real interest in you as a person. Getting you to sell this stuff is all they wanted. To achieve that they will feed your resentments, they will flatter your insecurities, they will isolate you from those who love you and when they are finished, they will throw you away like Mo has already done."

The chin came up again in preparation for

defending him.

"Where is Mo now? He is with Summer, the next girl on his conveyor belt. Do you understand that? There is no affection for you except for what you can do for them. Until you see that there is no moving forward!"

It's hard to watch a dream die or to teach a child of the light about the darkness in men's souls, but I did it then.

"Here is how we are going to move this forward. Is this phone the only way you communicated with Mo or Alfie?"

She frowned as if I was asking her to do long division in her head before nodding.

"My Mum sometimes uses my iPad and laptop in the house, so I didn't want to use those."

"Open it up and change the setting to "No Security". I am going to take it away with me today and have it professionally wiped of all traces of your boyfriends, WhatsApp, Snapchat, photo albums video files all of it. Do you understand?"

"It will be returned to you by courier tomorrow to the house. After that there must be no contact whatever between you and the others. Is that clear?"

She was about to say something, which was not Yes Sir! So I stamped down hard.

"I will leave a tracer on the phone and if I learn of any attempt at contact, I will send all of the information I have to the police is that clear?"

She nodded.

"I will take these drugs away with me today and dispose of them. Is that them all?"

She nodded again.

"At the moment I am all that stands between you,

your friends and the scumbags who got you into this mess all going to jail. Do you understand?"

Another nod. Behavioural conditioning at its best.

"I will not hesitate to put you all there at the slightest hint that you are not the perfect schoolgirl you should be with all your advantages. Clear!"

"I will tell your mum on the way out that you are upset about Summer running away and that I am borrowing your phone for today to try and find her. Alright so far?"

A slight dip of the chin

"I will tell her to keep an eye on you for a couple of days as running away can be contagious among adolescent girls.

I will make sure no-one contacts you about these drugs or the money for them. Fair? Anyone contacts you call me immediately. I will leave my number with your mum and put it on your phone under Jock. All clear so far?"

She was crying again as the enormity of her future problems piled up. The darkness was a fearful place when you have never seen it before.

"Right! Back to the job in hand for the moment. How long were you going out with Mo?"

"Since just before Christmas. Of course, he doesn't celebrate Christmas. They are all just about to enter Ramadan. That is their holy month, they don't eat or drink during daylight. Of course, they're not supposed to drink at all but that never stopped Mo or my Alfie."

Bad cop again.

"He is no longer YOUR Alfie. He is scumbag number two. Never to be spoken of or heard from again. I thought you said you understood. Don't make me ruin your

105

life just to find them."

"Sorry, it just slipped out. I understand well enough. Sorry!"

"When did he transfer his attentions to Summer?"

"Just a couple of weeks ago, though I think she was probably after him before that."

"Before or after you started selling their drugs for them?"

It was cruel but necessary if she was to properly learn the lesson. I watched the penny slowly drop through the slot machine of her mind and felt like the most horrible person in the world. The pain of realisation dawned across her broken expression.

"The same night. How did you know that?"

"A hard life spent among cruel men. Where did you go when you were going out together?"

"Usually to one of his shops if it was night-time or to one of his rental houses near the school if it was day-time. Once we went to his chalet in Porthcawl. The only full night we were together."

"Do you know where he is with Summer just now?"

"No! Honestly I don't. How could I?"

Honesty, for her, was a relative and elastic concept.

"Who has "your mother's phone" you or her?"

The emphasis on "your mother's phone" was unnecessary. Her guilt was written all over her face and she knew I had caught her in another big deception. With any luck Summer would have it and I could have tracked her using that phone. I was always lucky, but not that lucky it seemed. She walked round me and reached way down the back of her bed and pulled out a folding mobile phone even older than my bat phone.

I flipped it open and scrolled down the text messages. No security on these babies. They were all arranging time away for Summer. Seven in total over the last three weeks. I showed the messages to her and simply raised an enquiring eyebrow. Very Roger Moore, I thought, or perhaps Dwayne Johnson for the younger audience.

She nodded again. Fully conditioned for compliance now. I checked the call log. All from Snow White I presumed. A frantic fair few this morning and yesterday evening.

"Where would he have taken you on a Sunday evening?"

"We didn't go out on Sundays usually. Summer and I have choir in Llandaff, and we had to be there every Sunday. Besides, that was when Mo collected all his money from the shops and did his accounts. He usually bought me something nice on a Monday.

He liked showing off how much money he had. I used to visit him most Mondays. We only had PE on a Monday afternoon and his shops were usually quiet then. His restaurant was closed on Mondays and Tuesdays so we could go there too."

She was like a faulty tap; either full on or taciturn silence. It was hard to catch the diamond in the waterfall of words. I wished I had taped this interview. I had no real excuse except time pressure. I usually recorded my interviews to re-listen to them.

I picked up some intonations or word patterns on the second or third hearing that I had completely missed in live time. Well, not completely missed, the cold fingers of my subconscious usually tickled away at my imagination. It was doing it now. I knew if I left it alone to wriggle about it would come to me. If I looked for it, it would slither away into my dreams, possibly forever.

"…it was always nicer in one of his houses. There was always a proper bed and everything and his friends weren't around. We could never get time together when they were there; they always talked amongst themselves in Pakistani. One time…"

It seems that money didn't buy much of a cultural education. Pakistani men could converse in any number of related languages, and often in a mixture. That was what made it easy to spot outsiders. I knew all the words, but the jumble of languages and rhythms changed from valley to valley. Not unlike Wales in fact where different areas spoke different forms of Welsh.

The clock ticked on. This case was moving too fast for me today; between the hangover and the morning drinks, I seemed to be one step behind all the time. I would have to use the weekly briefing time to let my brain catch up. I suspected the answers were already in there somewhere.

"Where are they today then!!"

"I don't know. I really don't. I thought she would have phoned me by now but if you've got her phone, I suppose she wasn't able to. Not a Snapchat or TikTok or anything. She was supposed to call me last night, but she was probably having too much fun. If my mum didn't know she was missing, we were supposed to all go out together, but she never called. That is just like her. Not bothered about whether I wanted to go out…"

I let her see the anger now. She was normalising

the situation too much. I raised my voice a notch.

"Weren't you worried about her?"

The chin dipped and she cowered like a beaten dog, just as I intended but the spark of self-defence was still in her, or perhaps just a degree of self-justification.

"She was only with Mo he wouldn't."

"Mo! The drug dealing paedophile! And his drug addled friends, what could possibly have gone wrong do you think?"

The guilt flared again and not just in her eyes but in the childish pout and defensive posture. I made a note to scour her media before I erased it to see what was frightening her so much.

"Do you think they are in Cyncoed?"

She laughed. I hadn't expected that. The image hinted at the woman she might just become.

"They definitely won't be there. That's where his mother and wife live. That is the most out-of-bounds place there is in his world. I only know about it because Alfie had to drop something up there one night when I was in the car. Mo was raging that he had taken me there. Even in Pakistani I knew he wasn't pleased."

More bad luck. If it wasn't for bad luck, I wouldn't have any luck at all in this case. The easy solution was snatched away from me again.

"Where are the houses you visited with them?"

"There is one just down from the school in Pontcanna; that was where we would usually go, so that I could be back at four o'clock. There was one down the Bay, but I don't think he liked using that one. He said too many people knew him down there and there is one above his restaurant, but the people who work there are usually in there …"

"Start with Pontcanna! What's the address?"

"I don't know!" frown, smile "but I could take you there if you wanted."

"I thought you understood. You are not! Not now! not ever! to go near any of these places again do you understand! If you do all deals are off and all this goes to the police and all over the Internet. I thought you understood."

Repeat, repeat, repeat till it's the only message they remember. The mantra of army instructors the world over. Hopefully, she would remember the threat for a long time.

"How did you walk there?"

"I cut down through the park, so no staff see me walking on the road away from the school."

She looked up proudly as if I was supposed to be impressed by how clever she was. To me it seemed dumb to be walking across a flat empty field in plain view rather than a pavement where you have every right to be. That may be the soldier in me though, having never been a naughty schoolgirl.

"Then along Cathedral Road past the shops and then down to the left just opposite the café, before you get to it. It's only a short street so you go down there, and his house is on the right. On the corner just after you cross the first road you come to."

"Which flat?"

Houses down there cost a fortune so most had been carved into flats to provide young professionals with a prestige address they could afford.

"It's a house!! He owns it all. A couple of his friends live there. It's where I met Alfie actually. I think he

110

rents it from Mo. Mo is rich you know."

I allowed the anger to flood my features and lowered my voice to just above a whisper.

"The money for it is earned by making daft wee girls like you sell these for him."

I almost threw the bag at her and she flinched, seriously afraid now, as I had intended.

"Daft wee girls like you died to get him that money. This stuff destroys lives and kills people. Has that not sunk in yet?"

I thought I could find the house from her description. If not, surveillance wouldn't be that difficult with the Halfway and Conway pubs nearby as well as a couple of cafes to sit in and watch without being too obvious. Time to wrap this up now. Tick tock, tick tock.

"Right what have you got to do to get out of this mess?"

"Keep away from Mo and Alfie."

"What else?"

"I don't know what you mean!" Tears again.

"Not keep away. No contact whatever ever again is that clear?"

She nodded.

"No contact with Summer either until she is back at her mother's. Clear!"

She nodded again. At least I had taught her one good behaviour.

"No more of this shit," waving the bag, "and no more thinking that no-one loves you. Not when you live like this. Okay?"

The nodding continued. I handed her the phone. Change all your passwords to Katy0123. Facebook,

Twitter, Snapchat, WhatsApp, TikTok all of them.

A smile appeared through her tears.

"This is not a funny situation!"

"I am just laughing at you knowing about TikTok, I would have thought…"

"What that you and your friends invented communication. One of my associates made millions developing apps."

"Sorry!"

She looked as though she meant this one.

"Right. Chin up and wash your face before your mother thinks I beat this out of you. This is my card with my office number on it. Any problems from anyone about any of this and call me immediately."

"If I am not there it will usually divert to my mobile. I will tell your mother that Summer, not you, is the one on a bad path and has run away to avoid the consequences.

"I will tell her you are very upset about it all and blaming yourself you could have stopped her. I will tell her nothing of what you have been doing or what's on your phone. I will have your phone and Internet accounts emptied of all the dumb stuff. All understood!

"A year from now you will be a different girl and none of this will matter.

"Okay Clear!"

I picked up all the phones and put them in the carrier bag and rolled it down as small as I could. Distracted as she was by my flawless complexion, I felt sure Mrs. Price would notice that I was leaving with a bag I had not had when I arrived. I left Kat curled up in the corner of the sofa looking every inch the child that she was.

I tried to bound down the stairs, an exercise made as difficult as the ascent by the same spacing issues. I didn't want to topple over the unguarded edge. That wouldn't have been very Roger Moore. The morning drinks weren't helping either!

"Do you have time now for a coffee?"

This time it was neither my overactive imagination nor conceit, there was a hint of desperation in the plea. With the expectation of the privileged she sat down simply expecting me to join her. I was torn between the need to put her in her place, as I saw it, and the desire to help the youngster before I left. Thankfully for me, the good cop won out, but I could still hear the clock in my head ticking.

"I don't have time for a drink, but I would appreciate a quick chat, if that is alright?"

I sat myself down where I could look out over a view of the whole of Cardiff, in all its glory. A fair bit of Somerset as well, over the sparkling Severn estuary. It was beyond breath-taking. I had to wonder about someone who could sit with their back to a view like this. No matter how rich you were there should be no excuse for ignoring beauty like this. In saying that, it was improved by Mrs Price sitting in the foreground. It was enough to turn off the clock in my head. I could have happily sat there forever.

"How is she? I have been so worried about her recently. She really hasn't been herself?"

She demonstrated the extent of her worry by allowing the faintest of hairline cracks to cross her flawless brow. I realised she was awaiting my answer and pretended that my daydream was reflective consideration.

"She is very upset; she blames herself for Summer's disappearance. I don't have to tell you the

113

trouble girls can get themselves into."

Perhaps I did have to tell her, after all at Kat's age she was sowing the seeds of a multi-million-pound business not wild oats.

"Summer has run away with a boyfriend. She has been running around with a bit of a party crowd."

I hoped that was enough of a hint for her.

"Kat has been her alibi, covering for her with her mum. She thinks she should have stopped her. She sees now how dangerous this all is for girls their age. I know this is difficult for you to hear; God knows I am not a good example as a parent; but think how Kat feels sat between you, a stunningly beautiful successful businesswoman and Summer, every appearance of a true golden child."

"All those image issues and insecurities your charity deals with, are as real to her as they are to any child who calls them. Your money doesn't insulate her from those feelings. At heart she is a good child struggling with a bad event. This is probably the first time she has had to think about the consequences of her actions being less than perfect."

A single tear rolled down her cheek. I pretended not to notice for both our sakes. I could make a huge fool of myself with this woman. I did notice that it left no trail in any makeup though.

"She has given me a loan of her phone and tablet for a day to see if there is anything in Summer's messages which will help me find her. She really wants to fix things!"

She gave a faint coughing sound. Not for her the unseemly snort.

"You are truly honoured. I haven't seen that phone

114

out of her hand for months."

She struggled up a false smile.

"I will have them couriered back to her tomorrow, probably in the afternoon. I will have a better idea of what we are dealing with then. I have left Kat my card with contact numbers for me on it. If you can think of anything to help, or if Kat tells you anything you think could help me, please give me a call."

I heard the same glimmer of hope in my voice as I had in hers just moments ago. I stood to leave, and the movement started the clock ticking again. She rose awkwardly and called to my retreating back.

"Mister McLean!" She pronounced it properly to rhyme with "half a brain" as my father had always said about himself.

"Mister McLean! Will you let me know how it turns out for Summer please? I would like to help my daughter through this."

I was inordinately pleased that her thoughts were with the two girls.

"I will message you my private number. I suppose you can be trusted with such things."

She then took two quick strides and hugged me. To say that I was taken by surprise would be an understatement. I almost grabbed her and threw her over my shoulder in a jujitsu throw, just by instinct. She smelled wonderful in a soapy way, not a chemical overkill scent. Her breath warmed my ear and flooded my mind with thoughts that shouldn't have been there. My body did not too badly out of it as well. It really had been a while.

"Thank you for taking those vile drugs from her. I found them last week. I have been at my wit's end. I really appreciate the omissions in your story."

Not a multi-millionaire at that moment just another confused parent worrying about their confused child with no way of communicating between them. I really should apply some of that blinding insight to myself one day. I thought she had been listening at the door for at least some of my conversation for sure.

"I'll be in touch."

Leonardo DiCaprio at his smoothest, I thought as I headed for the door before my physical discomfort became apparent.

There was enough of a cold shower in the springtime breeze to return me to my normal taciturn state and I began to jog under the pressure of the ticking clock and to release some of the physical tension. The concentration needed in conversational interrogations was immense and some activity was required to loosen the muscles, which were always tense when listening. Then there was the other physical tension. A man could dream but any thoughts I had in that direction would have to wait until I really was dreaming later.

Thankfully my driver was waiting for me where I had left him in the golf club car park, nonchalantly reading the Muslim Times from last week. I knew it was last week's because I had read it last weekend. I tried to read it regularly to brush up my language skills.

I tapped the window before opening the door so as not startle him too much. Even as I climbed in, he was speaking;

"A few calls looking for you, boss. I told them I dropped you in Canton at that new brewery pub on the corner. Easier than just saying I didn't know."

"No problem. Don't worry you are still on for your bonus. Who was looking?"

"Just a couple of other drivers. They were promised fifty if they found you."

I wasn't sure if he was just bumping up the price, or if there had indeed been calls, when his phone rang. He pressed the Bluetooth in his ear with a well- practiced movement. He didn't know I spoke Urdu, so he had no reason to deceive me. I heard him tell the caller that he had not seen me since he had dropped me off as he had told them before.

When he hung up, I came to a decision. It would kill two birds with one stone; solving a delivery problem for me and keeping him out of the way for a few hours.

"I will pay you the fifty for keeping quiet, on top of the fare. How much would it be to go to Gloucester?"

To say that he looked suspicious was putting it mildly. I was lightly sweating from my jog, which didn't help.

"Just to take you there, or there and back?"

I didn't see what difference it made to him the mileage would be the same either way.

"Just to deliver something for me."

Wrong answer! The offer of unasked money followed by the delivery request was too much for any man to blithely accept far less a world-weary taxi driver. There wasn't much they hadn't seen or been offered most days. All human vices were on view in their place of work most days.

"I don't do that kind of thing. My cousin would do that for you though if you want me to give him a call?"

"It's okay! This is legit. It is just a phone I want

you to deliver. I won't even put it in a bag or envelope. I just need my colleague to have this phone tonight. How much?"

"Gloucester and back on a Sunday. The traffic back is bad as well."

I could virtually hear the pound calculator rolling round in his head.

"Five hours, easy! With this journey and the tip say four ton all in. How does that sound?"

I knew it was more than he had ever earned on a Sunday before, except on international nights perhaps, but probably still as cheap as a commercial courier. It would have the bonus of keeping him out of town for the next few hours. It was all the client's money anyway.

"Done! I will need a receipt though."

We both laughed. We knew a taxi receipt was about as useful as a used hankie, but it was at least some attempt at business-like behaviour. He dropped me back to the office with twenty minutes to spare before my four o'clock call.

I went into my office and got a big padded envelope and topped up the money I had taken at the Tesco with some notes from the expenses pile from earlier. I stuck in an extra twenty for good measure. Always too anxious to dispel the mean Scotsman myths. On the envelope I wrote as big as I could in felt pen;

ANNE
OLD NEIGHBOURHOOD INN
CHALFORD
GLOUCESTER

Thinking ahead for once today I then wrote ALFIE and MO on the back of the envelope and checked their numbers were in Kat's phone under those names. I kept a note of the numbers. I could trace those mobiles to save some time and effort. It may appear lazy, but I prefer to think of it as efficient. I went back out and placed everything carefully in the envelope so he could see there was no hidden "agenda" before sealing the envelope.

He had been whiling away the time talking to a couple of girls from upstairs who were taking in some fresh air before their shift began. A much better use of his time than reading a paper, I thought. He looked at me with a new respect.

Like most people he thought that my office was somehow connected with the sauna and sports massage parlour that occupied the top two floors of the building. How much respect would he give me, I wondered, if he learned that my flat was right below the sauna. Tearing him away, "You will find that easily enough on your satnav. It is the only pub in the village. Anne will be in the beer garden at six tonight. She will be watching for you. The car park is right next to the beer garden."

I didn't see any need for him to know any of my associate's names or where they lived. I was as sure of him as I could be but, in truth, that wasn't very sure at all. I could honestly say that only the taxman and I knew for sure who worked for me. What they told people was for them to decide.

"If you leave now you should be there in plenty of time."

It was a hint as well as an observation.

"I'll just grab a bite to eat at Sainsbury's and then

be on my way."

He looked as if he was just going to ask the girls to join him when a raised eyebrow from me stopped him. If he knew what they charged it would not even have occurred to him. Since the Assembly came to town within spitting distance of their establishment, prices had rocketed. I didn't think he had enough in the envelope for one of them let alone two. Even on a quiet Sunday.

Time for me to get on with business as usual.

SEVEN

The Paratrooper

Before that, I thought the plan forming in my head would require some physical on-site support and knew just the man for the job. Hired muscle was ten-a-penny in Cardiff, every gym was stuffed with boneheads pumped up on steroids and coked-out aggression, but your true fighting headcase was getting harder to find. Once a regular sight in every pub they had been lost forever like the unforgiving industries and cheap housing which had created them.

I preferred them in a fight. You always knew where you were with a nutcase, usually rolled in a ball on the floor listening to their laughter as a crowd kicked the shit out of both of you. It was never about the winning for a nutcase; it was about the Sunday morning story.

Fortunately, my frequent sojourns to most of the less glamorous pubs on the periphery of Cardiff meant that I still knew a few I could call. Like most endangered species they had retreated into small pockets far from civilisation; in the former mining towns of the valleys, where they appeared to thrive. From what I understood, the women up there still appreciated a "real man" where the Cardiff girls had largely driven the arseholes from their lives.

I thought I knew just the man, and this being a Sunday, hoped he was not in a police cell somewhere. "Shaky" Sam Stevens was a former member of the Paratroop Regiment, still the only line infantry regiment of the British Army never to be amalgamated or disbanded. He had been a sergeant in Number One Battalion, the infantry support for all British Special Forces and had been around many of the places I had.

Though we had never met "in the field" during his twenty-two years' service, we knew a lot of the same people. Of course, I knew their real names. I had drunk with him many times since moving to Cardiff. He looked like every Para I had ever met; a huge man with a face that spoke of as many losing fights as winning ones. He proudly boasted that despite several attempts, he was officially classed as too mad for the special forces. He thought that a compliment.

What he meant was that he had failed the psychiatric assessment. He was a good tool to have in your bag if you only needed a sledgehammer. He had some skills though to have lasted full term in a regiment as physically demanding as the Paras. He was great company until he wasn't. When he wasn't, a word or gesture out of place from someone in a distant crowd and all hell broke loose. There was no such thing as insurmountable odds for Sam.

He had become a fireman when he left the service but only lasted a short while. His version is that, "There was far too much sitting on your arse and not enough action."

The truth is probably that there were too many drunks who thought it funny to call him Fireman Sam for even him to fight.

His nickname "Shaky" came not from his need for drink in the morning though he had seemed to be heading that way the last time I had seen him. That was a case of the man becoming the nickname. No! It came from another of the great drinking myths of Cardiff.

He had always maintained that as a small boy his father had lived next door to the Barratt family in Ely, not the Cambridgeshire town, rather the Cardiff suburb famous for riots in the early nineties. He had adopted the teenage son of the family as a hero because he had a guitar and had followed him around.

When that boy became a star, he had looked to change his name and had used Stevens in tribute to his toddler admirer. Sam had told that story so often the squaddies started calling him "Shaky" Stevens because the details changed so frequently, ostensibly because as a small child Sam could not be expected to remember dates or addresses.

If only I hadn't heard a version of the same story a hundred times since moving to Cardiff substituting Shirley Bassey or Tom Jones with Shakin' Stevens. One embarrassing time in the Splottlands pub the barman had quietly pulled me aside and told me the old dear I was talking to really was Shirley Bassey's sister!

With ten minutes to kill, I gave him a call. He was in my phone as mad bastard one. I couldn't remember who mad bastard two was now. Sam was always my go-to guy. The phone rang out before cutting to voicemail. Not a good sign. I hoped he was not sleeping it off somewhere. It never even occurred to me that he might be in hospital, or worse. I left a short message asking him to call me back. If I hadn't heard from him after the team meetings, I could find out who mad bastard two was. I had been looking forward to seeing him as well.

I had just hung up when he called me back.

"Jock! Sorry I blanked you, my phone didn't recognise the number. I have to be careful with unknown numbers."

I had forgotten to switch my phone back to my personal SIM. Last I heard he was working as a bailiff, repossessing cars and such like. I suppose he had to be careful.

"Just a quickie, Sam. Are you free for some recce work on a search and rescue operation in Cardiff? Starts tonight into tomorrow at the latest."

"Is there likely to be trouble?"

He was the only guy I had ever met who reduced their price if it involved trouble.

"Not on the recce. I won't be doing the lift if it is too heavy, but there will probably be some light scuffling involved."

"I would need a ton for the recce tonight but if it goes into tomorrow it would need to be a monkey! I have an easy three hundred quid tomorrow morning I would have to let go."

Five hundred quid was a bit steep but seen as how I was charging five thousand for the same timescale I could hardly complain, could I?

"Could you bring the Transit down here by six? Any plates you like, just not your own. I'll supply any other kit we need. Dress for nightwork."

I think that covered it. I had all the cameras and microphones we would need and the two of us could cover

124

the restaurant and the house in Pontcanna if need be, or front and back if we knew where they were.

"No problem. See you later then. Office or pub?"

"Office, of course, I am working."

We both laughed, as I spent considerably more time in the pub than I ever did in the office and even then, most of the office time was spent napping. I was looking forward to seeing him again. It was nice to work with someone who knew all your methods and shorthand and he was brilliant company. Every week added another anecdote or two to his fund of stories. The night would fly by.

Still a few minutes left so I decided to spend another hundred quid of Mister Smith's money. Making sure my phone was on my personal SIM I called a guy I had regularly drunk with in the Blackweir after rugby training until four or five months ago. I was ashamed to say I hadn't spoken to him since the night I had taken to see a friend of mine, who was in Alcoholics Anonymous.

He had been at a low ebb and I felt I couldn't just have left him maudlin drunk. I had had enough of those nights to know the difference between self-pity and genuine despair.

I hadn't seen him back in the pub since, which I took to be a good thing. Then again, he might just have changed pubs or gone through with his threats to kill himself. We were not so close that I would know either way. I thought that DS Evans would have told me if he had killed himself. Sandra knew him after all, he was the police liaison with the mobile providers. It was probably him who had provided the map for Summer's phone.

I couldn't ask Sandy for this favour. She would be off duty by now having been on the early shift and I felt bad about asking twice on the same day. It could have put her in a bad position if   anyone checked.

"Fatboy, It's John McLean. How are you my man?"

"John. Great to hear from you. I've never had the chance to thank you for what you did for me. I got my hundred-day coin a couple of weeks ago. Everything is so much better now. Still a struggle every day but I am getting there. Haven't had a drink today and that is the most important thing. What can I do for you?"

"I don't know if you still do the phone finding but if you do, I have a couple of numbers I have to trace. Just where they are. No personal information or histories or anything."

"No problem John. For you anything. I suppose you need them in real time now."

"Well actually if you could give me a call at seven and let me know where they are, I would appreciate it."

"I have a meeting at seven I have to get to. I am nowhere near being able to skip meetings. Would half six do?"

"Ideal. Any help is much appreciated. Usually I would leave a good drink for you in the Blackweir, but I suppose that will be a while away yet."

I racked my brains for an alternative.

"I'll leave it in Wee Willie's coffee hut at the museum. You and the missus have a right good meal on me."

I thought he worked down there somewhere, which is why he drank in the Blackweir. Thinking about it he probably worked in the police station down there. Then again, that would be too sensible for Wales. I couldn't even

126

remember his wife's name. I only remembered that it was her who was causing his despair. Time for a panicked blind guess. This kind of conversation was much easier when you had both been drinking.

"Might help get you both back on track."

"There's no need but it is a nice thought. I think we are still a long way from on track. It couldn't hurt though. Text me the numbers and I'll track them till half six then give you a call."

"Thanks, Fatboy. Appreciate it. I'll speak to you later."

The good cop kicked in just before I hung up.

"Fatboy! Remember if you fancy company for a coffee or a burger or anything please don't hesitate to call. Anytime, day or night."

"Appreciate it John. For sure, I will drop in one day. Speak to you later."

The random kindness had choked him up. He had rushed through those last words as he hung up. Either that or he was trying not to laugh. I knew for a fact he had never seen me order coffee in his life.

Bang on four o'clock I plugged a little black box into my computer and the screen lit up. First up was Theresa in Gloucester. My longest serving employee and therefore she got first dibs on the time slots. She always had her family over for Sunday lunch and invariably took the earliest possible slot to give her enough of an excuse to cut her participation in the day short.

Her mix of blond and grey curls filled the screen. She looked like Hollywood's idea of a favourite aunt or near retirement head teacher. She had been a real-life spymaster before a scandal at GCHQ's listening centre had seen her resign, although no-one had ever suggested it was her fault. She was of a generation who recognised you could be responsible without being at fault. A long-gone generation, it seemed.

Their loss was my gain and for the last five years she had been a thorough administrator and reliable operative. It didn't hurt that her husband still worked at GCHQ with unofficial access to all the information that entailed. As far as I knew neither of us had exploited that relationship for actual information. Software was a different matter. As ever she was straight down to business.

"Any problems with the reports from last week?"

"Nothing on any feedback, so far. As usual they were good outcomes so I cannot see any problems."

"Some of the evidence on that personal injury was a bit iffy. The law is not yet clear on using deleted Facebook photos as evidence, the hosting company refuse to provide the necessary software trail for legal authentication."

"I spoke to the client about that last Tuesday, amongst other things. He wasn't worried about the technical side. He thinks the photos themselves would be enough to have the claim withdrawn. If necessary, we could always get witness statements to corroborate the activity, the pub looked busy. They can't all be his friends."

"I managed to clear some of the long-dated work last week as I only had one new case."

From anyone else this would have sounded like a rebuke, but I knew that if it was a rebuke, she would have started with it.

"I'm afraid that three of them will have to be paid, I actually think they are all genuine not just that I couldn't find evidence they were fraudulent. I'm sorry."

Like all my operatives she thought that our fees were based on how much we saved the insurance companies. None of them knew that our flat rate fee was what got us the work in the first place. Our core four clients, all insurance companies, were more concerned that we were correct in our determinations rather than motivated by a desire to prove everyone fraudulent. In fact, it helped their credibility if they could point to a pay-out rate even in any claim they thought fraudulent.

"No problem. Mark them down at a grand each and I'll see you get paid in the normal way."

Not that they didn't get a bonus from time to time. In fact, Theresa was one of three of my staff who were sharing a hundred grand bonus between them for smashing a crash for cash ring in and around Bristol. The three of them worked together to scoop up nearly forty individuals and three business owners involved in the scheme. That was the kind of work my clients didn't have the resources to put together. I was hopeful of picking up another couple of clients who were also saved money by our work. They had both seemed impressed by my presentation on the issue.

"I will be sending you three this week. All straightforward, I think. You still have those two public liability ones from a couple of weeks ago, how are they going?"

"Slowly but I am getting there. Some of the background work is taking a while to come in. I might need to call on one of our mutual friends I don't hear by next week. Would that be okay?"

"No problem at all. Always here to help. Save you

asking your man I suppose."

This drew a very frosty silence as it deserved to.

"No chance of that ever happening as you have been told before."

"Sorry! Theresa. Bad joke. It has been a long day. You know I would never ask that of you. I never have before, have I?"

"Never asked, no, but hinted strongly enough!"

Well if you didn't ask you didn't get. I didn't really need her man though. I doubted he could get anything we needed that my hacker in Swansea couldn't get.

"I have listed my expenses for the month. The only steep one is the two hundred pounds to use that old woman's front room for an afternoon. I think she robbed me."

"You should have used your inland revenue card on the way out and told her you looked forward to seeing it on her tax return."

"I did, but only after I had got the photos."

"Anything else I can help with?"

"Could I borrow your mobile blocker, please? I need to get that big personal injury claim to use the landline a bit more. I am one good statement away from winding it up. I want him on a nice clear landline associated only with him. In theory anyone can use a mobile."

"No problem. I will send it up. In fact, I might even bring it up myself if you fancy a drink one day. Once you get it just keep it. I will get another one made. I've told you before, it is more important to me that you have the equipment you need when you need it rather than saving a few quid by passing it around."

"That bit of kit is worth more than a few pounds.

It's better than HMG's version and theirs is supposed to be state of the art."

She may not want me to use her man, but she made no bones about me knowing how senior in HMG's war on terror he was. She didn't know that my boy from Swansea knocked it up for me in a morning for under a grand's worth of parts.

"Anything else?"

"No, I think that is me all up to date. Just the three cases on-going and the new three you are sending me."

"Good. Excellent report as ever Theresa! Before you go, I have a favour to ask. I am sending a mobile and tablet up to you tonight. Fourteen-year-old girl, daughter of an important client, got herself involved with some abusive men, I need her digital footprint cleansed of their presence. The password to all her media had been changed to katy0123 and that will get you into her cloud as well. The phone and tablet are unlocked. No sex drugs and rock and roll to be left so mummy can see it. Would that be possible?"

I knew it was possible. She had a wonderful seek and destroy software programme, which I knew she had used on a digital footprint before. She knew I knew as well.

"Why not just press factory reset?"

"I would like the footprint destroyed as far as possible into other platforms as well."

This would mean destroying images in other people's phones, tablets and clouds as well once they had been identified on hers. An immensely problematic undertaking. I waited while she considered it. I was asking a lot and we both knew her husband would have to help at some point.

131

"How important is this?"

A very fair question.

"In the grand scheme of things, not very important. She is just a daft wee girl who could have ruined her life forever over a man who is old enough to know better. You'll see when you look. I'll leave it up to you."

"I'll give it tonight. Anything more than that I will have to think about. I'll be able to clean hers up easily enough beyond that no promises. How good looking is the mother?"

"Gorgeous. You will see for yourself. Multi-millionaire as well but it is nothing about that. Anything you can do would be appreciated."

She had been teasing me. In truth I had no real idea how my associates saw me or what they thought I did with the rest of my time. I kept them in the dark on purpose.

"A Cardiff taxi will deliver it to the car park at the Old Neighbourhood Inn at six tonight. Take the old man out for a drink on me."

"He'll be sound asleep at that time or resting his eyes. Anyway, I like to keep him away from our work. What do you want me to do with what I find?"

"Keep a copy of anything that might incriminate the others but not identify the bairn and obliterate the rest. Anything you can do is much appreciated. See you soon when I bring up the blocker. Thanks Theresa."

I made a note to visit and take the call blocker against her column on my pad and put a note in my Swansea column to order another call blocker. I would do that in my next call.

So, it went on. Similar calls with my other four operatives. Problems resolved, payments arranged equipment organised, reports finalised and work generally organised. I usually left them all with a compliment to remind them about how valuable they were to me.

Theresa with unspoken access to GCHQ software, a retired detective inspector in Bristol with all his police contacts, the very young widow of a marine with two young children and a sister who had access to all MOD records, my hacker in Swansea with access to anything at all probably and a professional thief in Newport.

Between us we covered all of Wales and the west country for the investigations department of four medium sized insurance companies. We resolved an average of fifteen cases a week and the fee income from each job was split three ways. The operative got a third, I got a third and a third was eaten up in their cars, equipment and expenses.

All of them had earned well into six figures last year and seemed very happy with the arrangement. I cleared over half a million and couldn't have been happier either, at least financially. We were all well on track to earn a fair bit more this year as well. I was always careful that every pound we charged was matched by at least ten saved by the clients. I had it in mind that a ratio like that allowed them to justify using my company.

By the time I was finished it was half past five. Twenty-two cases resolved and reports filed, and sixteen new cases allocated. Half of my week's work finished. Tomorrow I would spend a bit more time discussing the reports with the clients over lunch and into the afternoon and then the rest of the week was my own. That was the me everyone in Cardiff knew.

Usually I would have headed into town for a few celebratory drinks in the Old Arcade or the Queens Vaults where the serious drinkers seemed to hang out on a Sunday. Usually I would seek out a karaoke or pub quiz to dominate, but tonight I had to dress for business before Sam arrived. Tonight, Matthew, I think I will be sporting mainly black.

On the dot of six I watched on my computer screen as Sam approached my door. If I hadn't been expecting him, I would never have let him in. He just looked like trouble normally but dressed for business he was particularly daunting. Like me he was wearing loose black cargo trousers, a tight black lightweight top and a black woollen cap. You could tell we had been trained in the same place. The only difference was that he was wearing black desert boots and I had my steel toecaps on. His were designed for stealth mine for brutality. A good mix in a two-man team.

I buzzed him in before he reached the door and he smiled as he saw me in the shadows.

"Thank fuck! I thought I was maybe overdressed."

I threw him a "Dwr Cymru; Welsh Water" high visibility vest to wear and I put mine on. It made us look a hairsbreadth less intimidating but more importantly it would be the one thing any spectators would remember about us.

I pressed F12 on my computer and a part of the wall behind me swung open to reveal a rack of shelves filled with surveillance equipment. I took a small crate from the floor below the shelves and put it on my desk. I began to fill it with what I thought we might need.

"This is a find and rescue op. Fourteen-year-old girl run away from home; now with at least one maybe more, much older men, probably in one of two locations, possibly drugs involved as well. I hope to have intel on exactly where at 18.30 hours tonight. If we can find her for sure we will do a recce and snatch her as soon as we can. If not, we will take a location each to recce until we find her."

"What are the locations like?"

"Three storey house, all one unit, in Canton. Lots of pub and cafe cover nearby, on-street car parking alongside, and big car park at end of street. Same degree of cover at other location, a restaurant with accommodation above in Albany Road."

"How good is the intel?"

"If it comes it will be spot on. I expect it to come."

"Why a snatch. Won't she come voluntarily?"

"Teenage girl who ran away from a millionaire lifestyle voluntarily, I don't think she will want to come with us."

Sam looked us up and down and shrugged.

"Guess not. Both busy locations with plenty of hostile eyes on though. Why not have the parents come and get her?"

He knew that the riskiest part of the planned op would be lifting the girl. Anyone seeing us dressed as giant ninjas carrying a possibly noisy girl would be certain to call the police or worse still try and intervene. I was pleased to see he had come ready for business with his working head on. I had been worried, given the late call up on a Sunday. I didn't think he had used anything to sober up either. He had none of the nervous tics, which would betray them. He caught me looking.

"I have been off the sauce for a few weeks now, Jock. New woman, new start. No more waking up in the jail, or the gutter, for me. I was pleased you called though.

135

Christ it's boring being good. No wonder you never try."

For the second or third time that day I was forced to take stock of how others saw me. This wasn't the snap judgement of a stranger either it was the view of someone I regarded as an acquaintance if not a friend. Perhaps I should add a sixth column into my Sunday evening to do list for things that I had to undertake to improve my image. Worth thinking about, I thought.

"I don't think she would go with the parents just yet. She has only just run away from them. They would risk driving her further away and deeper into hiding. A kid her age would probably rather suffer than admit she had made a mistake."

"Thank fuck you are not like that!"

Again, with the analysis. Today was beginning to feel like some mass intervention. Perhaps God was speaking to me seeing as how it was Sunday. A couple of swift rums would soon drive Him away till another day but given Sam's newfound sobriety I thought better of it. Later!

I loaded up night vision and infra-red thermal goggles, four remote cameras with two receiving tablets to view, two directional microphones and four single use sticky microphones, a couple of walkie-talkies, two remote digital cameras and two hand held cameras, a hand full of movement sensors and two earpiece sets tuned to the microphones and walkie-talkies. All stuff for external surveillance. I didn't think we would have the chance to use internal bugs and trackers. I added two comms microphones and concealed earpieces for good measure.

"Anything else you think we'll need just put it in!"

He lifted a couple of heavy-duty rechargeable hand torches and a couple of head torches and carefully checked they were working at full capacity before throwing them into the crate.

"Some amount of kit you have Jock," he said, examining the shelves, "did you bring this with you when you left the regiment?"

He was taking a smoke alarm camera and microphone apart to see what else was in it. While he was distracted, I pressed F11 three times then F12 twice while holding down the door lock button and a section of wall alongside my front door swung open. Built as an integral part of my indestructible shop front and with a two-inch thick steel door expertly masquerading as a wall, this was where I kept my good stuff, in bundles of four.

Four bullet proof vests, four stab vests, four Kevlar helmets with carry bracket for the lights and cameras, assorted lengths of knives and machetes and kukris and the eye-catching four Heckler and Koch G36C carbines and four Glock 17 pistols and two of the smaller, concealable Sig Sauer P230s all securely stapled to the reinforced concrete back wall.

For good measure there was also a box of the G60 flash bang grenades especially developed by the research bods for UK Special Forces. They were well past their sell-by-date, but I presumed they still worked. Curiously the most destructive thing in there was in an easily overlooked plain metal box bolted to the floor. C4 explosive. Utterly harmless unless it was paired with the detonators, which sat in a much smaller metal box in my office safe.

"No. The stuff I took then would be all out of date now. That is the best of gear. This is the stuff I brought with me!"

He did his best not to look impressed but failed.

"Fuck me. I thought I did well to keep hold of an M16 rifle and a Makarov pistol from the previous occupiers of Afghan. You must have needed a fucking truck. If ever there is a civil war, I'm coming to live with you. One thing about you fucking Jocks. You take your fighting seriously. When are you ever going to need all this?"

"Take anything you want from the top three shelves. If we need anything below that we are out. This is only bringing a wee lassie home, not rescuing the Queens grandson."

He was like a bairn in Santa's Grotto the week before Christmas; picking up and trying knives and axes and clubs before settling on an American Whiplash extending baton. I thought it was the push-down locking and release that intrigued him.

"This'll do for me. Too many weapons just confuse me. I was never one of you kung fu guys killing targets in all directions. I was more of a batter the one in front of you kind of guy. What are you taking?"

I reached to the back of the top shelf and pulled out my pride and joy for non-lethal combat, an object that looked just like a grey stick and was probably the least imposing item in the cupboard. It was, in fact, a pickled hippopotamus penis stitched into an elephant skin sheath with a shaped ostrich skin grip and retaining loop. All in all, it was about eighteen inches long, I guess they didn't use all the penis! And meticulously tattooed into the elephant skin shaft was the word KIONGOZI.

It had been presented to me by some irregulars I had trained in South Africa to fight in a kind of civil war in part of Zimbabwe many years ago. They had taken weeks to pickle the penis and tan and tattoo the leather. It meant

LEADER in Swahili, which at that time was the only non-English language we had in common. Most importantly it was shaped and fitted to my left hand, leaving my right hand free to hold and fire a gun or brandish a blade.

No matter how hard you hit someone with it, or where, it would not kill them. It crushed muscles, paralysed nerves, flattened faces and rendered unconscious but it did not kill and sometimes that was important. It was far and away the best cosh I had ever owned. The extending baton Jim had was capable of all that as well of course, but it broke bones and could crush skulls and break necks. With the adrenaline flowing and under the pressure of an attack it was not always, or indeed often, possible to control the force used. Still, each to his own.

"All that fucking kit and you're going to use a blunt stick!"

Without looking I flicked it backhand with a minimal force into the side of his neck. His flinch turned into a stagger sideways.

"Fuck me that was like being shot. What the fuck is in that?"

"A hippo's dick."

He laughed disbelievingly before noticing that I was deadly serious.

"Wait till I tell her I was nearly knocked out by a man hitting me on the neck with his dick. What an epitaph that would be. Give me a shot."

I handed it to him. He took it in his right hand and slapped his left palm with it.

"What a wallop. I'll need to get one of these. What's it called, a Kiongozi? African is it? You could do some damage with one of these. Not very comfortable for me this one. Probably the right size for your girlie hands though."

"Where else would you get a hippo's dick? Kiongozi was my nickname over there. The idea is you can do a lot of damage but not kill anyone."

That tempered his interest in it.

"It's made for the left hand to keep your killing hand free."

He swapped hand and slapped his right palm a bit harder than he had his left.

"Fucking ace! Want to swap?"

"No chance. You had the first dip into the pool."

Just to piss him off a bit more I reached into a small recess and withdrew a perfect commando dagger in a rubber scabbard and slid it into a custom-made pocket in my trousers before strapping the top round my right calf with Velcro. The iconic symbol of the Royal Marine Commando and the basis of the SAS badge. The legendary Fairbairn-Sykes Fighting Knife.

Mine was a World War Two original with its ebony ringed grip and silver crown hilt and I kept it needle pointed and razor sharp on both edges. Not a true dagger, more a stiletto.

He could see it was an original by the crown hilt, though I had had to buy-in the RMC sheath designed for wear underwater. It stopped it gleaming and rattling in the dark, and most importantly stopped me from stabbing myself.

"Aw c'mon. I never saw that. That's not fair you know where all the best kit is. Can I have yours if you die?"

"We're taking a wee lassie home, Sam. No-one is going to die. Hopefully no-one needs to get hurt."

Although I said that I could see that both of us were ramping up a bit with the selection of gear and dressing up. We were both as excited as each other at the thought of a bit of action. Like little kids on Christmas Eve. Made all the better as we knew there was no real danger of loss of life or being captured and tortured. In those circumstances we had both experienced the kind of grim focussed humour, which pervaded everyone in the final hours and minutes before kick-off. Now it was more like the final assessment exercise on a course.

"I'm taking this then!" he said petulantly picking up an American switchblade. There was something about that boy and weapons that extend at the press of a button. Soundlessly I swung the wall closed and clicked it back into place. So perfectly did it swing into the window return that I could not tell where the door began, and I knew exactly how it worked.

As a final preparation I unlocked my bottom desk drawer and pulled out a ridged brown chemist's bottle of chloroform and decanted some into a small square Tupperware container. I then folded a small square of towelling from underneath the bottle and placed it on top to soak up the chloroform before sealing the lid and placing it in the pocket at the bottom of my left leg. Everything had a place on an op, and it was important that we both knew where they were.

On major ops every pack harness carried all the equipment in a prescribed pattern so that ammo or explosives or first-aid equipment could be accessed in the dark by touch alone by the wearer or someone pillaging their corpse.

Our bodies began to subconsciously prepare us for

action just from the stimulus of touching the weapons. Long remembered instincts released adrenaline into our bodies. Not the best preparation for a night of inactivity watching the target, but we were both experienced enough and well enough trained to cope with the chemical messages. It didn't stop us glancing at my phone in its charging cradle on my desk every few second, wishing it to ring and get our operation underway.

Nonetheless, when it rang Sam gave a small start! I was, of course, the epitome of cool and completely unflustered. In fact, I had noticed the incoming call signal flash just before the ringtone, so was prepared when the noise came.

"Getting jumpy on your old age Shaky!"

He was embarrassed that I had noticed. I had no problem with it. For me it was a further indication that he was mission ready, if not eager. Always a good sign as far as I was concerned. I picked it up the phone. It was indeed Fatboy.

"Right on time, big man. No problems were there?"

"No. very straightforward, Jock. The two numbers are currently live and located somewhere just south of Cathedral Road either in the car park or Pontcanna Fields. They have been active down there since around three this afternoon both making and receiving a volume of calls and messages. It was easy because they both have their Internet and GPS switched on. A couple of gay boys out cottaging are they Jock? Or somebody famous out dogging?"

Again, what kind of business did these people think I ran.

"Something like that. Thanks a million, I really do appreciate it. I'll drop that gift in tomorrow afternoon. Take care big man. I meant what I said earlier. You can call me anytime you need company. I would imagine the nights are the worst. Don't hesitate, right!"

"Thanks Jock. It means a lot. I never know when I might need to take you up on that, but it is important that I know I can. Thanks. Try not to get sucked in by these guys now it's dark."

And with that half pun he hung up.

Shaky was eyeing me expectantly. I nodded and he practically ran to grab the equipment crate from the desk. He really was anxious for a bit of action. Before he could get to the door the phone in my hand rang again. Theresa! I knew she wouldn't be ringing for nothing. I was worried my messenger hadn't turned up and now someone else had Kat's phone. It was the risk I took earlier, that someone else would outbid me for the loyalty of the taxi driver.

I waved him back and indicated with a raised palm that we were waiting a moment.

"Hi. I saw your driver earlier. Before I start on the work you gave me, I think you should have a look at the output. I sent it to our secure cloud before we make any decisions. Call me back and let me know if you want me to proceed. Speak to you soon."

She was always very guarded in communications; never used third party names if she could avoid it and rarely, if ever, identified herself by name. You never lost the habit I supposed.

At her suggestion we never emailed confidential intelligence directly to each other but used a discreet joint cloud account to send and store information. She didn't know but I used the same system with each of my operatives now. If anyone knew how vulnerable electronic comms were, it was her. My hacker had approved as well. No greater praise as far as I was concerned.

"Make yourself a cup of tea Sam. This will take a couple of minutes. More intel. The good news though is that the targets are all in the same location so we can stick together."

He practically threw the crate back on the desk, frustrated by the delay. I plugged a second black box into my computer and clicked on to Theresa and I's secure cloud account. The password filled in automatically because I could never have remembered the sequence of symbols and spaces Theresa used. She would have been raging if she had known I used autofill. It took about a minute to locate for reasons, which I never understood but were something to do with secure routing.

I saw the file at once and clicked on to open. There were three folders. The first comprised dozens of selfie type photos of Kat and Mo with some of Kat and Alfie towards the end. They were mostly taken in a domestic setting, probably the house we were heading off to watch. I motioned Sam over to have a look.

"Target one and Target two. They are the ones with the girl we are retrieving."

"You never said they were ragheads! I owe those fuckers a thing or two. Can you re-open Alibaba's cave. I might want an upgrade."

He nodded towards the wall at the door.

"Whatever you owe, it will not have been these two. They have probably never been further east than Newport!"

"Target two is a big fucker, isn't he?"

While he was looking, I was opening folder two.

Judging by the distance these were photos presumably either sent to Kat or taken on her phone by someone else. She would not have wanted her mother to have seen these. She was naked, or nearly naked in all of them, performing sex and various other sex acts with Mo in the early ones, Alfie in the later ones and the two of them somewhere in the middle, so to speak. It was hard viewing knowing she was only fourteen.

"She's only a fucking kid for fucks sake. There is no way these cunts are getting off with a warning, I'm telling you that Jock. Fucking animals, the lot of them. It doesn't matter if they are over there or over here there's no excuse for that. They're fucking having it!"

In truth I shared his revulsion. I was updating my plan away from minimal damage that was for sure. I waved him away before I opened the third folder, labelled external. A dozen or so videos. I only looked at one. Four Asian men all in their thirties or forties "enjoying" Kat's naked body. There was something odd about her passivity and I wondered about her being drugged or unconscious.

In a deepening anger I snapped it closed and disconnected from the cloud. I unplugged the black box and replaced it inconspicuously in the pile of disused chargers and adapters in my desk drawer. I pressed the recall button on my phone. Theresa answered at once. She had been waiting.

"I have seen samples of them. You see why I want them vanished for her sake."

"They are already gone from her equipment and from anyone she sent them to directly. There are three difficulties for you;

"First; some of these, notably the videos, originated

elsewhere and without the back trace it may be difficult for me to wipe them entirely.

"Secondly; some of the videos have been shared in a twenty-five member WhatsApp group. Very difficult to infiltrate without direct ISPN access.

"Thirdly; I am loath to eliminate all the evidence. These bastards deserve to face the law for what they are doing to that child.

"Besides all of that, given the ethnicity of the men involved I think some of my former colleagues would be interested in speaking with some of the men. As you know, it is always difficult for us to infiltrate these communities."

She left it at that. I knew what she was saying. Our anti-terrorist guys would use the videos to blackmail some of the men into spying on their fellow Muslims. For that to be effective they needed the videos. A cynical man might wonder if that was why so few of the grooming gangs had been prosecuted in recent years.

"Leave the stuff in our cloud only, if possible. After we have finished you and I can discuss how to proceed with any external agencies. I am going to try and recover the next youngster in the chain tonight before it gets as far as more videos."

I pondered into the silence. I could hear both of us breathing.

"I have sent you the names of the guys in the photos. Their mobile numbers are in the phone under those names. Both are currently connected to the Internet. It should help with the stuff on their phones at least. I'll send you a third number, a colleague of ours, Geraint. He may be able to help with the ISPN and WhatsApp problem. Give me five minutes to brief him before you contact him.

146

Anything you can do is much appreciated, you know that."

"I can see why now. Sometimes, I think you are a good man despite yourself. I hope we speak about this tomorrow."

As soon as she hung up, I called Swansea.

"Mister McLean, you just caught me. I was just on the way out. Did I forget something, boss?"

I knew for a fact that he seldom left the house. All his work was completed electronically. Any legwork he carried out was done at his own expense by his younger cousin. The main reason he worked for me was that I never pressured him to go anywhere. I suspected our regular meetings in his kitchen were about as far as he ventured.

"No! No! Nothing amiss at all, Geraint. I would, though, like you to help one of your colleagues if that's possible. She needs help tracking down some ISPNs and accessing a WhatsApp group. It's part of a child porn investigation. She is ex GCHQ and her husband still works there but we don't want to leave any tracks here. Any chance you can help?"

"I didn't know we did that kind of thing. Normally I would say that WhatsApp encryption is uncrackable but with her background she would know that's a load of fanny. Happy to help catch bastards like that anytime, in fact I do a bit for a similar group in my spare time."

I didn't ask what spare time he had just as I knew he wouldn't ask why Theresa was doing what she was doing. I was hoping he would think it was a relative of hers. I knew she would never give anything away.

"Thanks. Any charges just put them on expenses. She will call you shortly. Sorry to spoil your night out."

I texted Theresa with Geraint's number and a

147

message that he was expecting her call and left them to it. Sam was perched on my desk, annoyingly clicking open and closed the switchblade. Having seen the photographs, he was more eager than ever to be going.

"Is that the girl we are going to get?"

"Sadly not! She is just another wee lassie who has suffered at their hands. Same age and colour as our girl though. The aim is to stop them before it gets worse."

"You know I've seen them over there with their child brides and that and never even given it a thought, but those photos are just sick. I hope they put up a fight, I can tell you that!"

"The aim is to get the girl. First and foremost. Our only mission aim! Understand! However, I agree if target one or two are in site there might be need for a bit of restorative justice, but it mustn't jeopardise the mission or our safety. Clear."

"Certainly are, Jock. Rules of engagement are crystal clear."

He winked at me as if one of the young subalterns was giving the briefing and we were nodding along with no intention of following the orders once we were out in the field. I could see why he had failed the psych exam so often.

"Nobody dies! Right. Under any circumstances."

I knew I had killed people by accident, usually by not paying attention or being too fussy about casualties, and I assumed he had as well. I didn't want it to happen here. Both of us had to take care and be precise in what we did.

"Yes, Sir!"

He clicked his heels which was somewhat wasted by the soft soled desert boots. We checked each other's kit and the contents of the crate, fitted the comms earpieces and throat mics and ensured they were covered by our hats and collars and we were off.

Shaky threw the crate into the back of his van through the side door. It was an unremarkable white van with only the faintest of marks where he had removed the magnetic identifier panels from the side. I knew he had several different company panels to choose from depending on his need for disguise. Tonight, we were totally incognito in plain white. I didn't have to ask if he had changed the number plates; I could see the shine of the top clips holding the false plate in place in the streetlight.

We fired up the van and set off on the ten-minute drive to targets one and two's location.

"When we arrive, try and park where we can get remote eyes on the front. Park illegally if necessary. We know targets one and two are there. You maintain front obbo, I will get ears on the property and check their security. Once we have a clearer idea of what we are up against we'll decide what to do next."

Almost by the time I had unnecessarily explained this, I was giving Shaky directions into the street. It was easy enough to find from Kat's directions and confirmed by the Mercedes with the personalised plates parked outside.

"I didn't even know these were here! I thought there was just the park behind Cathedral Road. Nice aren't they. Not cheap down here."

We parked right on the corner directly facing the target house. Not ideal. It meant we would have to spend time in the back rather than the comfier front seats, but it gave us a clear view of the typical Canton two storey brick house with stone details and bay widows. The front door was in an arched recess outlined in yellow brick to match the stone details. Many of the houses had filled the archway with a second door but this one was open. There were tens of thousands of houses like this in Cardiff, but not many as expensive as these.

One advantage to where we parked was that Shaky could set up the front door camera through the windscreen without much trouble as opposed to forcing it into the roof vent to give three-hundred-and-sixty-degree coverage. It also gave us second camera coverage down the access lane to the mews houses at the rear of the main properties on Cathedral Road. People paid hundreds of thousands to live in a converted garage or stables. In its own way it was a form of madness.

Leaving Shaky tuning the cameras and microphones into the tablets, I set off for a recce. The art to being unobtrusive was not trying to be unseen but rather to be unremarkable. Thus, Shaky tuned the tablets in full view with the side door of the van open and I set off in my high visibility vest unhurriedly pretending to talk on my phone. I filmed the front windows and door and all the way down the lane at the side including the wall into the back yard and then down the lane which gave access for the ashers or bin-men as they are known everywhere else in the world.

There was a seven-foot-high side and back wall accessed by a door-sized wooden gate to the rear lane, but I could film the upper floors. I walked the full length of the lane and could see that as I had thought most of the houses had been turned into flats or multi occupant houses judging by the number of rear-facing room lights which were switched on. The good news was that the wall was topped by a smooth red coping to match the house brickwork.

There was no glass to impede or wire to snag any intruder. Probably too unsightly for this area.

I could see hardwired cameras on the clothes pole at the rear of the property and the top corner of the side wall where it abutted the single storey rear extension. I presumed both covered the back door. As I was walking along a motion activated security light came on in the backyard then moments later a second one came on two doors down.

I heard the cat that activated them before I saw it gliding over the wall and into the rear lane. I counted the seconds the activation lasted for. By the time the light went off I had been too dazzled to look for the motion detector. No-one looked from any of the rear windows to see what had caused the activation. I walked back to the rear corner and added our own battery-operated remote camera to the back wall.

I strolled back and motioned Shaky into the front cab. We both sat and he produced sandwiches from under his seat. Good cover if we were spotted and excellent ham and cheese sandwiches. I plugged my phone into one of the tablets and talked him through the results of my walk around. He would not interrupt. Never interrupt the briefer only ask questions at the end. As my old commander had drummed into us; there are no daft questions only silly bastards who weren't listening the first time.

"No real problems. We have the front, side and entrance covered from here and an unwinking eye on the back wall. I will go back and place ears on the front bay widows; ground and first, being the only illuminated windows at present. That should give us as much info as we need as to whether she is in there and what we are facing.

They have two wired cameras on the back door and for safety we will presume one in the front door recess. There is a rear facing security light with associated motion detector which you can see from the footage is mounted directly below the light at first floor level. The whole set-up is amateur hour."

"Fucking ragheads the world over, too fucking mean to pay for the right kit."

I knew what he meant but silenced him with a sideways look. He laughed aloud for appearance sake. Just two workers on overtime having their sandwiches and a laugh in the van. The security gear looked as if it had been bought in B and Q. Shaky nudged me and surreptitiously turned the radio on as an elderly busybody dragged her fat bundle of white fur towards us along the pavement. Entirely unembarrassed she rapped on my window. I think she expected a salute. I slid the window down.

"What is the problem?"

No preamble, no excuses just the unswerving right to know of the privileged addressing underlings.

"The water in the Centre," I nodded towards the charity offices in the church on the other side of the street, "is discoloured and under pressured. We are just looking to see where the leak might be. It's probably just a failed valve in the lane somewhere. No problems on your side are there?"

"No! No! None! I would have noticed. Lady has just had a bath. Typical, you can come out on a moment's notice for those vagrants but if we have any problems, we must wait weeks for a response. How long will you be here? Your van is parked illegally you know this is a resident's only street."

152

The perennial "Me First" wail of the entitled. I thought she deserved better, so I gave it to her.

"We will only be a couple of hours at the most. We don't have any digging gear with us. We are only here to find out how serious the problem is. If it is the main pipe, the street and lane would have to come up. That could take weeks. These old lanes are murder to excavate. The last one like this we did in Roath we had to end up replacing all the cobbles with tar."

"Well you won't be doing that here. This is a conservation area. I will be speaking to my councillor in the morning. It's bad enough the new people don't contribute to the area without that. Make sure there is no noise after nine, Lady and I go to bed early on the Sabbath."

Unable to leave without a final instruction to the staff to keep them in their place she dragged the poor ball of fur back to her residence. Shaky was quivering with laughter.

"Well said, Jock. That ought to keep the old bat awake all night writing letters. Shame she saw your face though."

Shaky had kept his face turned away throughout the exchange, taking a sudden interest in the church opposite.

"Lucky if she could see the van, Shaky, she had cataracts the size of your balls. Back to business! It looks as if the light and cameras are all on the one power feed coming through the rear wall just below the far bedroom window. See it! We could cut it just in the way in or cut it now and let them get used to it being broken. Which do you prefer?"

"Do it on the way in. The sensor and light are

blocked by the roof of the extension. The ground floor rear wall would be in shadow and the detector would not be able to see anything low and close to the wall. The light coming on would dazzle the remote camera and deepen the shadow to hide in. There are pockets of dark all the way down the garden. Fucking ragheads. Spend thirty quid and make their security much worse. Just think how badly they have fucked up back home with hundreds of millions of American dollars!"

Time away from service had not blunted his analytical skills but then again, he probably still used them every day stealing back cars for the finance companies.

"Right just the ears to go on. Anything else you can think of?"

"Any chance we can recce an escape route out the back way?"

"Will do. Comms on from now on. Any movement or lights double click me."

I opened the door without activating the overhead cab light. We were both too experienced for that. We both turned our throat mics on.

"Comms check one"

"Comms check two!"

We both spoke in a low voice but normally. Whispers carried much farther than murmurs and we both had long experience of it.

I took two of the Italian made sticky microphones and retraced my steps from earlier. The bay windows were on the lane side of the house and I reached over the wall and stuck the ground floor one on the side bay window easily enough.

The second one I threw up and it stuck easily onto

the bedroom window. They were designed to look like bird shit, and I knew they did, particularly from the inside and at night. They had a two-or-three-hour battery life, like the rear camera, and then they dried out and dropped off the window. That should be plenty of time for us. I waited to see if there was any reaction from within. There wasn't.

"Monitors active and operational five-five reception."

Pleased with that I took another stroll down the back lane looking for the cat from earlier. I was going to throw it over the wall to activate the security light. As ever when you needed one there was none to be found. Instead I removed the yellow vest and folded into my right-hand top pocket and just hopped over the wall, rolling across the red coping to land crouched at the corner of the wall and the rear extension.

Helping me were the recycling bins left in a jumble below the kitchen window. They hid me from anyone looking out from the ground floor, either the windows or from the back door. For anyone to see me they really would have to come well out into the back green. I would back myself against anyone in those circumstances. Their security really was appalling.

I waited the thirty seconds for the light to go back out and straightened up slowly. Again, why set the light to the minimum time? Probably just how it came out of the box. Although I could just as easily jump the wall back, I eased the bins into a kind of stairway leaving a nest to conceal us if we returned. Blocked by the extension I could move relatively freely against the back wall. I hadn't seen one, but the bins covered me if there was an infra-red capability in the back camera.

Flushed with success I crawled along underneath the windows. There was all kind of crap on the ground; empty cans, soggy cardboard, plastic bags and the remains of a chair. As my eyes adjusted to the darkness, I could see the whole back green was like a junkyard. Good cover but trip hazards everywhere.

Rather than come back I decided to check out the escape routes whilst I was there. The kitchen window eventually revealed a slightly dated but normal kitchen with a worktop underneath the window on the inside and the bins and rubbish on the outside. The window was fixed with a small ventilator in it. The back door was further along, directly opposite the front door by my reckoning. It was a dated half glazed plastic door. It would only take seconds to smash through, either in or out, in an emergency. The door led into the kitchen and then through a second door, currently closed, into the hallway.

I knew that from there the stairs would be on the right and the sitting room on the left usually through a door but sometimes the wall had been removed to leave an open sitting room/hall opening directly on to the street.

It took me less than a minute to rake the door lock open using my lock picks. I left it at that. No need to lose all we had gained for a hairsbreadth more information. I crawled back and rolled over the wall back into the lane, landing on my feet and walking away immediately but unhurriedly refitting my yellow vest.

Crossing the street back to the van Sam was still sitting munching away on his ham and cheese. Rather than go into the van I walked round to the driver's door. When I got there, I noticed it was ajar. Shaky was holding it closed, ready to leap out if necessary. I was pleased to see him so switched on.

"Lock up and we'll go for a pint. No point in sitting here all night for all to see!"

"You don't have to ask me twice."

He picked up his tablet and looked enquiringly at me.

"I'll do the visuals and English audio you just need an earpiece for the raghead shit on your phone if that's okay?"

I noticed he had set up one of the directional stick microphones across the dashboard towards the front door. Sound thinking if you pardon the pun.

"No problem let's go."

Just as we were locking up, one of those cycle food delivery guys turned up and went to the front door. We both turned away and used the van as cover so we wouldn't be seen by whoever opens the door. I knew the equipment was recording it all so didn't need to physically watch in real time. We hurried across the road and down towards the main road.

"Halfway or Conway?"

Two well-known Cardiff pubs. If I knew them, I was certain Shaky knew them. The Halfway being just across the road we settled on that without further discussion.

"There's a girl in there. I heard her on the upstairs audio. Young and very posh."

Shaky was from Barry so everyone sounded posh to him.

"Probably her. Did you catch a name?"

"No, some Cardiff guy kept calling her Champ as if it was funny."

"That would be her."

We hadn't wasted our time then. We were in the right place and had eyes and ears on Summer. All we needed now was a plan to retrieve and return her and we were done. Piece of cake really and still only half seven. Cause for a celebration rum I thought. I had been craving one all day.

The Halfway was three quarters empty; a few remnants of Sunday Dinner parties in the booths and two or three couples hiding after the kids had gone to bed and that was it. Even the pensioners who escaped the nearby retirement home were absent. Despite this the two bar-staff went through an elaborate ritual of ignoring us. Not the sort of place for high visibility vests and overalls it seemed, especially standing where the cameras didn't cover.

"A large dark rum and lemonade please dear and a…" I looked round enquiringly.

"Diet Coke."

"Pint or half pint?"

"Pint please, love."

"Ice?"

"No Thanks."

"Lemon or lime?"

"No, it's alright as it is thanks. No wonder every bugger drinks. The fucking choices you have to make does your head in."

We retreated up to the mezzanine at the rear of the pub. For the second time of day I deliberately sat in a corner looking down on the pub to make sure we were not overlooked this time rather than overheard.

"What was with the Paddy accent Jock. Trying to seduce the barmaid?"

"I didn't want her remembering I was Scottish. There are not enough of us in Cardiff to make it hard to figure out who it might be. I thought Paddy went better with the vests and boots!"

"That was why I went with Caaaarrrrdiffff see! She'll never comprehend that I am from the Vale," said Shaky in his poshest voice, which was not that posh if truth be told. That was why I liked working with him; the more serious he tried to be, the funnier he was.

I stood his tablet up facing me and the screen showed four images; front door, front street, side lane and back garden and door. Ground and front bedrooms were lit and so was the kitchen but that went out almost immediately.

I tuned my phone to the front room mic, and I knew Shaky was listening to the bedroom mic. We looked very unsociable each with a single earpiece and me watching on the tablet. Five years ago, everyone would have been watching us, but I knew from my necessary research in various public taverns that this was how most youngsters socialised these days. I had even seen them texting each other whilst sitting at the same table!

"So how is the repo business going?"

"Great! But I'm getting fed up with it. Not the action there used to be. My insurers insist I am wearing a body camera and stab vest all the time. It gets a bit boring then. I miss trying to get Land Rovers off gypsy sites. That was some real action."

He knew we were only faking a conversation but still launched into a long and very funny story about setting fire to a car as a diversion only to find it was his target car. I was so busy laughing I found it difficult to listen in. God knows how he was managing. He abruptly stopped just before one of the punch lines and listened intently for around a minute.

"Bastard!" He looked up for me to indicate it was safe for him to proceed as I could see the room behind him. I nodded; a lot less suspicious looking than him looking around all the time before speaking.

"Target One is trying to talk the girl into going downstairs to party with his mates, or at least show off her body to them. He's just finished shagging her as well! She is resisting. Good on her. How does it seem downstairs?"

"Four hostiles, one of them is probably Target Two. One of them is called Arfan, which is close enough to Alfie to be likely. I am struggling with the dialect. It sounds like Dhakaiya. I can pick out phrases and words but am struggling to follow it all. Sounds like they are going to have a party once their business is finished."

"Fuck me. You are only here as a translator and you can't even speak the language. No wonder they made you a Captain, you are useless enough to be an officer! And to think they didn't even let me in!"

He was laughing and I joined in. I had known dozens of useless officers in my time but never an entirely useless squaddie. Another food delivery guy cycled up to the target. Must be a big party that was the second one in fifteen minutes. I watched as the delivery guy looked up into the corner of the door recess.

Hidden camera? I wondered. I could hear the buzzer in the living room and the cries of recognition. So, confirmed as a hidden camera to a screen they could all see. I frantically tried to retune to the directional microphone but couldn't find it on my screen menu.

Therefore, I watched silently as the door was opened by another giant Pakistani, not Target Two, mainly muscle-bound though. Even opening the door seemed awkward for him.

"Tell him... kitchen... Adnan... number ten..."

Was all I could make out. I saw the kitchen light come on and go out again a minute later just as the rider reappeared, dumped his insulated bag onto the panniers and cycled off into the night towards the city centre. Confirmed only four hostiles in the living room and at least one other upstairs.

"Another food delivery. Must be some party."

I nodded again to let Shaky know it was safe to speak. No-one was paying us any attention up at the back.

"Target One still wheedling away at the girl, trying to get her to take some ecstasy as well now. She sounds too clever for him though. He has taken a couple of calls in Raghead. Want to listen?"

"Not yet."

Too conspicuous sharing earphones even in a nearly empty pub. Another mistake! One that really would come back to bite me and the girl later.

So, we continued. It was probably the most comfortable observation I had ever carried out. I had another couple of rums and Shaky stuck to the soft drinks, we shared a bowl of chips. We could have stayed there all night when the pub began to fill with groups of young-ish drinkers and the barmaid approached us. I hit the kill switch blanking the tablet and phone screens

"You will have to put your phones and tablet away, I'm sorry. The quiz starts in ten minutes and you can't have those out."

"No problem. We are just off anyway. Thanks."

In truth the punters had begun to sit near enough our table to be able to see and hear what we were doing anyway. I swigged down my rum, Shaky left his yellowy orange syrup and we picked up our kit and left. Outside we headed across the road and stood at the edge of the car park. We were both still listening.

"How is it going upstairs?"

"I think she is weakening. She has taken a couple of tablets. She said they had swords on them. It seems as if she might be going downstairs with just a dressing gown on from what I can hear. Her voice is very slurred now and he wants her to take another tablet."

"I have four hostiles in the front room. At least two of them are big muscly fuckers. I don't think this is just a party for the wee girl. They have had seven deliveries in just over an hour and a half, all placed in the kitchen and all the messengers left with something. I think this is a drug drop. If it is, there will be guns there as well.

The front door is very heavy, and I recognise the effort the doorman makes to open it. I had to get mine motorised to make it easier. It would be hard to smash through. There is concealed CCTV from the front door recess to the living room so any intrusion that way would be expected. There is no indication of any security elsewhere that we have not spotted."

"What's the plan then, boss?"

I glanced at my phone. Three minutes to check-in time.

"We'll go back to the van. I'll report in, you can have a walk round. See if there is anything we have missed. Give me ten minutes. See if you can think of a safe rescue for tonight."

By the time we got to the van it was nine exactly. I keyed speed-dial one. It rang once before being answered.

"On time, I like that. How goes it?"

"I'm sitting ten yards away from her listening to her every word."

"Well done! I see the recommendations weren't misplaced. I'm impressed."

"There's two problems. She ran away herself to be where she is."

"Nothing to do with me, after all then!"

"No but the second problem is that this is less Romeo and Juliet and more of a Sunday and Susannah situation."

I let that sink in. not an easy thing for a father to hear far less an estranged one who used to perform the same role.

"Perhaps not even a Sunday and Susannah more a Sunday and anyone else. I don't think there is much male affection here."

"You are sure this is not related to me."

"No, her best pal was snared first. I am as certain as I can be that it is a co-incidence. Nothing to indicate otherwise at your end?"

"Not a word. I think you are correct in your assessment. How deep in is she?"

"Just with the hooker at present but that may be about to change. Drugs involved as well, recent though. Two or three weeks at most as far as I can establish."

"Get her out as soon as possible before this gets out of control. Try and keep her safe with you overnight. I will think about the way forward and let you know."

"I am just going to call her mum. I'll let her know she is safe and well and run away of her own accord. I will tell her I will bring her back tomorrow morning. How does that sound?"

"Always thinking of tomorrow aren't you. No bad thing. That sounds as good as we can manage. I will leave this phone on. Let me know once you have her safe and if there are any repercussions. I will think of what to do and say to her mother. Use any force necessary. I can arrange to have it cleaned up if need be. Do you understand?"

I understood fine but no-one was going to die here tonight. Five grand might buy that in his world but not in mine.

"Speak to you later!"

I hung up and speed dialled three. Not the Mum but Grampa. It was answered immediately.

"Is this bad news? Is that why you are calling me? Susannah is in the front room waiting for the house phone to ring. Where have you been? We have been calling you every hour. Please, we are desperate."

"Summer is fine. She has run away with an older boyfriend. I am sitting ten yards from her listening to every word she says. She is fine and well do you understand?"

He was shouting.

"She is alright, fit and well the Scotsman has her. She is alright sweetheart. Safe and well."

I heard the feet running towards him before Snow White was shouting at me.

"Thank You! Thank You Mister McLean. Thank You. Put her on. Let me talk to her! Thank You. Anything we can do, anything at all."

"She is not with me at the moment."

"What do you mean? Dad said you had her…"

"She is ten yards away from me. I am outside the house she is staying in and can hear every word she says. She is safe and well and in no physical danger."

Fingers crossed.

"Where are you? I can come and get her."

"She is with a boyfriend. She has run away to be with him. I will get her back but if we simply force her home now, she will run away again, and I might not be lucky enough to find her next time."

"What boyfriend? Is it one of those arseholes from the choir?"

I doubted she had ever called anyone an arsehole in her life before. It did not sit well on those pretty lips.

"I do not know how they met."

More fingers crossed.

"I will get her home by tomorrow morning. We will try and work out why and how this happened then, in the meantime try and think of how to stop her running away again."

"Bring her straight home. It doesn't matter what time it is. Please I must see she is okay. Please bring my baby back to me. Call me as soon as she is safe. Please! I won't be asleep. Call me please. Let me hear her voice."

"I have to go now before we are spotted. I will call later. Promise."

Shaky climbed back into the driver's seat as I finished the call.

"What's the plan then?"

"If she stays safe in her room, we wait till the deliveries are over. Hopefully a couple of the hostiles will leave, and we can sneak in during the night and snatch the

165

girl. Otherwise it will have to be a Blitzkrieg attack.

If she comes downstairs into the front room with target one, she will be in immediate danger. These bastards film themselves taking turns with the kids and put them somewhere on the Internet. We cannot let that happen. If she comes down, we will give it ten minutes, tops, to see if there is another delivery.

If there is, I will force through the front door when it is opened. You come in through the back door. It is open. The front room will be crowded. First of us through the door takes the furthest away hostile. Be aware for weapons. Then it is every man for himself.

If neither of these becomes the plan, after ten minutes I am going in through the front window. Noisy and messy and we would have to be quick.

Escape One is the van, leave the keys in the ignition, turn right and left and away but only with the girl. If we split, Rendezvous One will be the car park at the Severn Café in Canton every fifteen minutes.

Escape Two is over the back wall, left down the lane to the end-house, which is being converted to flats, over the back wall and in to hole up for a rethink. Worst case, back wall, left down lane and over the far wall straight into the darkness of the park.

No deaths! Clear!"

"Fuck me, Jock you don't half go on. Do they teach you that at Sandhurst? It's in, grab the girl, out and away! Is that about right."

"That's about it. We go on my call. I take the front you take the back. Faces covered, there may be other cameras."

"I might as well go around the back now. Give the

166

light time to go back off."

"Let's leave it until we know where the girl is."

"He is still trying to persuade her to party with his mates. Right evil bastard this one!"

We both got out of the cab and climbed in the back, out of sight. We didn't want anyone calling Welsh Water saying their two workers in Pontcanna were lazy bastards who had spent all night sitting in the van! We stretched out. As it was Sam's van, he got the yoga mat on the floor. He didn't fool me; he was bursting to get into action.

There was another delivery and it sounded to me like someone had shouted upstairs that there was only one left to come. They seemed to be moaning in the living-room about how it was always the same guy who was late every week. Although I couldn't understand all the words, I understood the tone well enough. Moaning was moaning in most languages. The universal language of the squaddie.

"Action Stations, Jock. He has persuaded her to come and meet his mates."

I heard the lewd comments at my end too. Shaky was already sat up, checking his laces and the equipment in his pockets. I did the same. We both clicked our throat mics on.

"Comms check one!"

"Comms check two!"

"Happy hunting, Jock"

"Ten minutes from now on my say!"

And with that he was off. Unrolling his hat into a ski mask over his face, he went over the side wall considerably more elegantly than I had. The rear light came on and thirty seconds later went off. No-one in the living room even commented. I checked my laces, the equipment in my pockets, loosed the scabbard on the commando dagger, the key in the van ignition and that all the doors remained unlocked. Then we both waited. I could hear them all cajoling the girl with wheedling tones and sharp commands. I may have to go in early if it kept up.

We were both lucky and unlucky. Lucky that the last delivery came when we needed it to; unlucky in that the delivery boy was another massive fucker.

"On my GO! Countdown!"

All I got in response was a click. No need to waste words. The adrenaline flooded my body and I breathed heavily to try and control it a fraction. I watched the messenger park his bike against the wall just where I had intended to go over it. The recess security light came on, the messenger pressed the buzzer and waved to the camera. I heard the buzzer in my left ear and the grumbling about whose turn it was to answer. They all wanted to stay and watch the girl.

I strode across the road. The door began to open, and time slowed right down as it so often did in the first phases of any action. I rolled down my ski-mask over my face. One whispered word.

"GO!"

EIGHT

The Rescuers

The doorman was the second big hostile. As everyone else had done, he reached round the door to push the front with his right hand whilst pulling the handle at the back with his left. The delivery boy blocked his view of me for the few seconds I needed. I hurdled the low gate at a full run and hit the courier with my club flush on the back of his neck, just below his cycle helmet. Rather than protect him, it gave rather a good guide to the sweet spot for rendering unconscious.

Maintaining my momentum, I pushed the courier as hard as I could into the door, turning to drive my right shoulder into the door for good measure. The courier's head hitting the door did nothing for his condition and his helmet split in two. The door struck the big hostile square in the middle of his forehead and whilst not unconscious he was disoriented. He was reaching for something behind the door with his left hand. A weapon, I guessed.

My hippo's dick was in the wrong hand for a telling strike so I butted him as hard as I could right on the side of his temple. He started to slide down the wall but was not yet out of the game. I kicked hard at him, adjusting

169

my aim to his jaw at the last split second. If I had kicked at his head, he would have been dead. As it was, I only broke his jaw and a few teeth on his way to Sleepy Town.

I heard a horrible crunch and looked up to see Target Two pitching forward into the kitchen past a smiling Shaky, blood pumping from a massive scalp wound. He must have been going to get the stuff from the kitchen when Shaky came in. It would have been a shock for him, I supposed.

Fewer than ten seconds and the three biggest hostiles were off the board. The living room door was at my end of the hall and I piled in through it. Keep moving forward, that was the plan at this point. Even with two occupants missing the living room was still crowded. Had I come through the window I would have landed on one of them. They were playing Call of Duty on a giant television on the side wall. As agreed, I went for the far hostile. Not an easy task as the girl was sprawled naked on the floor.

I didn't hesitate, no time for hesitation or thinking my old trainer had taught me, maintain the element of surprise. I ran right over the girl. I left two behind for Sam to deal with. If he failed, I was taking one in the back.

"GUN!!"

Target One was sprawled in an armchair at the far end of the room. On his right side, butt end resting on the threadbare carpet, was a full-sized shotgun. That became my sole focus. I knew, by where and how it was resting, that I was not dealing with anyone who was either trained or competent, but even the village idiot can blow a giant hole in you with one of those. I had seen them do it, as well.

He was trying to sit up and reached for the gun

with his right hand. Still three or four steps away I dived full length. Funnily enough, I had been trying to teach the women's scrum half how to dive pass, and this wasn't unlike that skill. He thought I was diving at the gun, but all I was doing was aiming to land on his forearm. I landed on it just as his elbow was on the arm of the chair. Fifteen stone of mostly muscle, and some bone if you included the head, landed square on his arm, folding the elbow into the most un-natural position imaginable and snapping several things with an alarming cracking sound.

He started to scream and there was nothing I could do about it. My weight was all forward, and I had to wait for my legs to catch up and get below me to allow me to manoeuvre. It seemed to take forever but it was way less than a second before the hippo's dick worked its magic again and ended his suffering, at least for the present. I was still worried by the noise though. I turned around.

Sam had taken the first guy on the couch with at least one blow to the face from his baton. There was a lot of blood again. The second guy had got up and was standing with his back to the wall under the television, waving a giant machete. They loved their giant machetes these guys. This one looked big enough to fell hardwood trees. He waved it at Sam who was standing between him and the door.

"Let me out or I'll cut you in two, Whitey!"

I don't know why but threats always sounded funny to me in Indian accents. Too much "It Ain't Half Hot Mum" as a child, I think. I was confident Sam had this covered and bent to check on the girl who had barely moved even after I had trodden on her. It must have hurt some I thought. My disregard infuriated him.

He took a massive backswing and lunged at Sam intending to fight his way out. It was the only realistic plan he could think of, though I would have dived for the window had I been him. The problem with long weapons in enclosed spaces is that you cannot swing them without hitting a wall or ceiling. Sam knew this, he didn't.

Sam shocked him by jumping towards him rather than away. Once he was within arms-length it was effectively all over. The hostile couldn't swing the blade into the short distance between them and, of course, Sam could now reach him, which he did. Ignoring the blade Sam grabbed both sides of his shifta, the loose-fitting shirt, and pulled him square into the most ferocious of head-buts. Even fifteen feet away, I heard the nose crunch and squelch. It is unusual to knock someone out with a head-butt, however, I guessed this wasn't the first time Sam had done it. The hostile dropped like a stone.

"Girl okay?"

"Just the drugs, I think. Clear and shut the front door."

Less than twenty seconds, one brief scream and it was all over. Six hostiles down and no injuries. Four hours of waiting, sixty minutes of planning and twenty seconds of action. About the usual ratios, I thought. Shaky came back as I was trying to wrestle the girl back into her dressing gown and park her on the couch in the space conveniently left by the guy with the machete.

"No commotion in the street! No extra lights on. I think we are okay."

"Well done Shaky! You were a bit quick in, weren't you?"

"I figured I was as well in the kitchen as out the

back if it all kicked off. The big fucker just walked right into me!"

Four hours of waiting, sixty minutes of planning and the Para just decided to start early. You had to laugh. "Thick tools for running head-first into an immovable object all day," that was how my old sergeant described the Paras. But still you had to laugh.

I could see two webcams recording in this room. They seemed to be focussed on the girl. Both cables led up through a hole drilled in the ceiling near the back wall. We were still masked so I wasn't too worried, but some of these guys had serious injuries. No sense in leaving the police a record of what happened. I pointed out the cables to Sam.

"I'll bet they all go to the same computer where the cable for the lights and cameras come in on the back wall. Probably in that back bedroom."

I didn't think they would run a power supply into the bathroom.

He didn't need telling twice. I thought about the girl.

"Try and find the girl's kit upstairs. She will have a bag of some sort. No point in leaving a trace of her."

With that in mind I set out to retrieve the hostile's phones as well. Bound to be pictures of her. I started with Target One. The bastard who had started it all. They would struggle to make his arm look normal again. I didn't think the arm and sore head were enough of a punishment, so I took the dagger and sliced off a fair piece of his nose. It would bleed but wouldn't kill him. I knew they could never reconstruct a nose without considerable scarring. Usually the skin graft was taken from the forehead and left a

173

distinctive penis shaped scar. He never even stirred.

I lifted his phone from the chair. His phone was on the left chair arm, where the gun should have been. Who leaves a gun barrel side up on their right-hand side? From there he would have had to lift it by the barrel in his right hand, change hands to place his right hand at the trigger end and only then swing the gun into the firing position. That was the time it took me to disable him. Amateur.

The machete guy's phone was still on the couch. It joined his mate's in my calf pocket. Couch guys was still in his hand and took a bit of getting out. His hand was in spasm and his breathing was poor. I think he was in a bit of trouble.

The doorman was stretched out where Sam had dragged him in by the collar. His phone was in his pocket. He had been reaching for another shotgun leaning against the doorframe near the hinges. Again, wrong side. He would have had to close the door to reach it and even then, it would have been in the wrong hand. It should have been clipped waist high on the opening side of the frame where he could reach it and use it through the open door. Beginners mistakes really.

I didn't need the courier's phone but rolled him over and took it anyway. I thought it unlikely he had photographs of the girl but why not take it anyway. Old intel gathering habit. Take everything you can carry. Good job I did. Right in the middle of his chest was a cyclists Pro Cam and I was smiling right into it. I lifted that as well.

Target Two had lost a lot of blood and his phone had fallen on the kitchen floor before being enveloped by the blood pool. I picked it up carefully and looked for something to wipe it with. As my eyes adjusted, I could see the deliveries from the couriers stacked up on a table beside the door. I opened one and it was full of cash. I presumed they all were.

Cash in; drugs out. I looked for the drugs. There were three waxed packets on the worktop like the ones inside cereal boxes. Even in dim light I could see the tablets in one and wraps in another.

In the cupboard underneath I found six large breakfast cereal boxes. They were totally out of place in that they were clean and neatly stacked. I looked in.

The waxed bag in the first one was filled with the violet tablets Kat had given me, as was the second. The third and fourth were filled by herbal cannabis and the last two, the grey crystals. I emptied the bin over the floor and put the six waxed bags from the full cereal boxes and all but one of the food containers filled with cash into it. I left the waxed bags on the worktop and one food container of cash for the police to find. It was heavy and tempted as I was to drag it across the floor, I did not want it going through the blood on the floor.

I broke open all their phones and added the sim cards, batteries and phones to the pile in the bin. I heard Shaky thump back down the stairs.

"Got the recorder and all of her kit, I think. I just threw all the shit in the bathroom into her bag. I lifted the camera off the back wall on the way in. Is that us?"

"We'll take the girl between us to the van. You stay with her and I'll get the rest of the shit. Let's get a wriggle on. Some of these will be waking up soon. Not the ones you hit right enough!"

"You've a bloody cheek. That guy's nose didn't look like that when I went upstairs!"

We both laughed. Shaky checked the street, scraped the mic off the downstairs window and brought the couriers bike in and dumped it in the kitchen. I lifted Summer and adjusted her dressing gown as best I could. I thought about the two of us lifting her. It would obscure her from anyone looking out but would involve a lot of faffing about at the door and getting into the van. I decided to go for me lifting and Sam checking the street and opening the van.

"I'll take her. You look out and get the van open. I'll come back and get the luggage. Okay?"

"You get the luggage and I'll reverse the van into the street before we load anything. Less overlooked ground to cover. How about that?"

"Better. Let's go."

Shaky strolled over to the van carrying Summer's bag, climbed in and drove it into the lane before reversing down to double park right at the target gate.

I scooped Summer on to my shoulder. She weighed the square root of bugger all. Shaky checked and nodded me forward. He opened the side door to the van while I walked out and placed Summer into the van. He was fussing around her making her comfortable on the yoga mat as I walked back to pick up the bin. If anything went wrong now, we still had the target in the van. The stuff in the bin was bonus. I almost walked into the old dear dragging her dog along.

"What did you find? You're not going to have to dig up the road, are you? I couldn't sleep for worrying you know?"

I moved to block her view and heard Sam slide the door closed. I prayed Summer would not choose now to

176

make a noise.

"I spoke to your colleague earlier and he thought it might be weeks."

She didn't even recognise me.

"No! I think we have it solved now. We will know for sure in the morning, but it looks all clear for now."

"Thank goodness for that. We would not have been able to cope with all the noise and mud and disruption. I hope you don't mind me saying but I noticed earlier that you had left your van open. You shouldn't really do that around here. It may seem a nice area, but we get all sorts visiting in there."

She nodded to the project offices.

"Well then, sleep well. I don't think there is much to worry about in the water."

She turned around and dragged the poor dog home without a backward glance. I took Summer's bag and the security laptop over and dumped them in the front seat. I then carried the bin balanced on my boot for extra support. The last thing I needed was for the bottom of the bin to fall out.

Before pulling the front door closed, I stood and went through my mental checklist making sure we had done all we could before leaving. I was satisfied. I pulled the door closed. Mission over and successfully completed. I hobbled over and lifted the bin into the back before climbing in after it and strapping it to the rear of the front seat.

"Drive on. Stop somewhere down Penarth Road for debrief."

And we were off and away clear. Halfway down Penarth Road we pulled into one of the dark side streets among a jumble of industrial units. I didn't need to check that we were away from any cameras I knew Shaky had that covered. Summer had barely stirred and was quietly snoring when we stopped. We piled out, removed the number plates and stowed them in a compartment in the back doors, stripped off the gloves and comms equipment and put them back in the crate along with the knives and clubs.

"Can I keep this please Jock? I was impressed with how it worked!"

I was less than impressed. I thought the metal baton had inflicted some terrible damage on the two hostiles it was used against. Then again, perhaps that was just Shaky. He might have caused just as much damage with his fists. In any event I would have been loath to use the baton myself having seen it in action close hand.

"Take it away with you Sam. Use it in good health."

"If I use it, it will not be my health I will be worrying about."

"Good job tonight, Shaky. That's as well as I have seen you work."

"Aye, the sobriety seemed to help. I miss the fighting though. I wish they had been a little more professional tonight. It all seemed to be over in a flash. Thanks for the outing Jock. I really needed it."

I reached into the bin and pulled out a food container.

"There should be a bonus in there for you Shaky. I think I will have to give the rest back to keep me square with the owners."

"I would have done it for nothing, truth be told, but

thanks for the thought. I appreciate it. I appreciate you thinking of me, big man. I know guys like me are ten a penny."

"Guys like you are priceless, Sam. Especially now you are not in jail every second weekend."

"Drop you back at your office, Jock, or are we taking the girl straight home."

"No! The office is fine. Her mammy can pick her up once she is a bit cleaner and tidier. It's a bit too obvious what she has been up to if I take her home like that."

"You're a nice man, Jock. A very nice man."

And off we drove back down to the Docks and home for me.

I clicked my roller shutter up and went through the rigmarole of opening the door before Shaky and I lifted all the gear into my office and finally the girl, still wrapped in her dressing gown and snoring away like a sailor. I laid her gently on the couch I had woken up on that morning. It fitted her a lot better than it had fitted me.

I would fetch her a pillow and cover once Shaky had gone and my door was closed and locked. I didn't want to have to explain why I had a naked fourteen-year-old on my couch. Shaky gave me one last hug then shot off into the night and his new life of tranquillity and light. I doubted it would last long given the gleeful smile on his face when he cracked Target Two over the head with that baton.

The door locked automatically behind him and I clicked the roller shutter down. There was no way of telling from the outside whether I was in or out now. Just the way I liked it really. Less than twelve hours from start to finish, the whole job. Who wouldn't be satisfied with that!

Three calls to make and then a celebration rum. I

was thinking about the rum when the order of calls came to me. I started by checking if any of the hostile's phones would allow an emergency call. As luck always had it, it was the one covered in blood. I put on my gloves again and keyed in 999 with a pen and hit the call button with the same implement. No sense in spreading more blood about.

Best broad Belfast accent again, trying to speak quickly, "Hello, police please. Hello, I was just passing a house when I heard a loud scream then all the lights went out. There is no-one answering the door. I am worried someone is hurt in there. No! I don't know this number; it is my boyfriend's phone. I don't want to be involved. My wife doesn't know I am down here. It's the house on the corner directly behind the Wallich Centre on Cathedral Road. Thanks!"

I hung up and turned the phone off before removing the SIM card and battery again. I didn't mind hurting them, but I didn't want anyone to die. Too many people knew I was looking for them. One was too many people to know as far as I was concerned. No police force liked a murder on their books. Drug dealers hurting each other was a far different matter.

Next I called the client. Time to 'fess-up about stealing a lot of money and drugs that ultimately probably belonged to him. I used my phone and the case SIM card.

"Hi, I have her now. She is sound asleep in my office, sleeping off whatever they gave her. There was no further interference with her as far as I can determine. I have retrieved all of the recording devices present, so hopefully we were in time and have captured all of the images."

"Well done indeed Mister McLean! Less than

180

twelve hours. I cannot thank you enough especially given the circumstances. Lenny will drop in with your fee next time he is passing. No need for an invoice. Let's hope she doesn't run away again."

"I've had a thought on that. I intend showing her the images before I destroy them. I want her to see what they intended for her. I have several other images of them with at least one other young girl. That should be enough to dissuade her of the romance of her situation."

"Great idea! The difference between just dumping her back and explaining her choices. Let her think of it for herself. I tried that with Susie before we knew she was pregnant."

The tiny maggot of a thought that had been crawling at the base of my brain just got a little fatter. I continued to ignore it.

"There is one problem left to deal with. One between you and I."

I could feel the frost down the line.

"We have no further business together, though that is not to say that I couldn't put some business your way. I really do appreciate how you have handled this matter. Even Gary was on your side when we spoke earlier. Quite an achievement, that is."

"No, this is an issue between us."

"Yes?"

"Yes! When I retrieved the girl there was quite a lot of collateral damage to her companions and she came with quite a lot of baggage which I presume ultimately belongs to you."

"I am not bothered at all by any collateral damage. I assume there were no civilians involved?"

"No. None at all, but half a dozen of our breakfast companion's friends will be eating hospital food tomorrow."

"Who cares? It's a hazard of the profession they chose for themselves."

"Our business was not their main concern. They appear to be traders on our friend's behalf. I'm afraid I caught them cashing up for the week."

He was thinking.

"How much are we talking about?"

"At least ten times my agreed fee in cash and probably a lot more in excess stock."

He was thinking a lot harder now.

"Did you not think just to leave well alone?"

"I left enough to make it obvious what they were doing but, I did not think you would want to lose that amount."

"So, you took it for me?"

"Certainly. I have no use for it. Get Lenny to arrange a courier pick-up and you can have it all, except my fee, of course."

"You know Mister McLean, there are not many people I would believe in this situation but, I believe you. I even trust you just to take your fee. Someone will call about the arrangements later. I presume we can keep this between ourselves?"

"Of course, who would I want to tell. It could cost me my balls, at least."

"What about your colleagues?"

"What colleagues? As Chairman Mao said, "a secret is only a secret if only two people know, and one of them is dead" this was a one-man job."

I knew I was alright because he began laughing.

"I look forward to our friend explaining this loss to me. Believe me I will make him suffer for this. I might just pop through to your city personally. This line will stop working now but you can always reach me through Lenny. You have made my day Mister McLean, in more ways than one. Perhaps I will see you soon."

And he was gone. I went over the conversation in my head and could think of no identifiers which would incriminate me if Theresa's husband's team were listening in. Just my name and Lenny's and a proper business transaction. He would get an invoice and there would be a file, just not one that mentioned the injuries or the money or the drugs.

My final conversation should in theory have been the easiest. Speed dial two and an immediate answer. The maggot's tickling gave way to a rush of butterflies in my stomach. Strange, I never felt those going into real action. Just phone calls with gorgeous women it seemed.

"Is she all right? Is she safe? Do you need anything? Is there anything we can do?"

"I have her travelling behind me with a female colleague right now, Mizz Gregor. She is safe and well and fast asleep. I will have her home tomorrow morning at the latest."

"Thank you! Thank You! Thank You! Please bring her straight home. Can I speak to her?"

"She is in a car immediately behind me and fast asleep. It would be problematic to speak to her at present, but I can assure you she is safe and well."

If you can invent a female colleague; you can invent a car, as far as I was concerned.

"Can we come down and be there when you arrive. Wait for you somewhere. Meet you at the services perhaps. Please! I just want to see her."

Instead of the easiest this was becoming the most difficult. It was like lying to my ex-wife. I was just getting in deeper and deeper. I was out of practice at this lying on the telephone game. I decided to kill two birds with one stone.

"If you could meet me at my office down the docks at seven tomorrow. We need to make sure she doesn't do it again. I may not be so lucky next time. We can try and decide a way forward. Do you know the address?"

"I very much doubt it was luck Mister McLean. You do not look like a man who relies on luck."

Be still my beating heart. I was like a little boy in school. If she could catch a man like Sunday Smith capturing me was child's play to her.

"I have your card with the address on it."

Inspiration came to me. I much preferred seeing her away from her stepfather.

"Please come alone. I know it will be difficult for Gary. Perhaps, he could wait outside in the car, if necessary, but I really think we don't want to overwhelm Summer. She may find it easier to talk about why she did what she did, to her mum. We all have to try and do what's best for her, for now."

"She would probably be happier with Dad. She has always been Grampa's little angel, but I take your point. I will see you at seven then."

"And Mister McLean, thank you! Take good care of my little girl."

And she was gone, like so many other women in

my life. What a maudlin thought. That was me coming down from the adrenaline rush of the action. I had always been like that, depressed after a mission. Looking at the veteran's mental health units. I did not think I was the only one.

The lies had given me an idea though. Score one for the sub-conscious mind, not to be confused with the unconscious mind, which is what I usually used through the week. One more call then.

NINE

The Madame

I picked up the office phone and selected the never-used line eight. It rang immediately.

"John. Everything alright?"

We had a simple code. If I wasn't alright, I would answer "Fine Thanks"; if I just wanted to speak to him, I would respond "can't complain". "Fine thanks" would bring a half a platoon of variously armed Vietnamese rushing downstairs to my rescue.

"Can't complain Mister Lui."

Mister Lui nominally owned, but without doubt ran, the brothel, which occupied the top two floors of the building. You could call it a massage therapist and sauna all you want but there had been a brothel there since the docks had been run by the Maltese in the sixties, probably even before that.

"There are no complaints about my end of the building, are there Mister McLean. No difficulties I must address."

That made it three calls in a row where I had been Mister McLean. I had finally become my father but without the unnecessary cruelty, I hoped.

Mister Lui was under the impression that I factored the building for the firm of solicitors who acted for the eventual owners, an invented company in the British Virgin Islands. Only my personal solicitor knew that I was that company, and it suited me to keep it like that, otherwise the people who owned Mister Lui would pressure me into giving them the property for next to nothing.

"No. No problems!"

We had invented the code because no matter how we laid out the entrance there were still people who thought my office was part of the brothel. On a couple of occasions individuals had come into the office to threaten, or even hurt me, thinking I was part of their security team.

I had dealt with them, but one time it had become a bit messy and friends of Mister Lui had needed to clean up and dispose of a couple of badly injured thugs. I hoped they had just dropped them off anonymously at some far-off casualty unit, but the reality was, who knew?

This incident had offended Mister Lui's honour and he had paid for my nice shiny new office frontage although I had chipped in the lion's share for the massive upgrade in security. In general, we rubbed along nicely. The rent was always paid on time, both the bank invoice and the cash portions and any maintenance or repairs were always carried out immediately. Unusually, I never had any problem getting tradesmen to make themselves available at a moment's notice to carry out work in the rooms full of scantily clad women.

"I was wondering if you had a woman available, I could have for the night?"

"Well, well, there is a first time for anything. I have always told you that such a service would be available to

187

you on the house at any time. I shall send one down immediately. No charge! But if you choose to tip that would be up to you."

"It's not like that! I have a drugged up, naked, fourteen-year-old, girl asleep on my couch. I rescued her from some very bad Muslims, and I don't want her to wake up and think I am with them."

I said Muslims to indicate that this would not cause any business problems for him, that the girl had not come from one of his rivals, or indeed colleagues, for all I knew. After all, I supposed he dealt in drugged up, naked, fourteen-year-old girls somewhere in his supply chain. Not upstairs here. Too close to the politicians and police for any of that illegal, forced labour kind of prostitution to be seen, but I had no doubt his people ran other less scrupulous establishments elsewhere.

"I will send down Mama-san. She is used to comforting young girls far away from home."

I knew Mama-san well. She often popped in for a chat and a coffee after she had done the shopping for the girl's upstairs or dropped down the cash portion of the rent. She always told me she had been too old and ugly to work the brothel but that she cared for the girls like her own daughters. I believed her.

She had been up there for the ten years I had been in business here, there had been five different incarnations of Mister Lui in that time. Either she was the real boss, or a spy for the real boss to keep the Mister Luis honest. I pressed for the roller shutter to go up and within seconds she was at my door.

"Mama-san thank you for coming."

"I am glad to get out. It is a very quiet night up

there. When we don't keep the girls busy, they do nothing but complain, complain, complain. Glad to be away from it. I brought some banh tieu. I made them myself. Get the good coffee on."

She placed a plate of what looked like Eccles cakes on my desk. They smelled wonderful. I went to the kitchen and put the expensive, clients only, coffee in the machine. I would add it to a mug of microwaved milk with six, yes six, sugars in it. That was how she liked her coffee. She shuffled over to the couch and examined Summer.

"Get a cover and pillow for this girl! She will hurt herself, all curled up like that."

There was no doubt she was used to giving orders. And having them obeyed at that. She was smoothing Summer's hair. I ran up the stairs and returned with the duvet and pillows from my own bed. I was pleased to note they were clean and smelled fresh. One up for Claudia, my cleaner. Of course, I hadn't slept in the bed since Thursday.

"She is very beautiful. Is she your daughter?"

The first person to imply anything the least bit complimentary about me all day. I could have kissed her.

"No. She is the daughter of a friend. I'm just keeping her safe here until her mother comes for her."

"Her mother must be beautiful."

"She is!"

"Beautiful girls never have to work for anything but when their beauty fades, they are lost forever."

There was no pain, no longing in her voice. Just a simple acceptance of the facts. I didn't know what to say.

"You should change. When she awakes, she doesn't want to see a soldier. The women upstairs may think it makes you handsome, but it will only frighten a

189

child."

Handsome eh! I was bouncing back from depression quite quickly. I put her milky syrup into the microwave and poured myself a mug of the good black coffee. I lifted one of the banh tieu and took a small bite. The smell was making me hungry, but I was always wary of Vietnamese food. You never knew when there was a killer blast of chilli in the dish, even desserts and cakes.

This cake was wonderful though. Like most of the food from that region it was sweet but with savoury overtones. What I had thought was sugar crystals on the top were sesame seeds. I realised how hungry I was and wolfed the whole biscuit whilst delicately pouring her black coffee down the side of her mug to hopefully settle on the bottom. I took another and scoffed that too. I was always hungry after a mission as well, I discovered.

"Go! Get changed. Have a shower as well. Look smart for when the mother arrives. Maybe the beautiful woman will be grateful. Then I can have one of my own cakes."

There was no mistaking the tone this time. I think she had tried to soften the command by teasing me at the end, but I couldn't be sure. I set off up the stairs to my flat leaving her to watch over my ward. When I returned shaved and showered and in a different, and more importantly, clean Cardiff City polo shirt and chinos she looked me up and down with approval.

I almost didn't recognise my office. She had moved a couple of side tables, relocated a lamp from my desk on to one of them set on the lowest level of light and covered the lamp that had always been on the other table with a red and yellow scarf she must have brought with her. The result was to create a warm, relaxing bedroom in the middle of my office. I thought I might leave it like that. It was, after all, far more often a bedroom than an office space.

"I left you the last two cakes. I am glad you like them. I see you like the changes to your room."

I made us both another coffee and polished off the cakes without embarrassment as we sat and chatted. I opened a bottle of a very lightly spiced rum from Antigua which a grateful client had brought back for me and we shared a glass or two. It was a little light for my taste, but she seemed to love it.

I knew the Vietnamese loved their drink. Every Christmas I sent a bottle of Ruou Can to both Mama-san and Mister Liu. I say bottle but it tended to come in a ceramic jug. And I say drink, but it looked like treacle to me. I had no idea what it was, but it cost a fortune. They both seemed to enjoy it.

"Go and get on with whatever it is that is bothering you! I will sit over there and watch over the child."

Another direct order. She was right though, I had a fair bit to do before morning, if you can say that at two in the morning. She pulled my comfy armchair over to face the couch and completed the warm and comfortable tableau. She turned her back to let me know she wasn't spying on me. As a cynic I knew she could see me clearly in the reflection in the glass, but I appreciated the thought.

The first thing I did was establish my alibi for tonight. I looked through my security footage on Sundays going back six months until I found one where I had arrived at four and stayed in all night after my works calls. I remembered that night. I was waiting for Karen from Asda to slip away from her husband and come and visit me. As so often recently, I had been disappointed, but it came in handy now. Everything happens for a reason apparently.

I rewrote the date on the image codes and cut and pasted sixteen hours from me arriving at four in the afternoon until eight tomorrow morning. I turned off the cameras for now and set them to resume at nine tomorrow morning. I could explain the hour time loss by saying I had turned the cameras off for a discreet visitor. It would also give me an explanation for any costume continuity errors. Job done. I would have this footage in the right place in the sequence and a taxi driver who would remember dropping me off.

Then I opened the Alibaba door and put my knives and a washed down club away. I wasn't sure how much forensic evidence you could get from a hippo's dick, but I washed it down anyway. I wasn't worried about Mama-san seeing my armoury. I was sure she had seen the plans before I had built it. She purposefully looked away in any case.

While I was on my computer, I took the hostile's computer from the crate. I had a choice of software programmes to overcome most basic security systems, courtesy of Geraint and Theresa. My power lead fitted, and I linked the two computers with a few other leads and fired it up. I didn't need any of the software I had, it just fired up and opened into the folders screen.

The first folder I found was security. I opened it and found it sub-divided by date for a couple of months. I opened the most recent as was surprised to find that as well as the ones we had found they had a camera in the attic or roof, covering the street. There we were driving up and parking. Full face, easily identifiable. Good job we took the hard drive. A triumph for belt and braces.

I deleted yesterdays and pulled the same trick I had with my own, cutting and pasting in from a Sunday two months previously. I copied the entire folder into my secure cloud. Then I began checking the folders with girl's names on them. I copied Summer's to my cloud. I would need it later. There was the webcam footage from that night including us bursting into the room. I deleted it all from just before that point.

I tried to open Katherine's, but all that was there was a jumble of code and pixels. Bravo Geraint. There were fourteen other girl's folders, all with stuff like the images I had seen of Katherine earlier. A random sample seemed to reveal that they were younger than Kat and Summer. It was sickening to watch, and I thought long and hard before transferring the files to my cloud account. I would go to prison for a very long time if I was caught with them.

There was a folder called chemist in which a basic account was kept of how much each messenger brought and what drugs they had taken away. Katherine's name appeared twice for very low amounts and I deleted those entries. Again! No security whatever. That was a folder I must have. Along with the money laundering notes I had in my safe, it was a big chunk of insurance against Marko and the ginger twins.

Having taken all I needed, I copied an innocuous looking icon from my home screen onto theirs and clicked on it. Geraint had assured me that running this would irrecoverably destroy a hard drive. I disconnected our computers and double clicked the icon on theirs. Millions of lines of script scrolled up across my screen. Presuming it would take a while I turned off my monitor. I didn't want to see those images again.

To fill the time while their computer hummed and clicked through its death throes, I emptied all the food containers onto my desk and began gathering the notes into piles. I could hear her softly chuckling at my efforts.

"You are not a cash business are you John? Would you like me to sort those for you?"

I nodded pathetically. I thought she was going to do as I had been doing grabbing and unfolding into piles. Instead, she just swept all the cash into my gym bag and announced she would be back as soon as possible. Summer was still snoring away, so I wasn't that concerned.

Twenty minutes later she was back. The money was sorted into bundles of a thousand, each carefully banded. One bundle seemed somewhat thicker.

"Thirty-nine thousand, eight hundred and twenty pounds in real money and two and a half thousand in fakes! She indicated the thicker bundle. We have machines for this kind of thing upstairs if you intend making a business of it."

"Thanks. That will save me a night's work!"

"I didn't know you had a cash business."

It was the kind of half question, which gave me the option of answering or ignoring without either of us being offended.

"It's not mine. I will be returning it tomorrow, today!"

"I hope you will be returning those as well." She nodded to the bin. "Treading on the toes of established businesses could get you in a lot of trouble."

There was no doubting the warning in her voice or

hard look on her face.

"No! They are going back tomorrow as well. I was just teaching the men who stole that wee lassie a lesson. They will be going back to their supplier first thing. The arrangements have been made."

"Ice and skunk have distinctive smells."

She was letting me know that she had not abused my hospitality and peeked into the bin. She held my gaze for a long time. She was not flirting or being my Mama-san now. Eventually she nodded.

"Good. I never thought you were a man like that. You are too good to survive in that business. No drug dealer would trust anyone with their money like you just did."

We toasted our accord with another rum. I had just poured it when Summer began to stir. Mama-san sat in the armchair and began to sing softly in Vietnamese. She motioned me away into the shadows of the kitchen area as far away as possible. No need for verbal orders. She continued to sing softly. Summer snuggled deeper into the duvet before wiping the cloud of hair away from her face, blinking like a surfacing mole.

Mama-san continued to croon away, like a radio left on low before speaking very softly.

"You are safe, child. Take a moment. You are safe, take your time."

Different concept, same technique. Repeat, repeat, repeat until it is understood. Summer jumped like a hooked fish, her head thrashing around trying to remember where she was.

"You are safe child. Your mama is coming to comfort you. This is a safe place, believe me. You are safe here."

Summer was suddenly aware that she naked underneath the dressing gown. Even from afar I could see the panic and fear grip her expression. She pulled the duvet up to cover almost all her face in the universal body language of defence, shame and guilt.

"It is alright. You are safe here. There is no-one here to hurt you. You are alright. It is safe. The man you can see is here to protect you. He was the one who rescued you. You are safe now. You are alright. I am going to get you a drink now. You will be thirsty, child! You have been drugged by very bad men. This man rescued you before anything too bad happened."

Mama-san rose and went to the fridge where she removed a bottle of water and a can of lemonade, I kept for guests to put in their rum. She placed them carefully on the table in front of Summer who was doing her best to hide under my bedcover. Mama-san went back into her repeat, repeat cycle without looking directly at the girl. She was almost like a trained interrogator.

"You are safe now, little one. It is alright here. These drinks are still sealed. No-one could have tampered with them. It is safe to drink. Once you have had a drink, we will see about getting you washed and dressed, ready for your mum. There is no rush. Take your time but please take a drink, some of those drugs can damage you if you do not drink enough."

I noticed that her accent was getting more and more Cardiff as she sought to tease the girl from her duvet cocoon. I wondered just how Vietnamese she really was? It hadn't even occurred to me that the drugs might damage her or that she might be frightened to take a drink from us. I had been treating her as rescued, Mama-san was treating her as if she were still a hostage. Hers was probably the right approach. I didn't feel bad about that; I was sure she had coaxed far more young girls than I ever had.

Summer reached for the water, being very careful to keep a tight grip of the duvet around her neck. I turned around to face into the corner watching only the shadow reflection in the tiles. I wasn't too worried. The roller shutters were down, and I presumed the glass was bulletproof from both sides. There was nowhere for her to escape to.

As she struggled to open the bottle, she needed both hands. She compromised by tucking the duvet under her chin. Once open, she used her free hand to lock the cover there. She swallowed the water with small lady-like sips but still managed to get through the bottle in no time at all before reaching for the can. That she could open with one hand and again she attacked it in small doses. Not for her the mouthful and satisfying belch approach. The water had lubricated her vocal cords.

"Where am I? Who are you? Where is Mo?"

Same as her mother, an unending list of questions. Too used to people dancing to her tune. Mama-san looked round to me. I watched her shadow head rotate from jet-black hair to pale face. She didn't know what to tell her and was looking to me for guidance. I wasn't dancing to her tune though I wasn't quite sure whose song I was singing now. I preferred missions that finished at the end not this kind of mess. I wasn't by nature a babysitter. Time for the strict cop. He had worked with Kat why not with Summer. After all they were essentially the same.

"Take your gear!"

I nodded to the bag Shaky had brought downstairs, "Go upstairs with her!"

No need for her to have a name for Mama-san. I don't think I knew it anyway.

"Get yourself sorted and when you are dressed and ready to go home, we will go over all those questions okay!"

It had all been going well until the end. As soon as I mentioned home the head had snapped up. It must be a teenage girl gesture. Kat had used it several times as well. Time to reassert dominance.

"Move!"

She thought of defying me, but the little girl in her won out. She stood, wrapping the duvet around her as elegantly as she could. She made it look like the sari of some fairy tale princess. Her face showed that she was going to become a truly beautiful woman, and her defiant expression that she was going to be a real handful. The exit was spoiled by the fact that she couldn't pick up her bag and hold the duvet at the same time. That and the fact that she couldn't find the stairs.

She looked around clearly expecting someone to solve her dilemmas for her. She also looked a little fearful. It occurred to me that she thought I meant for her to get ready here with me watching. I didn't want her that fearful. I nodded to Mama-san.

"Could you help her please? While I finish up here."

Mama-san smiled her compliance and picked up the bag and started up the stairs without looking back. Left with a choice of staying with me or following Mama-san, the girl virtually ran up the stairs. Hadn't lost any of my charm over the years.

They were gone almost an hour and it was after five when they came back downstairs. She was wearing her school uniform and her face was fresh and scrubbed of make up with her hair pulled back in a kind of ponytail. I recognised the clasp as the one Mama-san had been wearing. She looked about twelve and seemed tiny.

"Mama-san told me what you did for me. Thank you!"

It was said without any real feeling, but I was pleased it was said at all.

"I will leave you both to it. It was lovely to meet you Summer. Please listen carefully to what Mister McLean tells you. It is important for your future."

The last sentence was said with the hard face she had used on me earlier. It was effective. They had obviously been having a nice girly chat upstairs, being on first name terms now. Summer rushed over and hugged Mama-san as if she was holding on to a lifebelt in a stormy sea.

"Thank you!"

Mama-san fought her way clear but had to wait for the roller shutter to lift before she could leave.

I brought another can, of cola this time, over to the table for Summer.

"Could I have some water, please. I am still very thirsty. Tap water will do."

The way it was said made it clear that it would only do as a completely last resort. It didn't matter I had lots of bottles in the fridge. A legacy of my rugby coaching. I deliberately left her loitering near the door. If she was going to make a break it would be now. I was as far away as I was likely to get, and the first glimpses of daylight could be seen through the open roller shutter.

She wasn't to know that she would never be able to get the main door open. She sat back on the sofa where she had slept and unthinkingly hugged the pillow as a shield and comfort. It made her seem even younger.

I brought her two bottles of water and laid them next to the cola.

"Would you like something to eat?"

"No thanks, I was sick upstairs! Don't panic I got it all in the toilet! But it has left me feeling queasy. I don't want to be sick down here."

She performed the same trick as earlier with the first bottle of water. Finishing it quite quickly without appearing to take great gulps. She quickly opened the second.

"Who is Mama-san?"

"Good question. She is a friend of mine who is a kind of chaperone and carer for overseas students. I didn't want you to be frightened when you woke up. I don't know how much you remember about last night?"

She went bright red. How to make a beautiful girl even more appealing. The blush told me all I needed to know but unfortunately, I had to rub the lesson as deeply into her as I could to make sure she wasn't tempted to repeat the experience.

"You were drugged by Salim Mohammed and were about to be made to have sex with him and several of his friends."

She was a bright crimson and had pulled the pillow shield up to cover her face the way she had used the duvet earlier. I took pity on her. What kind of man wouldn't have?

"Don't worry. Nothing happened with his friends. I arrived just in time to put a stop to it!"

"They were taking photos of me though. I remember the flashes. They will send them to everyone. That is what they were going to do to…"

She tried to fool me by leaving it at that. I could see the realisation on her face about how horrible a threat that was.

"I know about Kat. It was her honesty that helped me save you from the same fate as her."

"I was horrible to her. Mo and I laughed at some of the photos. He told me we were different. Poor Kat. I suppose they will do that with me now, as well."

I was pleased she had worked some of it out herself. It saved me spelling it out. I pointed to the pile of phones on my desk.

"They won't be showing those to anyone else, anytime soon. That is at least one less thing for you to worry about. I don't think they had time to upload them anywhere as far as I can determine."

She was wary. I supposed the worry outweighed the relief.

"Are those their phones?"

"Yes!"

"Then thank you. It was more than I could have hoped for, but they filmed people as well. I saw the films of Kat. They were horrible. They had cameras there last night."

I was tempted to leave her worrying to reinforce the lesson but one look at the tears streaming down that angelic face of hers was enough to loosen my resolve. I pointed to the now silent workstation on my desk.

"Their cameras were linked to that hard drive. I have just obliterated it. Together with the phones I am as sure as I can be that there is no record of your activities last night."

She cried harder then let out a huge baby like sob. It was what my old aunt would have called a full snotter sob, the mucus streaming from her nose and blending with the tears. It was undoing all Mama-san's efforts to make her look normal.

"Th, Th, Th, Thank you!"

"Please go and wash your face. Your mum will be here soon. I don't want her thinking I have been torturing you."

She went to go back up the stairs before I re-routed her to the downstairs toilet. The last thing I needed was to be caught with a fourteen-year-old in school uniform on my bedroom. It seemed to take a while before she returned freshly scrubbed again. I hoped the towel was okay. I couldn't remember when I had last changed it. Her eyes looked as if she had put her contact lenses in back to front and then slept in them, but it was as good as it was going to get.

"Thank you so much. I can only remember parts of last night but none of them are very nice. I know what you saved me from so thanks. I really can't thank you enough. I was going to end up like poor Kat, wasn't I?"

"Yes, you were! That was the plan from the start! There was no romance for either of you! It is important you remember that! Very! Very! Important! These were very bad men exploiting the insecurities of very young women."

I changed it from children at the last second. I

didn't want her to be able to deflect from the lesson with an argument about her status. Like Kat I could see her chin coming up to defend the men. I was learning how to read adolescent girls. Fifteen years too late to save my relationship with my daughter unfortunately. I didn't leave her space to mount a defence. I fired up my secure cloud on my phone.

"I want you to look at these and understand who and what these men were. They were never your friends. You and Kat were the oldest girls I found on their hard drive. Look at this one! It was filmed only six months ago!"

I clicked on one I had found earlier and kept for this very purpose. It showed Salim Mohammed very clearly, undressing and raping a terrified young pre-pubescent girl. I doubted if she was ten. I couldn't watch it myself, but I made her look. She lasted about ten seconds, which was longer than I would have at the second inspection.

"Don't, please that is horrible. How can he do things like that! It is horrible! Horrible!"

Horrible seemed to be her most extreme reaction. I had a lot more extreme. If I had seen these before we went in last night, I would probably have taken the metal baton to the lot of them. Teenagers was bad enough, children really but with some of the attributes of a woman, but children. I shuddered.

"There are fourteen other girls in sets of videos like these; plus, you and Kat's."

She was crying again. I didn't think kitchen roll would cut it, so I handed her a tea towel. She covered her face with it. It took a while but eventually she stopped crying and scrubbed her face dry with the tea towel wiping

203

her nose with a flourish at the end. More washing. Claudia would think I was letting out my room if this kept up.

"I won't have to testify to the police, will I?"

It was a strange first thought. In one way it said a lot about her that she was thinking of bringing these guys to justice, but in another I would have thought that was the least of her worries. I supposed I was thinking as a father, not as a daughter.

"No. I have wiped all evidence of you and Kat from the videos. No-one will be able to tell you were there last night."

"Thank you. What about my mum?"

"She knows that you ran away with an older man. There was no getting around that. She thinks it was further away than Cardiff. What you tell her beyond that is up to you. If I was you, I would tell her at least a version of the truth. You will need someone to talk to about this, and perhaps help processing your feelings. She may be more understanding than you imagine. She only wanted you to be home and safe."

Again, the flinch in her eyes at the word home. The maggot was becoming a snake and wriggling into the front of my brain. I thought I could distract her with some goodies like at Christmas. I reached into my desk drawer and produced her laptop, iPad and phones. I left the one from the Chapter on top. That was what she focussed on.

"How did you find this? Is that how you found me, snooping through my stuff?"

"Truthfully no! I haven't opened them. You can check if you like, but if there is anything on there that would have led me to Salim Mohammed then you should delete it immediately. In fact, it would be better if you

204

copied the stuff you needed onto another hard drive and factory reset all your devices, including Kat's mum's phone!"

She smiled. "I can't believe you figured that out. No-one knew about it."

"Yeah. It was sooo clever!"

I did my best sarcastic adolescent voice. She laughed again. She really was stunningly beautiful. What a woman she could become. We were interrupted by a frantic knocking on the door. Summer looked alarmed and frightened all at once. I had the advantage of seeing that it was her mother, almost a full hour early. The stepfather was just getting out of the car. The luck of the wealthy finding a parking spot right outside my door. I buzzed Snow White in and rushed to block the door before he could follow.

"Girls only I'm afraid, for the moment. Summer wants to speak to her mother. Difficult time for the child."

"For God's sake I only want to see that she is okay."

He tried to push past me in the doorway but relented when I pushed back a good deal harder. I gave him my business face.

"You can see she is fine. Wait in the car. Don't make this harder for the two of them by us two rolling about on the ground."

Mumbling he walked round and returned to the car. Driver's side, naturally.

By the time I got into my office the girls were cuddling each other and both were in floods of tears. I fetched the towel from the downstairs toilet. I would have to visit the Home department at Asda if this kept up. Not really my kind of scene and I wasn't sure how to handle it. Finally Snow White turned and gave me a smile of such warmth I could have made my breakfast toast in its glow.

"I cannot thank you enough, John. You have no idea how I feel having my girl back safe. If there is anything I can do for you, please call me."

My heart genuinely gave a small lurch when she called me John and I wasn't imagining the stress on the anything either. Maybe I was getting better at hearing what women were really saying after a ten-year hiatus. My thinking was certainly a lot calmer and clearer fighting than flirting. That was for sure.

She picked up all of Summer's electronics and stuffed them into the bag of clothes and they both rose to leave. I was watching the mother when the daughter blindsided me. She rushed around the table and hugged me like I have never been hugged since I was a baby. She kissed my cheek and whispered,

"Thank you. I won't forget your kindness."

I prised myself loose and watched as they left through the narrow doorway, Mum carrying the bag, of course. Some things were still just taken for granted after all. I found myself wishing it was the mother who had hugged me. I noticed she had left her handbag in the jumble of towels and bedclothes on my small couch. I doubted it was a mistake. She would be back, and in the time it took me to figure it out, there she was smiling and waving at my door. I buzzed her in.

She strode forward purposefully.

"Forgot my bag!"

She hugged me as tightly as her daughter had done moments before, but it seemed as though she fitted better. It felt right and she must have felt the same as she relaxed into my grip. Abruptly she pulled away. No kiss then. I had been letting my imagination run away with me. Instead of leaving she sat down opposite me.

"What can you tell me that you couldn't say in front of Summer?"

"I didn't tell her anything about you and her real father. She was going down that same road but without the real love Sunday felt for you, but she shouldn't know you know that. I have eradicated any harmful images that were taken of her activities. She was sick this morning. She had been drugged when we found her last night so it may be that, but get a test done anyway. I don't think it has even occurred to her. Get her to an STI clinic as well. The guys who did this to her have been punished. Mister Smith has taken care of my bill although, in truth, it had nothing to do with his business activities."

She rose to leave, elegantly hooking her handbag over her shoulder whilst rising. I struggled to rise at all from that couch, so it was quite a feat of deportment. I struggled to hide my disappointment behind my business face.

"I want to thank you properly John! Could I take you out for a meal sometime? Somewhere really nice."

"Eh, sure, no problem, eh! Just let me know."

If I was getting better at reading women, I was still using a marker and moving my lips when it came to answering them. As smooth as a Welshman on his first date.

She came over and hugged me again. This time she kissed me full on the lips, and not a friendly kiss either. Soft and fragrant. It had been a long time. As she pulled away, she whispered, "That's just a small part of the deposit."

And she was gone; leaving only the buzzing of the door opener and a wisp of perfume in the air. I missed her going. One minute she was kissing me, the next the car had gone. I thought I would leave the lamps and couch as they were. I could buy another desk lamp if I needed one. My phone rang. Line 8.

"She was very beautiful. She would make a good wife for someone like you!"

Mama-san watching on their security system and having the last word. She was still laughing as I hung up.

TEN

The Lieutenant

I packed the phones and SIMs and the defunct computer into bag for disposal before the streets got too busy. I debated about the boots and trousers but settled on a long high temperature wash for the trousers. I couldn't face getting my dagger pocket sewn into another pair. I gave the boots a very thorough clean using bleach, before polishing to a high shine.

Good boots that were also comfortable were hard to come by. I cut the ski mask into pieces and put it in the bag. There had been too much contact in the head-but to be confident a wash would remove it from the woollen fabric.

I took a stroll around the neighbourhood with my bag and distributed its contents throughout a few filled skips that were awaiting collection. One of the advantages of being based in the Bay was that there were always any number of skips lying around in front of development sites.

At a pinch I could have used the skips behind the pubs and restaurants in the area, but these tended to be covered by CCTV. As I was passing Greggs, I took advantage of their bacon roll and a coffee deal, twice, for my breakfast. One to eat in the shop and one for in the office. Most important meal of the day especially if it was both the end of your day and the beginning.

I felt tired. Age was catching up with me and I considered a nap before setting out on Monday's business but the flashing light on the office phone forced me to reconsider my options. Three messages.

First message sent at 07.00 exactly was from Theresa. "Thanks for the help yesterday. Geraint is a bit of a whizz isn't he? He did in three hours what my old colleagues couldn't have done in a week, if at all. I hope it helped. I have couriered the phone back to you to arrive before 13.00 hrs. Hope that is okay."

Second message sent at 07.10 hours, "Mister McLean, I am just calling to thank you again for your help with Katherine yesterday. We had a long talk last night. It has seemed a long time since we have spoken like that. She told me what you were doing for her, or as much as she thought I needed to know. You have my private number, please give me a call and perhaps I can take you out for the evening as a small gesture of thanks. Please call."

Two of the most beautiful women I had ever seen had asked me out on a date within an hour of each other! I began to think that this was a rum-addled dream from the Saturday night. That I was yet to wake up on Sunday morning. There was nothing else to account for my sudden popularity.

The third call disabused me of the dream theory. Sent at 07.16, "Hi. I think you know who this is short boy! I hear you have something of ours. I will be over at eleven to collect it. Please try and find a way to get it to my courier without compromising any of us. Call me with the arrangements. See you soon."

When he said without compromising any of us, I knew he didn't mean the courier. They were disposable and the vulnerable links in any supply chain. I had better get a wriggle on to sort a safe way to drop off the drugs and money. I thought it might be best to do them separately. Better to lose half a loaf than all the bread.

I wrapped the drugs into three Sainsbury's carrier bags. Probably the most conspicuously coloured carrier bags there were, but all I had in the kitchen. I taped them all shut in as small a parcel as I could manage and put them all into my gym bag. I taped the bundles of money together less my five thousand, two hundred and added an invoice to Leonard Duvall detailing my five-thousand-pound fee, and the twelve hundred in expenses yesterday had cost me. Finally, I put two hundred in an envelope and marked it Fatboy. Always liked to dispel that mean Scotsman myth. Then I called Lenny back.

Like him I didn't use names. I told him I would meet him for a coffee when he suggested he was going to be through, at the small hut in the park opposite the museum. I thought he would be able to get parked near there and it was arranged. My first foray into drug smuggling was going ahead and I was considerably more nervous about it than I ever was about any action I had gone into.

I reviewed all that I could and decided I could have a two-hour nap before setting off to meet Lenny. I turned off the ringer on the office phones and my mobile before stretching out on the big couch. I was never so nervous that I could not sleep. The few rums with Mama-san were helping as well. By the time my security camera clicked back on I was sound asleep.

211

I awoke refreshed. I had needed the sleep. I took another shower and changed into my business suit but foreswore the tie. I would have to meet a couple of my clients after Lenny. We usually had lunch on a Monday anyway, to discuss last week's reports and let them gossip with each other about their industry. It was a routine, which had served me well.

I strolled over to the taxi queue and looked for my friend from yesterday, but there was no sign. He was probably taking the rest of the week off spending my money. I settled for the head of the queue and set off into the big city. Ten minutes and seven pounds later I was sitting at Wee Willie's with a coffee. I didn't have a panini as I intended to go for lunch but settled for a couple of pieces of chocolate chip shortbread. I knew his mother made it and it was as good as any shortbread I had ever tasted, including my Aunty Mary's. I left the envelope for Fatboy and Willie said he would make sure he got it.

I was still quarter of an hour early and I spent the time sitting enjoying my snack and watching the world go by. I knew that the bins in this bit of the park were emptied overnight with an occasional additional empty after lunchtime on hot, sunny days. It was a favourite spot for office workers and students to lunch on such days.

Today was not hot and sunny. It was warm enough when the sun came out and when you were out of the wind but otherwise it was threatening to drizzle between the sunny spells. I was the only one loitering in the park. I thought I was safe enough thinking the bins would not be emptied until tonight. I took the first package and strolled to the farthest away bin I could see from my bench at the coffee hut. I casually lobbed it in from a stride away. The bin was empty but for my package. On the way back I examined the other bins casually.

Two of them were also empty and each of them got a package at intervals of a couple of minutes. No-one paid me any heed though that didn't stop my heart from pounding throughout. I thought I would have rested easier after disposing of the drugs, but my heart rate stayed up. I didn't know why. There were very few places to overlook my disposals. That was why I had chosen this venue.

I had just returned to my coffee when Lenny and another brick shithouse West Indian joined me from the direction of the city centre. They were both wrapped up in Puffa jackets as if they were off to the North Pole. I insisted they both have a coffee on me, to keep warm.

"Bloody freezing here, Man. Could we not have met indoors?"

"I had to drop something off to the owner. Might as well kill two birds with one stone. I can keep an eye on your stuff from here."

Also, I did not fancy being left alone in a room with these two.

"As you look towards the museum your goods are in bins three, six and seven. They are in orange carrier bags. I presume you can have someone pick them up after we leave."

The other guy picked up his coffee and left without a word. As he got to the pavement he turned and saluted me with the coffee.

"Thanks for the drink, wee man."

Despite appearances he was as Scottish as I was. Lenny and I drank our coffees and savoured the chill breeze. I gave it a few minutes to see if his friend was reappearing.

"Your money is in the bag. Just under thirty-five grand and over two-grand in duds. I took my fee, as agreed."

Lenny eyed me up and down. He was a careful man and I could see he was thinking.

"Marko told us there was nearly eighty-grand taken. Did you take any off the top?"

It sounded conversational, but his eyes were clear and focussed on me.

"No! I took my fee plus two hundred for additional expenses over the thousand you gave me yesterday. It is all accounted for on the fee note. I left one package which was probably under five-grand based on the packages I opened. I could have kept it all."

"That would have been very dumb!"

He was still looking me up and down. I had had considerably worse examinations.

"I'm inclined to believe you. The pakis never weighed in that kind of cash before. What about the product?"

"There were six full boxes and some bits and pieces. I took the full ones, which you will shortly have and left the bits and pieces. One of them contained about a kilo of herb."

"Get you whitey! Herb! How do you know how much there was?"

"If the box can hold a kilo of cornflakes, I figure it will hold more grass. I left that as I thought it was probably the cheapest product in the shop."

He kept looking at me. I thought I might give him some tips after all this was done. I thought I was much

214

more intimidating at staring than he was. As we were speaking his colleague reappeared and passed him a slip of paper. I had watched the skateboarder collect the packages about five minutes ago from the corner of my eye. I didn't know if Lenny had been distracting me on purpose.

"Again, boy! You are about a quarter of what Marko said you took."

I let him examine me. I was not worried I had an ace in the hole after all. I had the accounts showing the monies and product in and out. Although I had believed her, I had checked that the money brought back by Mama-san tallied with the usual take. It hadn't been far away allowing for what I had left and the container I gave to Shaky.

"I have no interest in, or need for, drugs. What you have is what I took!"

"Again, I believe you! Marko is a dumb fucker. He can't figure out that if he had all the money then he should have had less of the drugs. He is claiming beyond the maximum for both. He thinks we are an insurance company."

He looked again at the slip and rocked his head from side to side as he did the calculation.

"The police didn't find any money or drugs in the property, you know."

"I didn't know. I had a busy night. I was having a kip. How many bodies did they find?"

"Five!"

"Then the sixth guy has taken them. There were six down when I left with the girl."

"Marko never mentioned the girl either. Describe the six."

"Salim Mohammed he's the gaffer, Arfan a big fucker, some guy called Adnan, another big fucker, a cycle courier and a wee guy with his face smashed in. If I had to guess I would pick the courier. I hit him the least amount."

"And you took the six of them? I heard there was a squad of you."

"Believe me! I would have taken a squad if possible. Have you visited that house? Yes? Then you'll know that there is not room to swing a cat. There were four of us fighting in the hallway and then four in the living room plus the girl. I don't think I could have got another person in there if I had tried."

He thought hard about it.

"Respect to you. You seem unmarked. Five of them are in the hospital, three serious. None dead though. I guess that was your idea?"

"That was why I left the money and the drugs. The police won't worry too much about a non-lethal fight between drug gangs, will they?"

"No! They will not. It's usually every man for himself then arrest the last man standing."

"Okay John. Thanks for all the stuff. I don't think we need any more from you. The police did find three shotguns and a pistol in the house. You were lucky!"

"Always."

His big friend just winked.

"We are going to see that lying little fucker, Marko. Want to come?"

"No thanks. Believe it or not Monday is my busy day in work."

"How did you get in through that security system and big steel door?"

"The back door was unlocked."

He laughed. They both did.

"Lucky old you. Eh?"

"You have no idea."

As they left, he gave me a parting shot.

"The papers haven't been kind. There is no mention of drugs or guns. You should have a look. Maybe you could sue them!" and they were gone.

I bought a Western Mail in the Spar in Queen Street, one of the busiest shopping streets. I used to buy its sister paper the Echo most days when it was produced in town and sold by a motley collection of addicts and alcoholics. Since they had moved the production out of town, I hadn't bothered.

It was probably months since I had read a "local" newspaper. I sat on some of the polished steel street furniture, as benches were now known, and there we were on the front page in huge letters, above a photo of the house we had watched all last night.

RACIST THUGS HOSPITALISE LOCAL STUDENTS

There was a sketchy story, short on detail except that three local students and their landlord and a local businessman, all Pakistani in origin, had been badly beaten at the house. Two were in a coma, two were badly disfigured and one required reconstructive surgery to his face where several bones had been shattered. Not just broken but shattered. No mention of drugs or money or guns or girls.

This would bring us nothing but grief. Local Imams were calling on authorities to act and find the culprits. Rather than drifting away, police interest would be stoked until someone was caught. I would have to do something about this before it got out of hand. We had been as careful as we could have been, but there would be a lot of pressure on this if it was permitted to go unchallenged.

Consequently, I could not enjoy my lunch at the new Marco Pierre White restaurant on the top floor of the hotel in Dominion Arcade with its views over the rooftops of the shops and offices down to the Bay. It seemed every bugger in Cardiff had a view of the Bay except me, and I lived there. I wasn't worried, exactly, but I was concerned. Too many people knew I had been looking for the girl and where. Everyone liked to appear "in the know" after all.

I left my lunch at three o'clock, as early as I had ever left before and much earlier than we usually called it a day. I told my companions that a night surveillance had left me exhausted. They lapped up that kind of operational drivel. I was tired, but I had to find a way to redefine the police investigation. I had a couple of thoughts on how. They relied on me finding one man in a big city.

Addy Davies was an ex-journalist. He had worked on many of the big London papers before sinking under the weight of continuous alcohol consumption to the obscurity of the Western Mail where he had been made redundant when they modernised their production.

Never a man to be downhearted he had maintained his alcohol consumption and funded it by selling cut price trainers in the pubs of Cardiff and occasionally at the market in Splott on a Thursday. Never on a Saturday because that was always the day Trading Standards raided the market for counterfeit goods.

Not that Addie's shoes were counterfeit. They weren't. They were stolen. His nephew managed a supply depot for one of the trainer shops out past Llanrumney somewhere. This allowed Addie to sell most major brands at half price, to fund his drinking.

I was a good customer. Every Christmas I would buy a selection of trainers for the girls upstairs from me. They spent so much time in killer heels I thought they would appreciate comfortable shoes for their off-duty times. I know Addie loved visiting to check the sizes and fittings. He was never that drunk!

That was what gave rise to his name. Addie, short for Adidas. Now I would have the onerous task of checking his regular haunts in the city to look for him. I started in the Old Arcade where he usually sat through the back in protest at its recent gentrification. He wasn't there so I swallowed my rum quickly and moved on. The Cottage, The Borough, Mollie's, The Duke of Wellington. No sign, but the rums were beginning to slow my search.

I thought I would give the Goat Major and Rummer a try on my way to Canton to search further afield. It was a struggle to keep going, but I was determined. I was trying hard not to stagger from exhaustion as I retraced my steps up Saint Mary's Street towards the castle just as it was getting busy with people returning from real work. It was as if God spoke to me.

"Jock! Jock!"

And there he was. I was looking for him and he found me. My luck again! He was sitting outside a kind of Mexican/Cuban diner in the last patch of sunshine on Saint Mary's Street. I had been focussed on getting to the Goat Major on the other side of the road and had walked straight past him. They had proper couches to sit in, not just those tiny aluminium seats so many bars favoured. I joined him.

"I heard you were looking for me. The boys in the Old Arcade said you were there about an hour ago! I knew you would look in at the Goat Major eventually."

"Why did you not wait in there?"

"Shut!"

"What! For good?"

So many of my favourite pubs were going down the closed then re-opened as fancy diners or wine bars route.

"I don't think so. I decided to wait here and watch for you. Lucky really. They have an excellent light Cuban rum two doubles for a fiver up until six."

The four empty glasses on his coffee table pointed out his consumption. I didn't want him drunk, but I felt like a celebratory drink myself.

"Say no more. Back in a tick."

It was a long thin bar with booths down one side and a bar on the other. It was empty. Not even bar staff as far as I could see. I had never been in there before, but I did like the Cuban dance music playing in the background. It reminded me of the old Toucan Club, now just another Irish bar. A mop of blonde curls popped up behind the bar. She didn't look old enough to be served in a pub never mind work in one. Getting old see!

"Four large rums please. Cuban if you have it and have a drink yourself."

She looked at me appraisingly. I think the drink for herself swung it for me.

"Are you sitting outside? I will bring them out."

"Drinks are on their way Addie! How's the world treating you?"

"Usual shit. Are you looking for shoes?"

"No, not today. It's your journalistic skills I need today."

"Been a while since anybody needed those Jock."

I knew he still sold the odd local story to the national papers, did some sports coverage as well, cricket and rugby mainly, largely for the free entry and hospitality.

"I have a story for you to sell. Drugs, police corruption, underage girls, immigrants."

I knew the immigrants line opened a much wider range of papers willing to print the story. I stopped talking as our drinks arrived.

"This is not like you, Jock. Fallen on hard times?"

"No! No! I don't want the money for it. You can keep it. It's a client of mine lives right next to it and doesn't like what the police are doing."

"It's not those Vietnamese up the stairs from you is it? If I write about them, they would cut my balls off."

"No! No! Have you seen the Western Mail today?"

"Only the website. I wouldn't give those bastards the shit from my neighbour's cat."

"Front page. Racists batter five Pakis."

"Something like that, yes."

"It was a drug den and the Pakis were abusing children in a big way, pre-pubescent children. The police found guns, money and drugs there but have said nothing. Probably don't want to offend Muslim sensibilities."

"Didn't think you were one of them conspiracy nut jobs, Jock. I would have thought a man who has been where you have would know better. Are you sure this isn't just the neighbours not liking the brown faces?"

"I can give you photos. At least four of the victims taking turns with a very small child. The same four taking drugs with piles of them on the table, guns visible in the background. One of the neighbours gave them to the police and they have been shuffled away. They are the victims now."

"Fuck me, Jock. That would be a goldmine. Who is the neighbour?"

"I'm not going to say. The last thing anyone wants is an intifada against them. You know how sensitive communities can be about perverts."

Addie was frantically scrolling through his phone to read the updates on the Western Mail website. He was smiling so wide it reached beyond the plastic of his dentures.

"A story like that would really stick it to those bastards. Teach them why they needed real journalists. Not that I doubt you Jock, but can I see the photos?"

This was a problem for me. I could have logged on and got them for him, but Theresa had made me promise never to access the secure cloud without using the black box.

"We'll have to go to my office, Addie. I need to download them from a secure cloud. I didn't want to take the chance of being caught with them. It would be jail time. They are that bad. I don't want my name or the company name anywhere near this story either. Once I give you it, it's all yours."

"Deal." He held out his hand and we shook. "Let's go!"

We nearly didn't finish our rums. They were lovely too. Smooth as oil. A waste really to glug them down like we did. Addie was on the phone all the way to the office in our taxi. I had never seen him working before; he was a different man. As soon as we were in the office, he was pacing around working the phone. If he was talking in money, he was rich. If he was talking in words, he was writing a book.

I attached the black box and located the files. I rummaged around for a memory stick. I had hundreds of them around the office, but, as ever, could not find one when I needed it. Eventually I found one advertising an insurance broker who had sponsored a rugby tournament I refereed.

I copied the video of the ten-year-old and checked that all four were clearly visible and identifiable. Then I found one that showed them giving a packet of drugs to a girl who looked about twelve after they had abused her. Significantly they were emptying the drugs from cereal packets full of the stuff. A Glock pistol was on the table and a shotgun was leaning against the wall. I closed and logged off from the cloud and put the black box back in the jumble of hardware in my drawer.

I indicated to Addie that I had it and he finished off his call. I plugged the stick into my laptop and let him view the content. He had to force himself to watch. I couldn't.

"Do you have any idea who the girls are?"

"None at all. The time says they should have been at school though."

"I didn't even notice that."

"The important thing is that the police know about all of this but have said nothing. Either they have switched the drugs and money, or they are protecting whoever's drugs and money it is. Ask them about the guns. I know they were taken into evidence. Drink?"

"I could do with one after that video, but I am

working now. Anything I do with this I will have to do in the next hour. Are you sure you don't want any of this Jock? It could be a lot of money."

"Would you want to profit from that Addie?"

He didn't answer.

"If time is important why don't you work from here? I am just going to have a wee lie down. It has been a long day. Use the laptop if you need hardware."

There was never anything important on it.

"Thanks, Jock." And he was off on the phone again. I was out on my feet so lay down on the big couch for the second time that day and let him drift away in the background.

ELEVEN

The Breakfast

"John! John! Wake up! The Japanese woman from upstairs is at the door. I don't know how to open it for her."

Unlike yesterday morning, was it only yesterday? I knew exactly where I was and could reasonably place the time at around ten o'clock in the evening. My mouth still felt the same dry, rummy way though. I rose and walked to the desk to use the secret door opener on my computer. I hated sleeping in my suit. The trousers were pure wool and were ruined by being crumpled and used as pyjamas. They didn't feel too comfortable either. I went to the fridge for a bottle of water. I would have to steal more at training later. The fridge was looking empty.

"Sorry Mama-san. I must have nodded off. This is my friend Addie. Addie this is Mama-san."

"Addie and I know each other well. He brings the shoes for the Christmas presents to the girls. He is one of the few men who is permitted to touch my feet. For free at least!"

She laughed coquettishly. I couldn't believe it. Mama-san was flirting with Addie. What was worse was that Addie was blushing. Some wonders shouldn't start at

225

all, never mind cease. I thought this was one of them.

"A parcel came for you today Mister McLean."

She put it on my desk. Kat's phone! I had forgotten about that. Too late now. I would return it tomorrow morning. I have to say the thought of seeing Penny again didn't fill me with any dread. I replayed her message in my head. I could say I was looking forward to it, in fact.

"Could I have a private word?"

She nodded out the door.

"It's okay. I have to go to the loo anyway."

Addie excused himself through the right door. I knew those doors were virtually soundproof by the number of times I had been caught by surprise by people appearing in the office whilst I was in there. Another virtue of the new shop front.

"We were visited today by some very nasty men. They were looking for a young girl who sounded very like the one you had down here last night. They insisted on examining all our girls and searched the rooms. Mister Lui let them. That tells you how nasty they were.

No-one mentioned your girl. Don't worry. We were a friend to you, just as you have always been to us. Besides they never asked about down here. I hear they visited all the establishments in town."

"Did you know them?"

"They are with the men who collect our insurance monies."

"Chinese."

"Yes. But not the usual guys. Higher up the chain, I think."

"Thanks. If you didn't tell them no-one else knows."

"The Mama and Papa know, the girl knows, and the people who had her know the girl. Someone always talks."

"Thanks. I appreciate the warning and your friendship. I really do."

I leant in and kissed her cheek.

"I could have Addie do that if you like?"

She thought about blushing. Score one back for last night.

"I see some Indian pimps had a bad accident last night. It would be most unlike them to be working with the Chinese, but it may be an explanation. We could not intervene if they were."

Her eyes were warning me the whole time. She was letting me know that silence was as far as they would go to help me, and perhaps not even that if they were asked directly. This situation was just getting more and more out of control. Mission creep as it was known.

"Thank you. I really am grateful."

Addie re-joined us, conspicuously drying his hands with last night's towel.

"You must come up for tea some time, Mister Davies. The girls always love to see you."

"That would be nice. I will give you a call next time I am visiting."

"Don't leave it till Christmas."

And I spared her further blushes by buzzing the door open for her to leave.

"Listen Jock. Are you sure you do not want a share of this! I might be on for six figures here. I am just waiting for a call back."

He was pleading but excited at the same time. I was

willing to bet he had never sold a six-figure story before.

"The money is nice, but really I want to stick it right up those bastards at the Western Mail. It's your videos that make it all work. Really the money should be yours."

"No thanks, Addie. You have watched them. I couldn't sleep at night if I made a penny from those images. It's your job, not mine and I am pleased about that."

Like all journalists, he had no shame about what he did and how he did it, so I knew I wasn't insulting him with my remarks. He gave no sign of taking offense either.

"The first instalment is on its way to print now, just backing the police into a corner really. They confirmed the guns but offered only "operational reasons" for not disclosing them earlier. Still no mention of the drugs or money though.

The big spreads will be Wednesday through to Sunday. There is a lot more money if I get the Sunday as well. Your photos, police turning a blind eye, possible corruption, fear of racism, vigilantes and to top it all do you know who owns that house?"

"Salim Mohammed."

"Partly. It is owned by a company whose two directors are Salim Mohammed and our good friend Marko. So, then we have links to organised crime, possible terrorism the list of golden targets is endless. They already have three other reporters working on the side stories. The incompetence slash corruption of South Wales Police is legendary. We can dig all those wrongful convictions up again as well."

The creativity was literally pouring out of him. He was back doing what he loved and if he wasn't my friend, he was at least a treasured companion. I was pleased to have been able to help him back on track, at last. I wished someone would reset my life like that. Even if only for a couple of days.

"I'm off home now, Jock. I have a lot of work to get through, but don't you worry I will do this story justice. I never lost the ability, you know, I just drowned the ambition sometimes."

Story of my life as well. I think there were a tribe of us in the drinking dens of Cardiff. I buzzed him out too. I was alone again, if not lonely.

I was thinking of the consequences of what was about to hit the papers and didn't want any of my Muslim friends too badly caught up in the whirlwind. I scrolled through my phone and called Tariq.

Tariq had been a friend of mine since I arrived in Cardiff. I had helped him with his classical Arabic to allow him to progress in becoming one of the leading Scholars in Cardiff. In return he had strengthened my midweek cricket team with himself and his friends, to take us to two promotions. I liked him. He would no doubt, in time, become an Imam, or leader, of one of the Cardiff mosques.

"Tariq, As-salamu alaikum, my friend."

"Wa alaikum assalaam, John. It has been a while."

"My friend, I wish to speak with you in English in order that your mother may not hear. My words are not for the market."

He laughed. I loved his mother. She knew the business of everyone in their community and loved that I spoke Urdu. She would gossip to me for hours when I visited, pleased to have someone who hadn't heard her gossip before. She had lived here forty years and never felt the need to learn English. I had often offered to teach her, but she insisted she had no time.

"How can I help you, John?"

"I want to help you this time, Tariq. Have you seen the story in the paper today about the five believers savagely beaten?"

"Yes. My Imam is very upset. Incidents like these are increasing daily. We are no longer safe even in our own homes."

"You know I support all you do to make your community safer for all, my friend, but in this case, I think you may want your leader to know that these men were not good Muslims."

"That is not for any man to judge."

"No. But tomorrow and the next day the national papers will be telling the story of these men abusing children, selling drugs, espousing violence."

"Those are the slurs they always use against us. We are an easy target because of the actions of the very few."

"I know this, Tariq, but they will have photographs of these men with girls of eight or nine, photographs of them posing with piles of drugs and guns. The house they were in is owned by Marko. You know what that means."

He was thinking. I could hear him reciting passages from the Qur'an. He knew it all off by heart. That was why I had been teaching him classical Arabic all those years ago. I knew he was seeking wisdom.

"I know you well, John. I think your heart is pure in these matters. I understand why you are concerned, and I will alert the leaders in our community to these developments. Forewarned is forearmed. Thank you. I'll see you at nets next month."

"You will indeed. Jazaka allahu khairan, my friend."

"More appropriate for you I think, John. Yours is the good deed."

Hoping I had helped put out that fire before it flared up. I turned my mind to the Chinese. I couldn't see why they were involved. I thought I might sleep on it. I was flicking through my missed calls, nothing important, when the phone lit up in my hand. Mad Bastard One. I answered.

"Jock, Glad I caught you. I phoned you a few times today. Sleeping probably."

"No! I have been busy, thanks. What's up?"

"Did you realise how much you gave me last night? I was quite happy with my agreed fee. There was nearly six-grand in that box. I can let you have it back."

"You earned it, Shaky. Keep it. I have already given the rest back anyway. Too late for refunds."

"If you are sure. The next couple of jobs are on me then. I quite enjoyed it. Did you see today's Western Mail? Fucking raghead cunts calling me a racist, one of them called me Whitey! You don't get more racist than that! Glad I rattled the camel-jockeys now."

"I saw it. Don't worry, you don't appear in any of the reports."

He laughed. Between us we could have lost count of the number of operations we had been on where our presence never appeared in the reports.

"The story will change in the next couple of days, no-one will be looking for us when the truth comes out. Too busy chasing bogey-men."

"I just wanted to let you know I appreciate it, Jock. Call me anytime."

"Will do, Sam. Take care. Try and stick with the new you!"

It was a bit late to call, so I sent Penny a text apologising for not returning Katherine's phone today, as promised, and telling her I would drop it off tomorrow morning before she went to school. Almost immediately my phone lit up. Penny!

"Hi. Got your text thanks. She will be glad to have it back, but I have to say she has not even complained about not having it yet. Quite an achievement for you. Speaking of achievements, I hear Summer is back home. Well done you. They are best pals again. I guess that was you in the news today. Please tell me those were not the men Katherine was involved with."

She eventually ran out of breath, I think.

"Nothing to do with me. Summer went home under her own steam and I have no idea who Kat was involved with. My colleague wiped all the information from the phone and the Internet before I got it back."

"Can you do that? Wipe all the information from the Internet?"

"I can't no, but my colleagues assure me they can. Not quite sure how legal it is, but it is done now anyway. Kat can check when she gets her phone back. See how many of her WhatsApp groups still have her in them, for instance."

"I can't thank you enough. Have you given dinner a thought yet?"

It was said casually, but I thought I detected a hint of strain in the voice.

"I'll give it a think later. Can I let you know tomorrow when I return the phone?"

"I'll probably be away by then. When do you intend to come? Do you fancy breakfast? Kill two birds with one stone? We usually eat before I leave around seven thirty."

I wondered if she was high, the way she was burbling on.

"I know Kat wants to thank you herself. She has been a totally different person since you left yesterday. It is like I have got my girl back. She hasn't stopped talking about how kind you were to her."

That was the bad cop me as well. Wait until she met the debonair, charming good cop. Then again, if it was working for me why change?

"I'll drop it back at seven then, if that's okay. I usually only have coffee for breakfast."

"That's a date then. Katherine will be thrilled."

I was thrilled as well. Date eh? Then again it sounded as if she might be trying to set me up with her daughter. That was a cruel thought given what Kat had just been through.

Admin done and up to date I decided against a nightcap in The Packet and set off for a relatively early night in my own bed. I hadn't been there for four nights now. I needed it. I showered and shaved before I went and set the alarm in my head for half six. I was sound asleep within a minute of getting under my duvet.

At half past six on the dot I was awake. I had been dreaming about the Chinese, but no new, quick solution had appeared in my head. What had occurred to me though was that I should have paid more attention to Salim's phone calls when I was observing. Too much presuming I knew it all. A common failing among men. It may not have offered up a solution, but it would have given me more intel to think of one.

I brushed my teeth meticulously, checked that I wasn't wearing too much after shave, brushed my hair and set off for my date with a little bit of nervousness. Before I opened the roller shutter, I checked on the sauna security system cameras that the street was all clear. It was. It was the careful man who survived to laugh at his cowardice. I never forgot that. I remembered the phone, which was the excuse for my visit and off I went to the taxi rank.

As ever I had a choice of taxis and set off, asking him to take me through Fairwater to Radyr. I stopped off at the bakers opposite the school in Fairwater and bought three bacon rolls freshly prepared and wrapped in tin foil. I still got change from a fiver. I would only have got one for that price down in the Bay.

I fell out with the driver after we arrived. I asked him to come and pick me up at eight and he began to hum and haw and think of reasons to charge me extra. In the end I told him not to bother. I would summon an Uber. It cost what it cost, but they were always glad of the work in my experience. I was right on time but my good mood of earlier had vanished. Probably make it easier for Kat to recognise me.

Kat, in her school uniform, opened the door before I even arrived. I was balancing the three rolls and her phone in one hand in preparation for ringing the doorbell. She skipped down the path and hugged me tightly.

"Thanks for coming. I'm glad I got the chance to see you again. I am so pleased you made it."

I didn't point out that she had my card and could have seen me anytime at my office. I guess what she meant was that she was pleased to see me without having to make any kind of effort. It was a jaundiced thought for a gesture of genuine appreciation.

We walked in together to the same kitchen area I had visited two days before. The view was still magnificent, the sun just rising across the city, and even more improved by Penny in the foreground in her business clothes. If she had looked spectacular on Sunday, today she looked like a film star playing a successful lawyer. She was sorting me a coffee from a complicated machine. I handed her the rolls.

"What are these? I thought you didn't do breakfast."

She smiled, and it touched me in places I hadn't been touched for a long time, if ever.

"Who doesn't like to start the day with a bacon roll?"

Almost David Niven like in my sophistication. The smell of the hot roll and then the bacon filled the breakfast area.

"God I'm starving. Can I have one mum?"

Another smile, another flutter.

"Go on then. I don't suppose one each will hurt us."

And she reached forward and snatched up the roll I had opened right out of her daughter's hand, before taking the daintiest of bites. Kat was not so reticent. She ripped the foil open and took a huge bite of the second roll like a squaddie after night stag. I was torn between the two approaches and waited like a gentleman for my coffee before taking a bite as big as Kat's. Mouth full of bacon, I slid the phone across the counter to her wordlessly.

She examined it to make sure I hadn't damaged it in any way. Perish the thought that a classmate would spot a stray scratch on the golden surface. A bit like her lifestyle I supposed. Then she turned it on. The chimes arrived much quicker on hers than they did on mine, but then again, I had no doubt hers cost considerably more.

Within seconds she was directing us for a selfie, half-eaten bacon rolls on the foil in front of us and the three of us squished together to complete the tableau. Another couple of her, eating her roll against the backdrop of the view from her window, and she was away again. The world had been suffering without her input for too long it seemed.

It had not been my imagination. Penny had not been quick to unsquish herself from me after the photo was taken. She appeared a bit flustered. I thought I would fluster her further.

"Is your husband away already? Not many people are up and away at this time."

Kat tried to answer but Penny got there first.

"Working away this week I'm afraid."

Her ears tinged pink delightfully. I had the impression that this was not the explanation Kat was about to give me. Trouble in paradise, perhaps. I wasn't going to raise Kat's troubles. I had told them it was sorted and that should have been enough. Kat, however, couldn't contain her curiosity.

"Was that you, battered Mo and his mates?"

I raised my best Roger Moore eyebrow at her. She ignored it.

"I saw it on Facebook. It doesn't seem fair calling you a racist. You didn't batter them because of their colour, did you? It was because of what they had done to me wasn't it. Someone should tell them. It's okay. Mum knows."

I loved her passion and sense of justice but thought I better head this off before she started spouting off on any of her social media accounts about what happened. I didn't need every schoolgirl in Cardiff thinking I was the Masked Avenger.

"It wasn't me. I just arranged to have your images removed to save you further embarrassment. Any further interest in this topic will only cause you that embarrassment. Do you understand? This was not me and certainly nothing to do with you. Is that clear?"

My tone had sharpened, and her chin dropped. Just like Sunday she nodded.

"Understood? Say it!"

"I understand."

"Who did it?"

"I don't know."

"What had it to do with you?"

"Nothing. I know nothing about it."

Rinse, repeat, repeat. Eventually the message will get through.

"You weren't this angry with Summer and she is as bad as me!"

"This is not a game. People are seriously hurt. You were going to be one of those people. So was Summer. Watch the paper this week you will see the hurt these people can cause. I had nothing to do with what happened. Saying I did could get me into a lot of trouble. Do you understand?"

Chin down. "Understood. It was nothing to do with you."

"Summer said you kissed her mum!"

I laughed. She was scandalised by me kissing Summer's mum the day after I had destroyed umpteen images of her participating in group sex with men old enough to be her father or even grandfather. Her morality only applied to others, it seemed. It was Penny's turn for the Roger Moore impression, this time.

"She said it caused a big row when they got home."

"Summer's mum kissed me. She was grateful for me returning her daughter. It was a brief thank you. That was all."

I was speaking to Kat, another girl whose values seemed to apply to everyone but her, but my explanation was for Penny. I could not read her expression.

"Still pretty disgusting at your ages. Summer was sooooo embarrassed."

I laughed and whatever Penny had been feeling she laughed too.

"Summer's mum is younger than me! Lady."

"I know. I would be mortified if anyone saw you kissing someone."

"Chance would be a fine thing. It's not likely to happen now you have to follow me around till your exams."

She shot me a look, which I was supposed to read. She may as well have spoken to me in Sanskrit for all the difference it made. I guessed the "follow me around" was the price Kat was having to pay for what freedoms she was getting in the foreseeable future.

All the while Kat was scrolling through her phone.

"Some of my contacts are missing!"

"Not anyone useful to your life going forward I

would bet. What else is missing?"

"Everything you promised would vanish."

"And I can tell you, it has gone from everyone it was sent to's phone as well."

"I know Summer told me. She thought you had done it when you had her phone."

"Leave her thinking that then! The people who helped me could get into a whole lot of trouble if anyone found out what they did. Understand!"

I didn't mean it to sound as harsh as it did. Her chin went down, and she nodded again. Conditioned reflex now.

"There were at least fourteen other girls whose photos I eliminated. Some of them appeared as young as nine or ten. Do you understand that! These were very, very bad men indeed."

She was crying again. I was ever the charmer, but she was getting on my tits with her golly gosh attitude to the adventure. This was assuredly not the Secret Seven or anywhere close. I could feel my resentment at her privilege boiling up. Jealousy was a terrible, terrible affliction. Penny was covering her mouth and crying as well.

"I had no idea it was as bad as that. I thought it was just a mistake, a girlie mis-step on the way to becoming a woman."

"I am telling you this, now, because I do not want any misunderstandings about how much trouble the girls were in. The papers this week are going to be full of what those men were, and what they did. If Kat can't put it behind her and behave normally, she could be endangering some of my colleagues and friends."

It was all true, but I didn't have to be so brutal in the announcement of it. Kat and Penny were hugging each

239

other now. I guess I wasn't going to be squished in to this one, somehow. I thought I really was becoming bad cop. I didn't think I had always been like this, but who knew. I didn't have many people left to ask how I had used to be.

"Perhaps she should stay off school and come to work with me until it all settles down."

"Probably a good idea. The reality for Katherine is a lot worse than it will be for Summer. I think she will struggle to deal with her reaction once she reads the realities."

"Hello! I am still here. I can hear you both. Much as I would like to spend another day with my mother, I must complete some work in class today. It counts towards my exam. I am tougher than you think. Not as tough as you Mister McLean, but I will manage not to break down crying and spill my secrets to the world. Do you think I want anyone to know what I did?"

The crying cleared up suspiciously quickly, I thought, and I was sure the "tough as you," was said flirtatiously, but what did I know. The more I thought I knew about women, the less sure I was about how to respond.

Penny wiped her face with a special scented wipe from a special container on the worktop. Who had special containers for their wipes? People who could afford houses like this I supposed. She gathered up the wipe and the tin foil the rolls came in and threw them into a bin I could not see.

"Right! I must be off now. I am in Reading this morning, sweetheart. I will be back to pick you up at the usual place at four. Thank you again, John. The more I learn the more I realise what you did for us. Are you sure there is no fee? What about your colleagues?"

"I have orchestra on a Tuesday mum. See you at six."

"Not any more you don't. Remember what we agreed yesterday. We will see where we are after your exams, not before."

"No! There is no fee. Summer's family covered it."

"Then you really must let me take you to dinner sometime, or perhaps I could cook for you here. I don't suppose you get much home cooked food."

"Not you as well mum! What is it with you old women? You can't even cook."

Penny's ears tinged pink.

"My God! You're blushing mother. How embarrassing is that. Of course, it might just be the menopause at your age!"

"I know. I am just sooooo old and dried up."

They both laughed, all the while working our way out of the door. Penny set the alarm from the outside using her phone. It looked flash and no doubt cost a fair few quid, but anyone with a scanner could have disabled it in seconds. Kat hugged me before mounting the huge Range Rover.

Penny hugged me too.

"Thank you very much. Katherine hasn't been like this for months. I meant it about coming to dinner. I will pester you until you come."

And with that thought she kissed me square on the lips and not at all like a sister. She tasted of bacon, which was remarkable as I doubted any of the roll had touched her lips. This must be how a normal family life felt on a workday.

"Muuuuum!"

"I know I am soooo shaming you!"

And with them both laughing they drove off. The last thing I heard was Penny.

"Remember John. Dinner! Soon!"

And they were gone, and I was left standing. They just presumed I had a car. No offer of a lift or anything. Stranded on a hugely expensive desert island in a village with no pub. I started walking down the hill to the train station. I had to be back in the office for my last two client check-ins and then the week was my own. A celebration drink in the Docks Conservative Club, perhaps a game of snooker and a think about what to do with the Chinese. Nothing had occurred to me yet.

"The best laid plans of mice and men gang aft agley," as Robert Burns once wrote. I had no clear idea what it meant but I thought it was something along the lines of men plan and Gods laugh.

I had just finished my weekly calls with my major clients; all happy, few further actions necessary, when a familiar number appeared on my works phone. Not the mobile.

"Could you meet me on the balcony in Wetherspoons please?"

Sunday Smith calling on Lenny's phone. I appreciated the please.

"Of course. Large spiced rum and plenty of lemonade, it's still a little early in the day, but I would be glad of the break."

"See you soon then."

I used the sauna CCTV before leaving, to check the street again. All clear. I walked past Wetherspoons to the end of the moorings and looked back. I could see Sunday sitting like the man from Del Monte in a linen jacket, panama hat and dark glasses against the spring sunshine. All he needed to complete the tourist ensemble was an "I Loves The 'Diff'" tee shirt.

There were only a couple of other tables occupied. They were in the hiatus between breakfast and lunch. I thought it strange he was alone. I waited and watched and eventually there was Lenny and the Scotsman from yesterday with a couple of other West Indians sat like a late rising stag party downstairs. I could tell they all had large breakfasts in front of them by the huge oval serving plates.

I went in through the patio doors and ignored Lenny and the boys as I headed upstairs and out onto the balcony. Sunday was on the wicker couches at the far corner. As far away as it was possible to get from other drinkers in Wetherspoons.

"You are a careful man Mister McLean! I like that."

He was letting me know that he had seen me checking him out.

"It is the careful man who survives to laugh at his cowardice. The Viet Minh taught me that and they were all still alive! Thanks for this."

I lifted the tall glass on my side of the table and took a mouthful. I was going to pace myself; I did not want to act disgracefully in front of this man.

He had a large jug of orange juice, which he had barely touched.

"I wanted to thank you for the work you did for me. Susannah tells me it all went well, and Summer is only too aware of how she could have ended up, all without finding out about her mother and me. Thank you!"

No kisses from him, I thought.

"Thank you too for the return of my property. Not many honest men about these days. I could pay you a finder's fee if you like."

I searched that black slab of a face for a hidden meaning but could find none.

"No. It's no problem. I presume the stuff was yours anyway. It is of no interest to me."

I think he was searching for a handle to control me. If I took his money, he could understand me better.

"I like the way you have handled the press as well. I presume there is more to come."

I hoped he wasn't going to lean on me to kill the stories. It was too far gone for that now!

"The usual child molesting terrorist shit, I think. Nothing linking to you."

"If I thought there was, we would not be having a chat like this, believe me."

In that moment I did believe him. I knew the key to intimidation was credibility and he had it in spades, no pun intended.

"You do have a problem though? Did you know that?"

"The Chinese?"

He laughed! The black slab split in two by an immense white smile.

"I told Lenny he didn't need to worry. A man like you would be on top of it. Lenny was worried about you. He didn't want you taken off-guard. Do you need any help dealing with them? I owe you a favour and I do not like being in that position."

"You owe me nothing, but if I need any help it will only be political. I have access to literally an army of trained help."

He laughed again. It wasn't that funny. The last thing I needed was to be in this man's debt. He had convinced me at the first meeting that he was a man who collected his debts. Neither of us could be sure of the other's agenda. We were dancing around and we both knew it. The man who said it was better to die on your feet than live on your knees had never had to make that choice. I took the squaddie's view. If in doubt, hunker down and hope it blows over.

"Marko is extremely upset. His meeting with Lenny and Big Peter did not go well for him yesterday. He owes me a lot of money for his losses of cash and stock. I do not trust a desperate man, and neither should you. Also, some of the merchandise was not from us. That is not in his agreement. He couldn't explain why he had Chinese drugs mixed in with our stock. Three of the men you overcame were his best men, he tells me. Well done!"

"Den and Donnie wouldn't be pleased to hear that!"

"No! I don't suppose they would. Do you want to tell them?"

"Not to their faces. No."

Both of us laughed this time. My rum was finished. I nodded to his drink.

"Want something to put in that?"

"No thanks, I would appreciate it if you could wait a few minutes for a refill. I don't want to be here too long."

I hadn't thought before, but he had made himself extremely vulnerable out here, away from his protectors and very visible. I should have appreciated it more.

"I suspect I will be dealing with Marko before long. He is attracting too much attention, not on top of things enough. He has been buying from the Chinese. I don't think you will have to worry about him for long."

"I wasn't worried about him at all. If I was, I wouldn't have taken his stuff to give back to you."

"He is threatening all sorts to whoever raided his property."

"He won't find out who raided his property. There were no criminals involved. He will be looking in the wrong places. After tomorrow's papers he will be too busy clearing up his mess. I do not know how much he knew about the kids. I think Salim was selling them on to the Chinese for drugs. I don't know if that was a solo enterprise or under Marko's orders. Either way, the press coverage should come as a shock to him tomorrow."

I was fed up dancing around. He had said he had limited time. I was taking a chance getting right to it.

"Taking a chance there, John are you not? How could you know the girls weren't for me?"

"If they were, you could have told me where to look for Summer. In fact, you probably wouldn't have needed me at all."

"You know I run girls though."

"Of course, I do! I live underneath a brothel. How could I not know who runs women in Cardiff? That is the point, you run women not girls, certainly not children. The jail sentences are too long if you are caught with under-twelves. We both know that."

"You took a big chance on your view of me as a man."

"I've always been lucky."

"How do you know about the other girls who were involved? Susannah says you showed Summer images of little children being abused?"

We were getting to it now. He wanted to know what I knew, and more importantly, what I could prove.

"Like their physical security, their electronic security was shit. They kept all the images on the same computer as they kept their security footage and were dumb enough to keep it on-site. We removed it to take away the security footage and bingo! There were the videos and photos."

"Was that all that was on the computer?"

No smiles now! We were at the coalface with nowhere else to dig. Time to decide; lie and keep the insurance or give it up and perhaps be owed a favour. I gave it up. I didn't want to be looking over my shoulder waiting for them to come and find it; or to burn me to the ground to destroy it.

"They kept their accounts in it as well."

"Where is the computer now?"

"Completely overwritten and smashed into half a dozen skips."

"How much did you copy?"

"The images of the girls and the accounts."

"A careful man indeed. I knew Marko had lost something more than money and drugs. He blustered too much. I presume you will give me a copy of the accounts. They will tell me how much business he has been doing with the Chinese. I have no interest in the images. As you say the jail time for just looking at them is too great."

"Do you want them sent to Lenny's phone?"

"If you could do that soon I would appreciate it. I would like to see them before I head home today. The less time I spend in this shit hole the better as far as I am concerned. Thank you for your honesty. A lot of men would have been frightened to admit they had that kind of knowledge."

"It was only an insurance against the kind of accusations Lenny hinted at yesterday. Had he insisted I took more than I gave, I could have showed him the figures."

"You know you are a lot smarter than you like people to think, aren't you? I like a man who isn't greedy. They are hard to find. Thanks!"

"I hope Salim was working the girls as dealers on his own behalf and selling them on to the Chinese for his personal benefit. I don't think Marko knew anything about it until yesterday. If he did, he is in even deeper shit. It's his job to know things like that. You figured it out in three hours. Either way the Chinese were dipping their bread in my gravy. I will sort that out."

He was rising to leave. The maggot in my brain kept crawling about. It was time to get it out or leave it there, crawling about my subconscious, keeping me awake at odd times. Let's find out how much he owes me.

"Can I have a minute please?"

He sat back down again without protest. I liked that he respected me enough to at least listen. It was a good sign. Where to begin was the difficulty, and not just because he was a gangster, but because he was a father, and so was I. Who wanted to hear this?

"Summer is fourteen. She ran away from home. Susannah was fourteen when she ran away from home, as

248

well. You hooked vulnerable girls for a living. You were good at it. You will know that one of the major factors in teenage girls running away is to avoid sexual abuse by a father or more often a stepfather, usually just after puberty.

Gary Gregor treats Susannah like a wife in public. His arm is often around her, holding her. She is very childish in his company in a way that she is not when she is alone. Summer was afraid to go home yesterday. Every mention of home caused her to flinch.

I have shared these suspicions with no-one, nor will I, but as a father I will leave it with you to consider if you want that kind of level of involvement in Susannah and Summer's lives and whether you want to face the kind of anger that raising the issue will bring.

I am sorry to put that kind of suspicion in your mind where none existed, but be assured nice houses, good schools and big cars do not stop that kind of thing happening. I am truly sorry, and I am by no means certain, but I am sure enough to tell you I worry about it happening."

His expression never changed. He wouldn't look at me. To demonstrate how serious the situation was I joined him in drinking straight orange juice. Had he known me better, he would have realised that this was a once in a lifetime serious for me. He looked up. There were no smiles now.

"You are one of the few honest men I have met in recent years. You are a clever man and a very careful man. Sitting here, listening to you, I realised that you were not introducing a thought into my head. You were digging a thought I had buried back up.

When Gary called me at the weekend, the very

thing you spoke of flashed through my head and disappeared. I will have to think about it. I can tell you I have enjoyed speaking to Susannah again in recent days, though I hear she has been kissing other men."

It was a poor try at a tease and his voice and face were strained as he attempted it. Neither of us laughed. It was not really a time for laughing. What I had suggested was a horrible thought for any father. I was even adopting Summer's vocabulary now.

What I left unsaid was the thought that perhaps Summer wasn't even his daughter. The light coffee colour would suggest not. I did not tell him that that had been the first thing, which had occurred to me when I saw her photo. Sometimes it was shit pretending to be a detective.

He rose and shook my hand.

"Thank you, John! For everything. Remember I owe you a couple of favours now. Don't hesitate to call on me if you need anything. Send those accounts to Lenny as soon as if you can, please?"

Another please for me to appreciate. For all his money and power, I pitied him at that moment. Anyone can make good business choices, life choices were a bit more difficult, but usually quite clear. Family choices, however, were the hardest of all to understand or explain. I didn't envy him his. I didn't envy me, mine either.

I went back to the office and sent a copy of the accounts file to Lenny. That tiny trickle of information started the avalanche, which engulfed us all. Who knew?

TWELVE

The Hostage

I regarded the long screed of works emails on my computer and thought about whether to set about clearing them up or have a quick half hour on the couch. It was a close-run thing, but I had been in bed all night last night and hadn't touched the emails since nearly a week ago.

Time to earn the big bucks. The recycle bin was going to take a pasting I knew that going in. I promised myself that if I finished by four, I could have a night in The Packet to celebrate. Look for my shoe at the same time. It still hadn't turned up. Some detective! Couldn't find his own shoes.

Two out of every three went straight into the bin, half of those that remained went straight to file with no action required, that left me about twenty I had to think about and reply to. If I stuck at it, I could be in the pub by three at this rate.

Just as I started my office phone and mobile struck up at the same time. Lenny on my office phone, Penny on my mobile. No contest really.

"Penny how…"

"John! John! Thank God I got you."

She was shouting and hysterical. The panic and fear in her voice set off a primitive response in me to match her alarm.

"They've taken Katherine, those men. They've taken my baby. They want a million pounds for her. Please. Please tell them I'll pay it. I'll pay anything. Please John Please help me. Tell them not to hurt her!"

"Take a breath please Penny. Don't speak and take a deep breath. Hold it for a moment and exhale slowly. All right! Now listen to me! Focus on my voice and your breathing."

I had seen panic often. The key was to make the sufferer assert some form of control of themselves. Their words or their breathing or their movements. The control eventually knocked the panic into shape.

"Who has taken Katherine?"

Soft, calm and measured. I could not allow my anxiety to creep into my voice. I was already thinking of the Chinese. I had been expecting something, but aimed at me, not the girl.

"I don't know. They sounded foreign. They said if I did not pay them a million pounds, they would harm her, and I would never see her again. Please you've got to help me!"

"How did they sound foreign?"

"The words weren't right. They had an accent."

"Where are you now?"

"I am on the M4 on the way home. I have to try and get a million for them. I don't think…"

"Breathe, hold it for a moment and back out. They know you can't do that today. Crashing won't help anyone. I want you to come off at the next services. Do you have any idea where they are?"

Softly, quietly, distract and control. Force the mind to focus on something it can control. Find control that way. Getting her to do this was distracting me from my panic.

"Leigh Delamere. I am sure I saw a sign. I am near Bath. Yes, there it is. Services five miles."

"Pull into the left-hand lane now. Drive behind the trucks. Let them set your speed. Do not miss the services. You are in shock. Focus on the truck in front and your breathing. Slow in and hold. I can only help if you are in a fit state to help me. I cannot do anything without your help. Do you understand?"

"Yes. I am in the left-hand lane now. God these things go slow don't they."

"Yes. They do! Breathe now. Slow in and hold. Use the time behind the trucks. Control your breathing. Nice and slow. I want you to find a quiet place in the services and park. Is that clear. Do you understand?"

Emphasise her control. Slow her breathing. Distract with simple tasks. Confirm her understanding.

"When you are parked speak to me again. I have things to check before we speak again. I will answer you immediately. Do you understand?"

"Don't hang up please John."

"I am not hanging up. I am leaving the line open. I want to hear your breathing. Slow and steady until you are safely parked. You absolutely must be safe for Katherine. Do you understand?"

The call waiting bleep was going berserk and my office phone was ringing out for the third time in a row. Both from the same source. Lenny. The urgency made me doubt it was good news. I put my mobile on the desk on speaker and with the volume as high as possible. I hit the recall button on my office phone. There was no salutation.

"The boss wants to speak to you. Hold on!"

Direct order, no niceties. Sounded as if he were driving as well.

"John. Fucking Marko has gone off his fucking head. He has snatched Summer and wants a million pounds for her, the stupid cunt. Says he knows what she means to me. Did you tell him?"

"I most certainly did not, neither do I know anyone who is privy to that information. I need you to calm down Mister Smith. Tell Lenny to pull over a moment would you please?"

"Will I fuck. I am going to rip that fucking golliwog head of his right off his shoulders. I should have done it this morning when I had the chance. Big, ginger cunts or not!!"

"Lenny. Can you hear me. Please pull over this is a trap! Can you hear me? A trap! Please pull over."

"You've got a minute John. After that I think the boss will rip my head off. Leave the line open. I had enough trouble getting through there."

I had my mobile and office phones both busy. I was at a loss what to do. I rummaged in my jacket pocket for the bat phone. I had to look-up Snow White's number in my mobile. Penny heard the beeps.

"John! John! What's happening I'm almost there now. Don't hang up. Please."

"I'm not hanging up. I am still here keep taking your time breathing. Slow in and slow out."

"We all know how to breath, you prick. Stop fucking us about. What is the problem?"

I was losing track of who I was talking to whilst trying to key the number into the bat phone with my thumb. A very tentative voice answered;

"Hello. Who is this please?"

"Susannah. It is John McLean."

"John. I am so pleased you called. I have been hoping to hear from you after the excitement of yesterday. Is this your private number?"

I was still a bit thrilled that she called our kiss excitement given what was going-on on my desk. I walked away to the kitchen where neither of the phones on my desk could pick up my conversation. I felt like a schoolboy when she spoke to me.

"Is Summer with you by any chance?"

"Yes, yes she is! I let her bunk off school. We are having afternoon tea as a matter of fact. Do you want to speak to her?"

"No! It's okay. I was just a bit worried when she wasn't at school."

"God that's so sweet, you checking to make sure she is alright. When are we going to dinner?"

"I will call you about that soon, I promise. I am glad everything is all right. Sorry to interrupt, enjoy your afternoon tea. Remember no cakes till you finish the sandwiches."

She was still laughing as I hung up. I picked up the office phone.

"Mister Smith!"

"This better be fucking good news, John. Ordering my fucking driver around."

"Summer is safe and well and having afternoon tea with her mother as we speak."

"What do you fucking mean? Marko told me himself he had her."

"He has the wrong girl. He has taken Summer's best friend Katherine Price. I have her mother on the other phone right now."

"Fucking useless twat. Are you sure?"

"I spoke to Susannah less than a minute ago."

I could hear the laughter in the car as they decompressed from the tension of moments before.

"That doesn't mean they won't come back for her though!"

"Trust you John. Always thinking of tomorrow, aren't you? What do you propose apart from me ripping his head off?"

"Where are you now?"

"Just coming up on to the motorway."

"M4 or M5?"

"M4."

"Would you mind turning right and heading to London. At, I think, junction seventeen or eighteen, turn around and go into Leigh Delamere services westbound. You are looking for a big white Range Rover. There will be a woman in it. Stunningly beautiful. She will probably still be crying or at least looking upset. If you could stay with her and keep her safe, I will deal with things at this end.

Keep your boys out of it for now. At least then if I need you, you will have cooled off a bit. I think this is probably related to me anyway."

"Will do, John. Lenny is taking us there as we speak. Do you think this is the Chinese?"

"Who else would it be?"

"That slimy cunt has taken up with them. Does he

think he can sell off my business?"

"Where else could he turn? I'm guessing you backed him into a corner this morning."

"If he had a brain cell it would die of loneliness. He is only my representative. He has convinced himself that he runs Cardiff. Twat! Sort this out for me for now, John, and I'll make the problem disappear permanently tomorrow."

"Will do. My only priority is to get the girl back safely then we will see where we are."

"Okay. Tell the girl's mum we should be there in about twenty minutes. Tell her not to be frightened when she sees us. That Lenny terrifies some women."

And with that they were off on the mission I had invented for them.

"Did you hear much of that Penny?"

"I heard the stunningly beautiful bit. I won't forget that!"

"There will be two big African men coming to you within the next half an hour. They are there to protect and reassure you. I will get Katherine back just like I got Summer back yesterday. Do you trust me to do that?"

"Yes! But they said I will never see her again if I do not pay them. Do not risk her life, please! I beg you."

"I would never do anything to harm either of you. You understand that don't you?"

"Yes, I trust you."

Repeat, repeat, repeat.

"I will get her back. You believe me, don't you?"

"Yes! But I can pay. I will give them the money. It would be no problem."

"Listen to me. They have taken the wrong girl. They think they have taken Summer. It is her father they want the money from, not you!"

"Does Gary have that kind of money?"

She wasn't thinking straight, but subconsciously she had seen the same as me.

"Gary is her grandfather. Her father has that kind of money."

"She doesn't know who her father is?"

"No! She doesn't, but I do, and this is about him. Perhaps it always has been, including dragging Kat into it in the first place, to snare Summer. The kidnapper doesn't know the girls, he has taken the wrong coffee-coloured girl."

"Do you think so?"

"Possibly. Anyway. There is no way anyone could raise that kind of money at this time of day. If they call back tell them it will take you until lunchtime tomorrow to raise as much as you can, but it will be nowhere near a million. I should have it solved by then. Whatever you do, do not mention Summer! Do you understand that. There is nothing to be gained by endangering her as well and it could make the problem twice as hard to solve and ten times as likely to go wrong. Do you understand? Do not mention that they have the wrong girl."

Repeat, repeat, repeat.

"I understand. You will be careful as well, won't you?"

"Always. I rely a lot on luck too, of course, but only for my personal welfare. I will get Katherine back safely. Of that I have no doubt."

"Neither do I, but please keep yourself safe."

Second time in a week someone was worried about me. It could get quite tiresome, quite quickly.

"Call me if they get back in touch. Remember tomorrow lunchtime. Any more thoughts about the accent?"

"I know this sounds strange, but it sounded like a someone from Cardiff pretending to be Chinese. Does that make any sense?"

It made too much sense. It could be Cardiff Chinese or someone trying hard to blame them. I would know which it was soon enough I supposed."

"Do you have the number they called you on?"

"They called on Katherine's phone. The one you brought back this morning."

Bingo! My lucky streak continuing.

"Have you spoken to your husband about this. Is he on his way home?"

"I doubt it. He ran away with our bookkeeper nearly a year ago. We haven't been able to find hide nor hair of them since, nor the two and a half million pounds they took."

I couldn't help myself. I laughed out loud. I had sorted an identical problem only last week, for a bit less money, admittedly. I was also relieved that she didn't have a husband. Somewhere, flirting with a married woman had bothered me, now it was fair game.

"It's not that funny. Katherine was very upset by it. She had to have therapy."

"That's not what is funny. Do you not realise that is exactly what I do for a living? Finding people like that. LOCATION SERVICES."

"I thought you worked with film studios and such like."

I couldn't moan, that is exactly what I wanted

people to think when they saw the brass plaque at my office.

"Anyway, I am not that fussed about getting him back. He would have probably gotten a lot more in a proper divorce so, more fool him. Please just concentrate on finding Katherine and keeping you both safe."

"I will. I will call at nine to let you know how I am doing."

I called Sunday Smith as soon as I hung up.

"We're nearly there. Traffic is murder at this time."

"It's not that! I think you should call Susannah and have her and Summer stay somewhere safe and out of the way for a couple of days"

"Ahead of you there, John. Already done. They are on their way to the Berwick Lodge Hotel just north of Bristol for two nights at my expense."

"Could you take Penny there too please? I don't want to rescue the child to have the mother disappear or any unwanted visitors to their house."

"No problem John. Do them both good to have familiar faces around. Thanks for sorting this. It's another one I owe you. I can't believe I listened to that mongrel. How dumb am I. How fucking dumb is he, taking the wrong girl. Thick as shite, both of us, if you need anything or anybody give me a call. I might just hang around the hotel, just in case. I'll text you a number for the next couple of days."

"I haven't told Penny who or what you are, just that you are there to protect her. If you are going to be hanging around you had better think of what Susannah might tell her."

"Will do. Watch yourself. These guys might be a

bit more serious than the pakis. The big ginger bastards were carrying heavy this morning, and the Chinese love their MAC10s."

Too many Jackie Chan films. That was the problem.

"Call you later!"

Time for another miracle. This one would perhaps be the easiest of the last few days. Before I had returned her phone, as I promised, I had added one of those invisible tracking apps to Kat's phone. Not that I didn't trust her, but why take the chance? I fired up the app and there she was, clear as day. A flashing red dot on the only buildings for miles. I tapped on my Ordnance Survey App and there it was.

The map had PH beside the building indicating it was a pub but given that the only other building for miles was a church, I thought it likely it was closed. It was on top of a hill overlooking Treforest Industrial Estate about ten miles north west of Cardiff. Perfect for them, difficult for me. There was nowhere to linger inconspicuously around there from the looks of it. It was just far enough away that it qualified as a Cardiff pub I hadn't been in. There were very few of those.

I went back to her phone tracker and clicked on the link to operate the camera. It was evidently in someone's pocket or didn't work. What did I expect? It had only cost £3.99. The microphone did work, however, and I could hear muffled voices. Then I could hear one voice very clearly, Marko's. Her phone must be in his pocket.

"And I'm telling you he can get a million in a heartbeat. I earn him more than that every few weeks. What do you think he does with all that cash? It's probably just lying about somewhere. Don't talk shit Donnie."

I left it on low for now, I wanted to focus on thinking about how to get the girl back safely. Three choices really. Pay, retrieve or snatch at the handover. I didn't want anyone to have to pay. If they did it would just become a recurring problem and I didn't really want to wait for a handover. If they were smart, there would be too many people around for a snatch, particularly if they were as heavily armed as Mister Smith had indicated. That left retrieval.

While I was figuring this out, I was also listening to her phone. I estimated there were two others in the room with Marko. Donnie and one of the Chinese probably. I was just going to turn the app off to save the battery for later when I got lucky again. Two new voices appeared and two made the sound of people leaving. Marko again.

"Told you! They would need a helicopter to come here. We don't need lookouts. We can see the road from here."

The reply didn't please him.

"Well don't expect me to stand out there. You don't keep a monkey and dance yourself. You guys will need to learn that if you want to run a city like this."

What a dick. He couldn't have told me more if he had been on my side. I would have loved to see Donald's face at being called a monkey. If you have a pointy stick you shouldn't keep poking the gorillas with it. It would cost you in the long run.

Marko and two others in a front room facing the road, another two outside on watch. It was doable, but the key was not allowing the girl to be hurt. If she was in the room with Marko and the others there was always a chance of her being damaged. If she was locked away somewhere else that would be the defining bonus. I could clear them all with impunity.

"Give it five minutes and I'll call again. We'll have that money tonight, you'll see."

I called Lenny. It was picked up immediately.

"Just arrived. Christ you weren't kidding when you said beautiful were you? All she goes on about is you. Pissing the boss off already, I can tell. He usually gets the attention."

"Could you put him on please? Its urgent."

"John. Everything okay? I am taking you off speaker."

"Yes. I have located the girl. Marko and the Chinese have her. They are going to call Penny in a couple of minutes. They still think she is Summer and are expecting the money to come from her family. Could you play along please? Tell them you can arrange the money for them tomorrow, first thing. I should have it sorted by then."

"You are a juju man. A suspicious man might wonder how you can know these things so quickly."

"I'll tell you another time. I can hear everything Marko is saying, for now. That is how I know he is just going to call Penny. How is she?"

"She is fine. She can tell by my smile that everything is all right. Big fan of yours, by the way."

"Could you just tell her to play along. I will have Kat back sometime tonight. I will call when I can, but Kat is safe and well and I know exactly where she is. In half an hour I will be watching over her directly."

"Stay safe Mister McLean. If you need anything call Lenny."

He was cutting me off before I implicated him in any wrongdoing in front of a witness. He was also telling me that there would be no more speaking to me direct. Lenny was the cut-out. Too many mafia movies. All these gangsters loved their on-screen heroes.

"John, Lenny here. I have left them in the car for now. Do you need anything?"

"Not for now, thanks. I'll let you know later once I have a plan."

"I think you always have a plan. Just so you know the Boss spoke to the Chinese on the drive here. It seems their local guys have gone the same way as our local guy. Fucking mad! Officially, no-one higher up the chain is very pleased with them. Unless they succeed, of course. No-one wants a war. If you succeed that will be the end of it as far as they would be concerned."

"Thanks. Last thing I need would be having to tool up to fetch my supper of an evening."

Lenny was still laughing as he hung up. What he hadn't said was that if I failed, they were on the road to nowhere, and not for very long either. Big stakes for such a little girl.

I turned my tracking app on her phone off. I wanted to save her battery in case I needed it later and I didn't know what her screen showed when the app was actively listening and watching. I should have checked that when I installed it. I was dying to hear Marko's call but couldn't take the risk.

One thing I needed urgently was transport. I fired up Mad Bastard One on my phone again and was pleased when Shaky answered.

"Twice in a week, Jock, people will say we're in

love. How can I help you? Don't say you want your money back; she just booked a big holiday with it."

"No. I told you. It was yours to keep. You were well worth it. How do you fancy another dig at it?"

"When? We are off at the weekend to some swanky resort in the Caribbean."

"Tonight. Straight retrieval. Young girl. Same organisation as the other one. Bit better organised and armed though. Full kit for tonight but you would just be the lookout and driver unless it goes really pear-shaped."

Letting him know what the risks were.

"I owe you from the weekend anyway, Jock. No charge for this. If you let me go in while you drive, I would probably pay you to be honest."

"I can't have you going on holiday in a cast and bandages, can I? I have never met your new bird and I'm frightened of her, as it is."

"When's the go?"

"Soon as you can get here. Same van as Sunday, if possible, if not anything will do. No obbo on this one. Quick recce, then in and out. This girl knows and trusts me so we should be okay there as well. Bring full kit with you but arrive in a white shirt, black tie and flowers. You are going to a funeral on the way."

"Mine or yours?"

"Hopefully nobody's! How long to get here?"

"I am in Barry just now. Say half an hour. Give me time to iron a shirt. I presume you are opening Alibaba's Cave again?"

"Yes. No problem. My job! My kit!"

"See you then. No identifiers on the vehicle."

I didn't expect there to be CCTV at the site. If there

was, they wouldn't need to keep watch, but thought this might be an all or nothing escapade and there was only one road. Any police investigation would be able to trace vehicles near the entrance and exit. One end of the road was just above Pontypridd Town Centre.

That would be the in and out route. Enough traffic on three or four busy roads to provide cover. The alternative was behind the giant GE aero engine works at Nantgarw. I would bet they would have CCTV covering the back of their site. Why take the risk?

If all else failed there was a path down the hill into a housing estate, then on to Treforest Railway Station. A fair alternative, though the contours indicated the hillside was quite steep. It wouldn't matter too much. We would be going downhill.

While I waited and got changed into my cargo trousers and Lycra top a thought crept into my mind unbidden. Worth a try, I thought. I scrolled down my phone and there she was. The possible solution to my troubles. Couldn't hurt I supposed? Press Call here goes nothing.

"Mrs. Peters. John McLean. How are you?"

"Mister McLean. I haven't had the chance to thank you for the flowers and chocolates at the weekend. They were lovely. The flowers still look beautiful. I said to Donald that I get more gratitude from you than I ever do from those two. I mean, I love them, but they could take lessons from you in grace."

Score one for Lenny. Always easy to overlook the small details, but he hadn't, and I was hoping to reap the rewards.

"I hope you didn't mind me giving the boys your private number. They seemed desperate. They haven't been themselves for a couple of weeks now!"

"No! No problem. We try and look out for each other, as you know."

The good Lord strike me down dead. The trouble that one call had caused was multiplying every hour.

"That is why I am calling. I don't tell tales out of school as you well know, none of us do, but I hear that Marko is getting the boys into a lot of trouble."

"They've always been in trouble, those two. People picking on them because of their size."

In my experience few people victimised the huge. Quite the reverse, in fact.

"This is a bit worse than their normal work though, Mrs. Peters. I know where they are and what they are doing, and it might get them killed if they are not careful."

"I never liked them working for that man. He is a weasel. You can see it in his eyes. The boys will look out for each other. They will be safe enough."

She sounded confident, but I could hear the doubt and fear in her voice. Frightening old women now, what was I becoming?

"I know they will try to. This time, though, I think Marko is about to sell them down the river. I think he has been working up to it for weeks."

First rule of interrogation, listen and re-use expressed opinions. I was using her own observations to support my case.

"They have been worried, recently. I know that, the number of times they shut up when I come in, and Dennis is off his food. That's never a good sign."

Given that he had eaten enough for a small village in my office, a couple of days ago I would have hated to

267

see him hungry!

"What can we do to help them Mister McLean? I presume that is why you are calling."

"Could you give either of them a call, please? All I want you to tell them is that I can help them, if they want help. Please have one of them give me a call when they are on their own. That is all. I like the boys. I want to try and get them out of the mess Marko has left them in. before they get seriously hurt, or worse."

I watched for the Lord striking me down again. Adding lying to threatening an old woman. What was I coming to?

"You are a good man Mister McLean I know that, but if this is a trick, I will let the boys fight over your bones, I promise you that.

"Thank you, Mrs. Peters. Save me a coffee crème or two. I hope we can all laugh about this tomorrow."

"I don't think they make them any more Mister McLean. Like so much else they are lost in the mists of time. I will call Dennis. It will be up to him if he calls you."

"That's all I wanted. I hope to hear from him."

If I could persuade the boys away, it would leave three against one. I fancied those odds. I fancied five against one as well if necessary. This wasn't going to be a fist fight. I fancied my chances in a firefight because I had decades of training and practice in them. I was sure they hadn't. Watching films and playing Call of Duty didn't count.

I watched Sam arrive in a small blue van on the sauna CCTV just as my phone went. Dennis! I buzzed the door open and answered.

"You're a right bastard, Jock! My mum is worried

sick now. What did you tell her you were going to do? And you took credit for the flowers and chocolates. The grief Donny and I had over those. I know it was Sonny that bought them as well."

"Den! I didn't tell her I was going to do anything, but I would like you to listen to me."

"Why the fuck should I? You've no weight in this. We've got Sunny by the balls. We took his daughter at lunch time."

"How alone are you just now Den?"

"Completely! Why?"

Just to check I turned on Kat's microphone. I could hear Marko in mid rant. I couldn't hear him in the background of Den's phone, so at least he wasn't near Marko."

"Did you hear that Den? That was Marko! I am listening to everything in that room."

"What room?"

"The one at the front of the pub."

I took a flyer.

"Don't look round like that. You will break your neck!"

"You really are a fucking ninja aren't you, Jock, all that kung fu shite and all."

"Please, just listen Dennis. What colour is the girl you think is your ace in the hole?"

"The colour of Marko, why?"

"What colour is Sonny?"

"You met him, He's the colour of coal."

"Think about that for a moment, Dennis. Marko has taken the wrong girl. She is not Sonny's daughter because he doesn't have a daughter. I was looking for his niece. I know you have the wrong girl because I rescued Sonny's niece from that house in Pontcanna on Sunday night. She is safe and miles away from Cardiff. Sonny's niece is much, much darker than the girl you have taken."

"What a fucking dick. He told us he had her pictures with Sally and the guys."

"I'm sure he does, but that was weeks ago. She was the girl before Sonny's niece."

"Why are you involved then?"

"Sonny doesn't want to have to worry about his niece ever again. He wants me to clean up the mess once and for all. Do you know what I mean?"

"We won't be as easy as Sally and his boys, you know? No matter how big your army."

"Who said I had an army. You have been in that house, how many men could you fit into that hall, or the living room. I did them myself."

"Anyway, we are ready for you. Come if you dare."

"You don't think you are going to stop me with those Chinese knock off MAC10s do you?"

"How the fuck do you know what they are? I don't even know."

"Look just behind the trigger guard on the right-hand side. There is a long number. It starts with M-A-C-1-0. Military Armament Company Model 10. MAC10 Anyway take my word for it Your brother and you and two Chinese won't be enough to stop me. If I wanted to, I could drop you and the other Chinese now, before I even go in. You won't be counting on Marko for much when the chips are down will you?"

"Like fuck you could!"

"Bang! That would be you dead, Dennis. Bang!

That would be your pal on the other side of the building. End of story, forever. Your Mum crying at your funeral and asking me why I didn't help you."

"What do you want?"

"I don't want to hurt you and Donald. At heart, I don't think you are child killers, but that is how this situation is going to end. You will have to kill Katherine. Even if she doesn't know your names, she knows all your faces. There aren't two other guys like you and your brother are there? I don't want you dying for Marko's stupidity. I bet you didn't like being called a dancing monkey quarter of an hour ago. Did you?"

"How the fuck did you know that?"

"I told you, I can see and hear everything. Have a quiet chat with your brother. Marko is a dead man walking, so are the two Chinese fellas. Do you think the bosses like to see the foot soldiers getting uppity? No matter what happens here, those three are dead men. They are not taking over Cardiff. Bristol or London or Manchester are going to swallow them whole. Don't be part of it. Marko is off his fucking head."

"We are stuck here now. He won't let us leave, even if we wanted to."

"I will let you leave, but only if you do not raise your weapons when I come in. I give you my word on that. One twitch up with the guns and your mother will be burying both of you. I promise you that as well. What do you say?"

"I'll talk to my brother and get back to you."

"No need. I will call you five minutes before I come in. If you are out of the game just say, not now Nico!"

271

A little Velvet Underground reference for my late father there. Hours of music education not wasted on me!

"If I don't hear those words then all bets are off, but you'll need more than that shitty replica to fight me off. See you soon Dennis. Use your head here."

Sam was standing quietly at the door waiting for me to finish before letting him in. he looked smart in his shirt and black tie. Like a chauffeur. The neighbours will think I am going up in the world.

"Fuck me Jock you looked grim there. Who were you giving the message to?"

"Maybe taking half the opposition off the field before we begin. Worth a shot, at least."

"This is becoming a habit. Maybe you need a partner. I could just do the fighting for you if you like."

"Or maybe I could buy you a nice peaked hat and you could be my driver."

I pressed open the door to the armoury and selected two bulletproof vests, two sets of night vision gas masks, two of the H and K G36 carbines, two of the Glock 17s with shoulder holster and a couple of the low intensity G60 flash bangs. I checked the magazines in all the guns. I didn't bother with spares. If that wasn't enough firepower we were fucked anyway. I packed them all in a cricket holdall with a giant Kookaburra printed all over it. I stuck the commando knife in its special pocket.

"That's me ready. What about you? Briefing on the way."

"Bit more serious than last time eh?
No jokes now.

"They might know we are coming. Four guys with full MAC10s and a fifth with unknown capability."

272

"No comms."

"Not needed. Confined location two defined exit routes. The visuals should make the state of play obvious."

He just nodded. Just when I thought he was worried, slowing down because of his new lifestyle, a huge grin spilt his face.

"I never thought I would get to handle a G36 again. Thanks, Jock."

Fucking Paras. They could never surprise you with their attitude. I drove, simply because I knew where we were going, and he didn't. Didn't even ask, just sat with the flowers on his lap waiting for his briefing.

"Going to retrieve a fourteen-year-old girl being held hostage by five heavily armed hostiles in an abandoned public house, miles from anywhere in open countryside. One road passing the pub. We are going in and out the same road to avoid cameras. Are the plates okay for reading?"

He nodded. I really was teaching my Grandma to suck eggs, but time diminished all capability and it never hurt to check. Always better to hurt his feelings here, than his wife's at his funeral.

"You will drive in and turn the van to go back the way we came in. There is a church next to the target property. It is the only structure for miles around. Visit a grave and have a quick recce. If safe, walk along as if you are going for a pint at the pub, checking if it is closed. Back to the van and report by phone even though I will be in the back. The hostiles know me by sight.

To date they have been operating a two out; two in guard roster. If that still holds, I will take the two outside and then go in behind a flash bang to finish the job. You will be second man. You will go in behind me only if I am down. Otherwise you will stand in reserve. All well I will bring the girl out, into the van and away.

Anything wrong, the secondary route is cross-country down the hill. There is a footpath into a housing scheme. Keep heading down and right and a train station should be visible ahead.

There is a chance two of the hostiles will become non-combatants. We will know just before going in. They will be the two big ginger cunts. All Clear."

"Easier if we take a guard each and I throw the flash bang and find the girl while you do the clear up. Too much for you to do dealing with the hostiles and trying to protect the girl. You know that."

He was right and I had thought of it, but we were going to kill people here today. I didn't want Shaky involved in that. He had a normal life to go home to. The truth was I didn't.

"This is going to be no-holds-barred. You have a life to look forward to. No need for both of us to go to jail."

"No fucker is going to jail, Jock. These cunts have kidnapped and terrorised a kid as well as all the other stuff. Fuck them. I won't lose any sleep over them if you don't."

"I would lose sleep over anything happening to you, Shaky. That would be my fault and there is no need of it."

"Come on Jock. You know I am going to follow you in anyway, you might as well use me in a structured way."

I knew all right. Planning and the Paras. Never a good mix unless it involved flat out action from the off. After a bit of back and forth I relented. New plan.

"If the two gingers are off the board, I will take the outside guard. We will go in together. You flash bang the room and protect the girl, covering fire only if needed. I will deal with the two remaining hostiles. If all deals are off, we take a guard each, you flash bang the room and have responsibility for the girl but take as many hostiles as you can. Does that sound better?"

He couldn't wipe the smile off his face. If we both go from the off, can I borrow the commando knife. I have wanted to use one of them since I was a boy."

"I bet you bought the comics, didn't you?"

"Didn't everyone? Anyway, can I borrow it, please?"

I couldn't see me ever having to find out who Mad Bastard Two on my phone was. That was the last thought I had before we stopped, and I climbed into the back to get ready and hide from prying eyes. Sam drove on up one of the steepest hills imaginable laughing at my attempts to hold on in the back and within a couple of minutes he was turning into the church.

"You were right the pub is boarded up. There is a big ginger cunt walking down the side of it. Wish me luck," and he was off, wielding his flowers like a shield.

I lay in the back wriggling into my vest and attaching the carbine sling to the webbing, so it hung in a firing position on my right. I checked the pistol and holstered it in the quick draw position for my left hand. Neither of the weapons had safety catches. They were for killing, nothing else. I laid out Shaky's gear for him. It would be cramped in the back. Easier if I slid out and left him to it. Satisfied I called Dennis.

"Not now Nico!"

Sam was getting in the van. He phoned me from the driver's seat. No-one looking on would think he was doing anything other than calling home.

"Two outside guards like you said. Chinese guy on the far side, next to the old pub bay window, big ginger fucker this side, just took a call. Life in the front room facing the road. All ground floor windows boarded up. I think they are using a side door about halfway down this side just before a big modern extension. Any word?"

"The big gingers are off the board. There will be one upstairs as well. Don't shoot him by mistake. His mother would kill me."

"Let me take the outside Chinaman then! It would be easier for me to approach dressed like this. You would fucking terrify him."

And he was off. He knew I was trapped in the back for the moment. I watched out the back window as he strolled past Dennis and rattled the front door for effect. The Chinese guy came around the bay frontage to see what the fuss was and Shaky broke his neck. Just like killing a chicken. Cupped right hand straight up under the chin, left hand pulling the right shoulder towards him as sharply as possible.

If that hadn't worked, he would just have turned it into a stranglehold, right hand continuing across the face, left hand twisting the victim round in front of him. Lock the right hand in the left elbow and squeeze. Just as deadly, just as silent but a damn sight more painful and slow.

He had just eased the guy into a sitting position almost hidden by the hedge when a tractor rolled past. Shaky simply stepped into the hedge and vanished from sight. The tractor rolled past and away. The driver didn't even look round. Shaky strolled back without a care in the world and let me out the back.

"The big guy just waved me through but keep an eye on him would you."

I watched Dennis while Shaky shrugged on the vest. He didn't bother with the sling and holster. He jammed the short in the right armpit of his vest and picked the carbine up freehand in his left. He unpinned the flash bang and held the detonating lever down by gripping it in his right hand. Masks on and ear-defenders in and we were away.

This was our only vulnerable moments, getting to and from the van dressed like killers and armed to the nines. We doubled over to the pub where Dennis was obligingly holding the door open for us. He looked more at home doing that than he would have done beating a young girl, I thought.

"Donald is in the toilet. You better not be fucking us about Jock!"

I went up the stairs first. It was an old building, a coaching house probably and the steps were stone and therefore silent. I went first. I could hear Marko holding fort. Probably shouting because he was talking to the Chinese guy, even though he had a Cardiff accent too.

We could probably have managed without the flash bang, but they were a bastard to re-pin and anyway Shaky desperately wanted to get that rifle into his right hand and firing. I kicked the door and the grenade followed immediately. It did what it said on the tin. Big flash, loud bang, room filled by noxious fumes. I was through and the Chinaman was dead in less than a second. Left-hand or not, two to the head. The product of countless hours of ambidextrous practice.

Marko was lounging in a big armchair. He was blinded, deafened and disoriented. We could have taken him alive, but that would only have been passing the problem down the line. He had a big shotgun across his lap. I looked to Shaky. He was gleefully lifting his rifle to the fire position. I reached across with my left hand and stopped him.

He looked so disappointed. I lifted the MAC10 from where the Chinaman had dropped it and handed it to him. It was set on full auto. It would fire all thirty rounds in its magazine in just over a second. I think Marko thought we were playing a video game. Shaky delivered the whole magazine at and through him with one squeeze. It made a sound like a faulty zipwire. He did well to keep his aim, usually it rose up with the force of firing so quickly.

He was still smiling. I could see it in his eyes through the mask. I knew he was going to ask if he could keep it. I would tell him he could have the guy down the stair's gun. That should keep him happy. There wasn't much left of Marko except a pulpy mixture of him and chair and a fine red mist in the air. His legs were intact though. He didn't even have time to piss himself. I helped myself to his shotgun and let the dead Chinaman have both barrels to the head, hopefully obliterating my bullets. It must have done there wasn't any head left.

Donald emerged from the toilet and nearly had to go back in. He was white as a sheet and trembling. Not really cut out for the real dirty work then. I asked him where the girl was, and he nodded to the door at the far end of the landing. I told him to go and get the other Chinaman and leave him in a heap at the bottom of the stairs.

I stopped Shaky leaving and made him put the MAC10 back in the Chinaman's hands and rub his sleeve and hand all over the dead man's hand and sleeve for the residue. I should really have made him hug him because the MAC10 had a blowback system and the residue got everywhere. There was so much crap and bits of body in the air, I didn't think it made much difference I picked up the carcase of the flash bang and that was as clean as we were going to get. I pulled the door closed and set off for the girl.

I was just about to go in when Sam grabbed me. He motioned for me to remove the mask, just as he was doing. Good thinking really. When you are kitted up you forget how scary it must look to civilians. I tried my best smile and opened the door. Kat was spread-eagled naked on a bare single bed, wearing only a double pillowcase over her head. She started screaming through a gag as soon as I opened the door. Deal or no deal I was going to kill the brothers if they were involved in this. Behind me Shaky said, "Don't feel as bad now. We should have taken our time."

"Katherine, Katherine! Katherine!!" progressively louder.

"It's John, Katherine, It's John, Katherine! It's John, Katherine!! From Sunday. I had breakfast with you this morning. Remember."

Gradually she stopped wriggling and screaming,

"You are safe. I am here to help you. You are safe, do you understand?"

She nodded and tried to speak.

"You are safe. Do not try to speak. I am coming to help you now. Do you understand?"

279

She nodded again.

"It is daylight. When I take the hood off it will be bright. Don't be alarmed. You are safe."

Taking a leaf from the book of Mam-san.

I cut her feet and hands free and she sat up immediately rubbing her hands and feet. They were blue from the constriction. If they didn't hurt now, they would as soon as the blood started flowing again.

I eased the hood from her head. The gag was her pants stuffed in her mouth and held there by gaffer tape. Her eyes were raw from crying. If I could have, I would have gone back and killed them again. I hugged her and stroked her hair.

"You are safe now. Those men won't hurt you again. They won't hurt anyone ever again."

Behind me Shaky had stripped off his kit and was handing me his white shirt. Incongruously I noticed he had only ironed the front. I helped her into it. It came to her knees. It would have to do for now. I couldn't find anything else to protect her modesty. Shaky led the way.

We both slung the carbines across our backs to hide them slightly from view. We had to jump over the Chinaman at the bottom. Katherine stamped on his face as hard as she could. It broke his nose for sure. I heard it crack. I don't think she realised he was already dead. Shaky went out the door first and signalled to wait. He was checking it was safe to leave, but also making sure the brothers weren't waiting to ambush us. I hoped he was also bringing the van round to the door. He was.

"Them two have fucked off. Good job and all. I want a word with them after."

Me too. I noticed he had had time to lift the other

MAC10.

"Pile in now and we will sort it out down the road."

Still kitted up I lay in the back. Shaky guided Kat to the front seat as gently as he could and climbed in the driver seat. Uncomfortable with a safety less carbine strapped to his back. To say he drove carefully on the bumpy country lane would be an understatement. Eventually he stopped in a layby just before a signpost for the golf course.

The two of us stripped the kit and put it back in the cricket bag.

Kat sat in the front seat intermittently crying. I went around and crouched by her open door.

"I am just going to call your mother, let her know you are safe and well. She was just going to pay a million for you, you know. That should help get a raise in pocket money if nothing else."

She tried to smile. It was a good try.

"I could try and remove that guy's nose bone from your foot if that would help."

She laughed out loud at that one.

"Can I not just go home? Please."

"Not right away, sorry. I had your mother taken somewhere safe, near Bristol, in case they came for her as well. I didn't know what was going on and thought it better to be safe than sorry. Would you like to speak to her? Then we can arrange for you getting home. What do you think?"

Head down, she nodded slightly. I pressed the Call button.

"John! Is she alright? Have you found her yet? I told them I would pay. They said they would call soon with the arrangements. Do you think you can get her back? I don't trust them."

"I have her. She is safe and well and unharmed. Would you like to speak to her?"

"Oh! Thank God! Thank God! Put her on please. Are you sure she is alright?"

"Mum! Mum! I'm alright. John came and got me. Yes! I knew he would find me. He told me on Sunday! Yes! He's fine as well. I don't know. We have only just stopped. I don't know where. I don't know. Muuum I don't know. Talk to John!"

She thrust the phone back to me, petulantly, I was still warming in the glow of her asking about me.

"She keeps asking me all these questions."

"Hello. We are near Pontypridd. No, she is fine. No, it won't happen again. She just wants to go home. No, they won't. Yes! I do know that. Why don't you take a minute or two to gather yourself then we can plan?

If you must, meet us at my offices down the Bay in an hour and a half. Yes! I know, but we have a couple of things to do first. No! She is fine. I will see she is fed. My offices in an hour and a half. Yes! Yes! Yes! Me too. See you then."

I rolled my eyes as I hung up. She laughed.

"She does go on, doesn't she?"

She was bouncing back already. The resilience of the young. Shaky was watching from the back of the van. He had done the checklist and wanted a word.

"I think we are clear. If the police were coming, they would be coming up this road from that police station."

He nodded to the big blue sign on the other side of the river, bright in the falling darkness.

"What is our story? I don't like that those two big ginger cunts and her, have seen us."

"None of them know anything about you. Nothing. We left nothing behind that will lead to us. By tonight I will have a video alibi and she will have an electronic one. I presume you will have a loving one. The place was a pub. There will be nothing but prints and DNA. The dead guys are the top kiddies in organised crime in the area. There is nothing to link us to them. We were never here and anyone who says otherwise is a criminal and a liar or at worst a severely afflicted child. Happy?"

"Fine, as long as we are clear. You spoke to me today about debt recovery for some of your insurance clients, costs, timescales, things like that and I met you for a coffee and a chat. Okay."

"Okay."

He removed the fake plates and climbed in the back leaving me to drive us back to the office. We would have stopped and got Kat some clothes, but as standard practise neither of us had any money with us. He thought I could help Kat back to normal better than he would have.

As we approached the Square, I clicked the roller shutter up and opened the door. Kat looked fabulous in Shaky's shirt except for having no shoes. On her it was a knee length dress. I turned on the same lamps as Monday morning, and showed her up to my flat for a shower. All I could offer her in the way of clothes was a John Martyn tee shirt far too small for me and a pair of cycle shorts with a bib and brace. It wasn't much but I had been a bachelor for a long time.

I went back downstairs where Shaky had made us both a coffee and was on the biscuits. The body always craves sugar after action. It is a reaction to the adrenaline. I opened the regular office safe, not the one hidden underneath and pulled out about half of the five thousand I had from Sunday night. I handed it to him.

"Have a good holiday on me, mate. I appreciate your help."

"Don't embarrass me, Jock. I owed you one, at least. Besides, I got that lovely machine pistol for a souvenir. I can't tell you how much I enjoyed it today. I look forward to you phoning, I really do."

"Buy the new missus something nice then. On me. Please take it."

"Alright then. But only because I don't want you squandering it on a week of debauchery upstairs."

The whole amount would have, just about, got me a night of debauchery, if I didn't tip.

"Remember to tell her it's from me. I want her to like me when I eventually meet her."

"Oh! Don't you worry about that, John. She loves you. The action she gets when I get home is about as good as it gets, from me at least."

Another side effect of the adrenaline. And with that he was off, leaving me alone with another naked fourteen-year-old girl. I couldn't call Mama-san a second time. What would she think of me? I got to work, putting away the kit out of the bag. I made a mental note to clean all the weapons tomorrow. I wanted it all filed away before I had any visitors. I replaced all my cricket kit into the bag and dumped it in the kitchen area.

This time the trousers and shirt would both have to go. Too much body matter and debris floating around in the air. The mask and gloves could stay. They were in the armoury. If it hadn't been for the mask, I would have had bits of the Chinaman and Marko in my hair for weeks. I stuffed the clothes in a carrier bag to go the way of Monday's stuff, later. I stuck on a pair of gym trousers and a cricket top and set to work on my security footage, again!

It was considerably more difficult to find footage of a Tuesday when I was home all day. Usually I finished my business meetings and headed out for the day to celebrate. I settled for a Thursday about five months previously when I had the flu and was lounging about downstairs all day feeling sorry for myself and worrying that my hangovers were getting worse. It was the best I could do. I turned off the camera and timed them to come on at six tomorrow morning. I wouldn't be up before then. It had been a busy few days.

I was just putting my phone back together, idly wondering how long it took Kat to have a shower, when it rang. Lenny's phone but Mister Smith calling, no doubt.

"Mister McLean. I hear you have the girl back successfully. Well done. Just four hours, start to finish. I thought the recovery of Summer was extra-ordinary, but this is truly astonishing. You told Penny there was no need to worry about a repeat, is that correct?"

"One hundred per cent. Not just a tale to reassure her."

"And her captors gave her up peaceably?"

"No! Some had to be persuaded to leave the board entirely. I hear there is a sudden vacancy at the top of your organisation. Difficult to fill as well, because your nearest rival has two vacancies there too."

"You really are a remarkable man, John. I cannot thank you enough for clearing up my mess for me, I am sure my rival is grateful as well. I spoke to her just before I called you. No worries there at all, for either of us. Did you clear the board entirely?"

"No, I did a deal with the brothers. I kept them available to you. I thought you would need someone to keep the business going, even if only in the very short term. I wanted you to have that choice."

"Excellent. Always thinking of tomorrow aren't you. Truly excellent. I would like you to think about applying for the job, John. Don't answer me now. Take tonight to sleep on it. There could be a huge financial package for the right person, and I think you are the right person, John. Who better than an honest man, after all!"

My luck again. Most people would kill for an opportunity like that, and this one just landed in my lap. I supposed I had killed for it, though.

"How are the girls?"

"To be honest, John, I have left them with Lenny. They were doing my head right in. Never go back, John. It just isn't the same. It really is a foreign country. Besides all I heard from the three of them was how kind and handsome and clever and dishy and funny John is. Honestly, it was the kind of shite you would hear if you came back from the dead at your funeral and listened to your favourite aunt talking about you. You have some fan club there.

I am buying Susannah a house though. Anywhere she wants. Time to get them both away from the Downs, I think. She jumped at the offer. I think she has become as suspicious as you. Summer is some girl though, isn't she? Pretty, clever, brave, fearless she has it all."

"Beginning to sound a bit like one of my aunties there yourself. Did you tell her who you were?"

"Didn't have to. She figured it out herself. Like I said, clever."

He sounded smitten. He may have moved on from the fourteen-year-old Susannah, but I though he was going to have a struggle getting away from the fourteen-year-old Summer. Daughters are born with that ability. I know mine was.

"Anyway! I must go. Business goes on. Put out one fire, move on to the next. That is why I need someone like you. Someone who makes sure there are no fires. Could you meet me tomorrow, please? Same place as today. Say eleven o'clock. We can speak then about my job offer. Thanks again, John. At heart, I am as big a fan as the girls."

Just like me on a Sunday, I thought. Leave them with a bit of positive reinforcement. A cheap psychological trick. Cheap but effective, nonetheless. He hadn't even waited for a response. A man used to being obeyed.

Just as the call ended Kat finally made an exit from the shower. She came downstairs, looking ridiculous in the cycling bib and tee shirt combo, made worse by the towel wrapped around her head. God my towels were taking some punishment this week. I would need to leave a bonus for Claudia, I thought.

"God John, not only do you not have a hair dryer or straighteners, I couldn't even find a hairbrush."

She made it sound as if I was in the Flintstones. Why would I have any of those things. I had a couple of combs, that did me for hairdressing. On a real red-letter day, I would maybe use a little gel someone gave me for Christmas once. I may not have them, but I knew someone who did. Line eight again! I was becoming a bothersome neighbour.

"Mama-san. No! No! No! No problem like that. I know you will not see those two again, certainly I will not be worrying about them. This is another girly problem I am afraid. I don't quite know how to ask, but could I borrow a hairbrush, hair dryer and straighteners for half an hour please. Yes! Yes! I know. Nothing Mama-san, I know nothing about what a young girl needs. Yes! I will. Thank you!"

"Have a seat, Kat. Someone will be down with hair things in a moment."

"You don't get many women visitors, do you John?"

I was saved by the bell, or belle in this case. Kristina, the most beautiful of the upstairs girls, was at my door, dressed to kill and pushing a trolley. She looked magnificent. I buzzed her in. Kat's mouth fell open. The trolley turned out to be a set of drawers on wheels. I had a comb in my pocket, why did they need a trolley for fuck's sake! Then again, I never looked like them.

"You were saying, Kat?"

Kristina turned to Kat and gently removed the towel.

"I have to leave in half an hour, Mister McLean. Is that okay? I have an important appointment."

"Of course, it is, Kris. I only wanted to borrow a hair dryer."

"Mama-san knew it wouldn't be for you."

Kristina started opening drawers and pulling out bits of kit and nozzles and sprays. She appeared to have more kit there than I had in the armoury.

"Please sit here, love."

She had worked hard to lose her Cardiff accent but

occasionally the phraseology just shone through if you knew what you were listening for. Kat moved into my comfy armchair and Kristina plugged in an extension lead and began assembling enough equipment to fuse the National Grid.

"I can't believe you know a hairdresser who can come at a moment's notice at this time of night. It's so cool. I must get your number for my mother."

Despite all she had been through, she was still incredibly naïve and innocent. Kristina winked at me and carried on.

"What did you use on this hair, babe. It feels like a ship's line."

"John didn't have anything up there except shower gel. It was all I could find."

"Let's see if we can fix it up a bit. Do you know John well?"

She was fishing to tease me. The girls upstairs often commented on my lack of female visitors. I liked to think of it as flirting though I supposed it was just old-fashioned human curiosity.

"He is a friend of my mother's."

"Really!"

Two syllables, twenty meanings the way Kristina said it. I didn't think her raised eyebrow was as good as mine though. She was massaging foams and sprays into Kat's hair. Then she laid out five different brushes on a pull-out table on top of the trolley. I thought she was opening a shop.

Only after about five minutes of that did she start to dry the hair. I had to keep half an ear on the conversation. I didn't want Kat talking about what I had done for her. So far, I was her mum's boyfriend. That was good enough for me on several levels. Then the hairdryer started up and a variety of appliances were installed on to the nozzle. Brushes were selected at random, to my untrained eye, and there was a flurry of actual hair drying.

There were a couple of implements plugged in to heat up as well. I was sure one of them was the same tool I had seen used to torture prisoners in Syria. It certainly hadn't been used to do hair on that occasion. Wrong end, so to speak.

Quarter of an hour later they were finished. She even had a giant mirror. It slid up out of the back of the trolley. Kat was ecstatic.

"It is easy to do hair like this. It is so well cut and in such wonderful condition. I envy you this hair, I really do. Would you like me to do your make-up?"

Visibly swollen with pride at the compliment, Kat assented. The trolley rotated and make up was produced from the rear drawers.

"Oh! My mum makes those. I can get you some if you like?"

"Your mother makes these. They cost a fortune."

"Do they? I don't know, I suppose we get them for free."

The truly entitled indeed. Kristina was trying to catch my eye and nodding to the bottles on the trolley. She needn't have bothered.

"I'll get her to drop some down here for you. You could pass them on couldn't you, John?"

She wasn't yet anywhere near the level of my daughter, but she was certainly getting there with the commands. A few sweeps from one of another forest of paintbrushes and they were done. Kat turned around. She looked lovely. Still obviously a child, but with a lot more of the woman she would become on show.

"Wow! You have made me look like the other girls in school."

"I used to do the other girl's make-up at the beauty contests. I did a bit for the BBC, as well. Now I only do the girls upstairs. It has been nice doing yours. You are such a beautiful subject. I must go now, John. I cannot be late. You! Go upstairs and put your nice dress on. You will be the prettiest girl there, I promise you."

"Thanks Kris. I appreciate it."

I buzzed her out just as Penny was arriving, another one who could magically find a parking spot outside my office. I guess I wasn't always lucky. It kind of balanced out sometimes. The two women faced off in my doorway, looking each other up and down. I was pleased to see that Penny had had time to re-organise herself after the ordeal of the afternoon. I was even more pleased to see that there was a tinge of green in Penny's gaze. Kris turned for the last word.

"And I always appreciate the shoes, John. See you tomorrow night!"

She had right of way seeing as how she was pushing a big trolley. I could see one of the Vietnamese lads was waiting to carry it upstairs for her. As Penny came through the door, Kris raised a discreet thumbs-up behind her and laughed. I had had more beautiful women and girls in here in the last two days than I had in the previous ten years.

"John! Thank you, thank you."

She strode over to hug me at least as tightly as she

had that morning. I thought it was as much a reaction to Kris's presence as anything, but the look in her eyes hinted at more. She turned to Kat.

"Katherine! My God! What have you done! I thought you would be wretched. I was terrified you may have been hurt, or worse. You have no idea what I was imagining. Look at you, you look great. You look as if you have been to a spa."

Kat rolled her eyes at me and smiled. Christ! I was even having private jokes with her now.

"John's friend Kristina did my hair and make up for me while we were waiting."

"Did she really! Lucky she was here."

Girls, women, I was back having no real idea when the teasing ended, and the sharp comments began. Just when you think you understand you realise how much you do not know. I was back at the squaddie approach. Hunker down and hope it passes.

"What are you wearing?"

"I was covered in blood. Not mine, the guys who were holding me. We had to destroy the clothes so as not to link me to the scene. John was brilliant rescuing me, but this was all he had that fitted me."

Good on her. She had obviously been doing more than washing in the shower. I suppose all that money spent on education bought you something after all. Clever girl indeed. If she wasn't going to say anything, neither was I.

"Do you know he doesn't even have a hairbrush in his flat. Kristina is his neighbour. She did my hair and make-up. I think she took pity on me. I promised you would send her some make-up. That was okay wasn't it?"

She was talking too much to cover the lie. A

common trait among inexperienced liars. She also sounded very like her mother when she prattled on. I rolled my eyes, but it was a private joke just for me it seemed.

"I don't think John gets many visitors, especially females."

"Well he better start getting used to it then, hadn't he?"

They both laughed.

THIRTEEN

The Social Worker

Two weeks later I was sitting in the old bank building, just along from the new police station wondering who Anne Gaye was and why she had called me. She had insisted on meeting me and I had insisted on a locally owned coffee shop rather than one of the many chains and franchises in the Bay. I always liked to keep my money local, if I could.

I was early and playing 'guess who' with the customers as they arrived. I was only on wrong guess number three when I chose her as a probable. She walked in, smartly dressed, straight to the counter. Ordered without hesitation and chose the homemade tiffin bar as a side. She balanced the saucer with the cake on the cup with her coffee and came straight towards me.

Clearly, she was someone who came here regularly and who knew the tiffin bar was better than most. Everything about her was no nonsense. Short in stature she made up for it with an aggressively good posture, square on, shoulders back, chin up. I didn't think I had seen her before. I would have remembered.

The entire left side of her face had been burned. By heat, not chemicals, I thought. Patches of it had been grafted to pink and shiny but it looked as if they had given up the ghost with the rest. It remained stubbornly ridged and brown, or almost maroon, in colour. Other than that, she was quite pretty. Her eyes sparkled as I looked at her and I liked the way she carried herself.

"Mister McLean, Anne Gaye. People call me Patchy. Thank you for agreeing to see me. Thank you too, for not looking away at my scar. That's not why I am called Patchy, by the way."

"No problem. People call me Jock. Seen a lot worse, if I'm honest, usually on good people. I have one much the same on my side. Want to compare?"

"What caused yours?"

"Stray bullet hit a magnesium flare in my harness, melted the lining of my body armour onto my body. We stopped carrying them on the harness after that, yours?"

"Pimp. Held my face onto a cooker. My wig melted on to me."

"A career ending injury, then."

She snorted a laugh. It was quite endearing.

"Not quite, but near enough."

I could have sat there and just enjoyed my coffee with her until the pubs opened, but I thought I should appear business-like. If I had learned anything it was that you could never judge who could be a lucrative client. I had met the representative of my first insurance company in the toilets at Sophia Gardens. He was covered in vomit and had somehow ripped his shirt to the navel. Not the buttons, but the actual front of the shirt. I had never solved that mystery either.

"What can I do for you?"

"Nothing. Why would you think you could do

something for me?"

"That's usually why pretty women call me. I am not on Tinder or Plenty of Fish. It's usually business."

"I appreciate the effort at flirting, I really do. There is nothing I want from you I just wanted to meet you. Is that strange?"

"What, in a kind of "saw you across a crowded room and wondered" kind of way. That would be strange. In fact, I don't think it has ever happened to me before. I knew I hadn't wasted fifty pence on that aftershave. I must buy another gallon soon."

She was laughing. The burn had caused nerve damage to the left side, and it gave her smile a kind of lop-sided look, but her eyes made up for it. The light of her laugh sparkled and danced, flashing in her eyes like fireflies on a pitch-black night. I could have watched it all day, or at least until opening time.

"I wanted to meet you because I am always careful about who gives us money. I run the Sanctuary charity in Butetown. Have you heard of it?"

I had a vague recollection of a sign in the high flats just up from my office, near the PDSA. I thought I had read something about it at a Cardiff match, as well. They were having a bucket collection last season sometime. Anyway, I didn't have to be much of a detective to figure it out from the name and her previous occupation.

"Just up the road. Works with prostitutes. Tries to keep them safe and get them out of the life and away from drugs and drink?"

"That's the one. It's my charity."

"Are you looking for a donation? Is that it? Happy to help. You know where my office is don't you? Most of my best friends are prostitutes of one kind or another."

"We call them sex workers now, but I don't suppose that makes much difference to a man your age does it?"

I didn't quite see what she was saying about me, but I didn't think it was very nice. Before I even realised, I had done it I had lifted my chin to argue my corner. Too much time in the company of adolescent girls recently. She laughed.

"Got you! The girls don't worry too much about what they are called either. A few of them know you, and your neighbours speak very highly of you indeed."

She was teasing me and seeming to enjoy it. I was quite enjoying it myself.

"I don't need another donation from you. The one you gave will keep us in business for well over a year."

Without question I was going to have to give up, or at least cut back on, the drinking. I had no idea what she was talking about. I hoped I hadn't promised some of my cash nest-egg to her when I was pissed. Joe the Toff!

"I see you don't know what I am talking about. Do you know Alan Davies?"

"Possibly, I know lots of Davies'. Lot of them about."

"This one is a journalist."

"Oh! Addie! I know Addie quite well, as a matter of fact I was talking to him only last week."

What a job he had done for me. The child sex ring was front page news for a week, the police corruption coverage was still on-going. There was a parallel scandal in social services as most of the girls had come from care homes. The local police and crime commissioner lived just three doors away. He had also done a spread on Marko disappearing abroad after the arrests of the five guys we had battered. Nobody was looking for us anymore for the beatings at least. As far as I knew the bodies still hadn't been discovered in the pub.

Either that or Sunday had literally buried them for me. He had taken my refusal of his job offer with good grace. Perhaps he had taken it upon himself to remove the evidence, or perhaps the Chinese had. I didn't know and certainly wasn't going to look. That was why I had been with Addie last week after the Birmingham match. I fed him the stuff about Marko, and he tried to get me to take some of his fees.

He was a different man. Smartened-up he had been on the television news nationally as an expert on what had been happening. He told me he had also filmed an episode of a TV series about Britain's violent cities with one of those bad actor hardmen who fronted such series from time to time.

I had seen one filming in Syria once, as if he was on the front line. Strangely, they never showed all the abuse he had endured from active troops. He took it in good part though. I didn't suppose he had much choice. He only played the part of a hard man after all.

"He made a six-figure donation to my charity in your name. He said it was your dues for his stories on the child sex ring, but that you wanted nothing to do with that kind of money. Is that correct?"

"Yes, largely. I told him I didn't want to profit from that kind of misery. It is all his money. It is him you should be thanking."

"I did, and I will be again. It might seem like

tainted money to you but to us it is a lifeline. I just had to be sure it wasn't an attempt to control us or shut us up."

"Not from me. Use it in good health! I meant what I said about contacting me if you needed a donation. Not that kind of money of course, but better than buying a flag."

"Nobody sells flags now. I bet you can't remember the last time you gave money like that!"

I didn't even have to think.

"I'll bet you the coffees."

"You're on."

"Poppy day last year!! People do still sell flags then. You'll have to buy the coffees."

I could have afforded to be generous but wanted to get one back for the quip about my age. Mister Smith had brought with him a ten-thousand-pound gift from the Chinese for sorting their problems without unnecessary fuss or attention. I think that embarrassed him into matching it for solving his problems, though in fairness, Lenny had told me that the drugs I returned were worth over a hundred grand wholesale on top of the thirty odd thousand in cash.

Lenny was popping in to see me regularly now when he was through supervising the brothers. I think he was pleased I hadn't taken the job. How could you settle in a job knowing someone like Lenny coveted it? And there were dozens more like him.

"What were you thinking just then? I could see you day-dreaming."

"I was thinking how nice this was, sitting here with you. Just passing the time."

And I was. Her scarred face and haunted eyes were a familiar terrain for me. The two of us had seen terrible things and I had certainly done a few, but we could still have a laugh. That was where I was most comfortable, exchanging war stories, remembering the darkness and heading towards it, and oblivion. Not the bright sterile kitchens inhabited by beautiful people in The Downs and Radyr.

Villages without pubs or troubles, what kind of existence was that? Certainly not one I was destined for. I still hadn't found my shoe.

I hope you enjoyed JOCK OF THE BAY enough to look forward to its sequel, JOCK OF THE TOWN, available now on Kindle. To whet your appetite here is the opening chapter of JOCK OF THE TOWN, the next adventure for Wales' latest anti-hero John McLean.

ONE

The Ambush

It was, without question one of the worst attempts at an ambush I had ever seen. Had it been a training exercise run by anyone in my squad, all the participants would have been doubling a route march with full Bergens until they collapsed. It was shambolic, and that was with me making it easy for them.

I had set off for an early morning run when traffic was at its lightest. I deliberately chose a route with a long straight to provide good visibility for the mobile component of the snatch. I turned along the barrage to provide a long straight approach by the snatcher, with good visibility and few witnesses.

There was a point at the barrage car park, where the pavement tapered in and pedestrians had to travel through a narrow gate. I could not have given them more perfect terrain to perform a textbook snatch and they totally fucked it up. There could be no real excuses either. There had been a sustained drizzle throughout my run so the wet road couldn't have been a surprise. I presumed they had been briefed on elements of my background. The only unknown to them was that I knew they were coming. That shouldn't really have made a difference.

The first mistake was following too close in the van. Twice they had been forced to pass me and circle around to come back into position. A blind man would have noticed it at that time in the morning. They hadn't even made any effort to disguise the vehicle as a delivery truck or works van. The engine had a distinctive rattle in third gear as well. I could place them behind me without looking round.

Secondly the runner had set off too early from the opposite side of the barrage. I could see him all the way along and he had stopped twice to avoid arriving at the best place too soon. This was a common mistake amongst the inexperienced or untrained. No-one wanted to arrive at the action already out of breath from sprinting into position and it was a natural human reaction to give yourself a bit of leeway with the timing.

He was dressed wrong as well. He was wearing running shorts and medium priced, but specialist running shoes and compression socks. All good cover and fitting for an early morning runner. But he was wearing a loose tee shirt. I was forced to presume he had a pancake holster on his hip and needed a long shirt to cover the gun and allow easy access. A real runner knew that loose cotton rubs your nipples to points of agony especially in damp conditions.

The runner has no need of a gun in any event. The weaponry should all be in the van behind.

In truth, I knew it was amateur hour for a long way before the event and was tempted to make them suffer by running a short loop up the hill into the cliffs of Penarth for some interval training. I decided against that because I could not be certain that I would have arrived at the ambush in optimal condition to thwart them. Ten, or even five, years ago my fitness would not have been a consideration.

I rehearsed the event in my mind as I approached the turn onto the long barrage. The standard operating procedure for a street lift would be for the runner to approach me from the opposite direction on my right-hand side forcing me towards the road. As we ran past each other, the van should pull up alongside us with the side door already open. The driver's door should open to block my path with the driver looking to intimidate me either with weaponry or by physical size.

At the exact same time the rear doors open and man three exits to block any retreat and to clear up any debris from the lift such as shoes or bags or hats. The fourth man should never leave the van. He is there to subdue me once in the vehicle usually chemically by an injection of Valium or a pad of chloroform. If it all goes wrong, he is the spare driver.

The technique is simple. An old army rule. The simpler it can be made the less there is to go wrong. The runner simply shoves the victim towards the open van door. The driver and rear man heave him in, and the van man subdues him. The runner keeps going to a prearranged rendezvous.

The driver closes the side door and hops back in

and the rear guy jumps in the back closing the door after himself. Done properly the entire action occupies less than three feet of pavement with seventy five percent of the view obscured. It should all be over in fewer than five seconds, start to finish, and the runner jogging past without paying any attention casts doubt in the mind of any witness that anything has happened.

That is the procedure in an ideal world and ideal conditions, and I had truthfully done my level best to provide those. There was not a single part of their process which went to plan.

Firstly, as I knew this was likely to happen, I had armed myself with my favourite cosh. A length of pickled hippo's penis sheathed in elephant skin, and with a custom-made ostrich skin grip and wrist loop. It had the Swahili word KIONGOZI tattooed into the elephant hide, meaning leader. It had been a gift from some insurgents I had trained in southern Africa somewhere. It was the most effective non-lethal weapon I had ever owned. There was no need for any serious injuries today. This was just a preliminary joust after all.

As the runner approached. I heard the van accelerate to reach us as we crossed. Again, poor training. That aural clue would be enough for even civilians to look round to see what was happening. I moved to the very right-hand edge of the pavement to force the runner to pass between me and the van. He would have to grab and throw me from that side.

In the stride before we crossed, I pulled the cosh from my right sleeve and lifted my right hand as if to wave to someone behind him. I could hear the van braking but had to focus entirely on the runner. If I didn't deal with him adequately, I would not have the chance to proceed to the occupants of the van.

The runner could not help himself. On the wrong side from his anticipated version of the event, he was already mentally off-balance. The movement of my right hand distracted him into following it with his eyes and the thought that there might be someone behind him checked any decisiveness in his actions. As he tried to reconcile all these thoughts my cosh struck him about half power on the temple. He went down like an Italian heavyweight boxer.

Meanwhile, the van had overshot the crossing point. A combination of the acceleration to catch up and the greasy road surface had pushed it beyond us. The back-door man sprung out just as his colleague, the runner fell unconscious at his feet. It takes a special kind of training to stamp on a fallen colleague without looking down and he hadn't had it.

By the time he had glanced down and tried to avoid his fallen colleague the cosh had done its work again. A full downward swing to the crown of his head just as he began to look up again. The hippo's dick made a pleasant hollow thump when in full swing. It was strangely satisfying.

At this precise time, the driver had no clue as to what was happening. He would have been focussed on stopping and opening the door. The overshoot had delayed him slightly, and all the action had taken place behind him, largely in the blind spot of his mirrors. He had jumped out ready to deal with closing the side door and perhaps lifting any stray legs or arms into the van. Instead he found me only a stride away and with two of his friends on the ground.

He panicked. There was no training or thought in

his lunge towards me. Really, he deserved all he got. Between the overshoot and the mad rush, it was a particularly poor performance in a disastrous team effort. I stepped forward and butted him full on the bridge of the nose. I was acutely conscious that I was now framed in the side doorway and must beware of the fourth man.

The headbutt had broken his nose and he could not see for the tears rolling reflexively down his cheeks. I could have put him out of his misery humanely using the cosh in my left hand, but I wanted to move away from the line of sight of the fourth man as soon as possible. Instead, I pulled him forward and down by his collar allowing me to retreat a step or two. I had to be careful not to fall over the bodies on the pavement.

Once he had a bit of momentum, I brought my knee up square in his face. I gave him a second knee for good measure. It was important that he learned from his mistakes. His next victim may not be as forgiving and merciful as me. I pulled him forward on to the pile. The fourth man did what he should never have done. He got out of the van. It is a golden rule for a reason. If he doesn't get away, who reports what has happened?

He didn't come out of the van alone. He had a small Sig Sauer P30 in his right hand. Three beginner's mistakes in the same movement. He shouldn't get out of the van; he shouldn't threaten me with a gun he cannot use. If they wanted me dead, they would shoot from the side door of the van on the way past without stopping. The point of a snatch is to bring in the victim alive and relatively undamaged.

Finally, the gun was in the wrong hand. I was behind him; I could have stepped behind the van and he would have been stuck with the gun along the side of the van rather than in a position to shoot around the end from his left hand. It didn't matter, I was going to take it from him. I deliberately stood on the fingers of the driver, trying to put as much weight as possible through the heel of my running shoes. It was enough to draw a scream from him even in his semi-conscious state. Lack of training again. Almost criminally amateur, in fact.

The gunman looked down. Not even just a quick glance either. There was a lot of blood by this time. It seemed to hypnotise him. I skipped forward to keep my weight on my right leg. I left the cosh to dangle on its retaining loop and locked both hands around the wrist of his gun hand. My right hand, driven by the weight on my right leg was pushing the gun up and away. My left hand was forcing his wrist back and twisting like an Olympic rower in the recovery stroke. The result was a satisfying crack as the wrist fractured and the gun dropped to the pavement. His scream quickly drowned out the driver's.

Not wanting the screaming to draw attention. I brought my right elbow sharply down and across onto his jaw. The screaming stopped immediately. He looked like a pile of wet clothes on the pavement. I should have bundled them into the van and left them somewhere inconspicuous to recover, but I couldn't be arsed. I was so disappointed at how poorly they had performed. It was truly shocking. A real "nil points" performance if ever there was one.

It was particularly disappointing that three of them were carrying Sig Sauer P230s, the concealed weapon of choice for British Special Forces. If this was the modern definition of special, they had fallen a long way in the years since I had demobbed. I doubted it, somehow.

I left the four of them on the pavement and took the guns and the van. I couldn't be bothered finishing my run. That was how depressed I was at how easy it had been. I took the guns home with me and left the van next to the Sennedd building where the Welsh Assembly sits. Hopefully, Special Branch would call the bomb squad out to it and embarrass the idiots who had sent them after me. I hoped so anyway.

Being careful to avoid the multitude of cameras and looking out for any police returning to the nearby station I crept home. I didn't want to be stopped carrying three unlicensed pistols in my running shorts. I was struggling to keep them on under the load.

I would give them back later. I knew this was only the first gambit and they would come for me again. Hopefully a bit more professionally this time.

Published by
www.publishandprint.co.uk

Printed in Great Britain
by Amazon